Long-Legged Rosie

Murder in Myrtle Beach
A Frankie McKeller Mystery

Long-Legged Rosie

Murder in Myrtle Beach
A Frankie McKeller Mystery

by Troy D. Nooe

Last Call
PRESS

Last Call Press
Myrtle Beach, SC

Cover painting by Gail E. Haley
Frankie painting by Joe Burleson
Book design by Luci Mott
Originally Published by Ingalls Publishing Group, Inc

ISBN-13: 978-0692581919
ISBN-10: 069258191X

Library of Congress Cataloging-in-Publication Data
(from Ingalls Publishing Group, Inc. edition)

Nooe, Troy D.
Long-legged Rosie : murder in Myrtle Beach / by Troy D. Nooe.
pages cm. -- (A Frankie McKeller mystery)
ISBN 978-1-932158-38-0 (trade pbk. : alk. paper)
I. Title.
PS3614.O64L66 2015
813'.6--dc23
2014021052

Dedicated to Emily, Greg and Andrew,
my three favorite people in the world.
Even though you don't get how cool your Dad really is,
I love you anyway

Long-Legged Rosie

Murder in Myrtle Beach
A Frankie McKeller Mystery

Chapter One

I'd have recognized those long legs anywhere, and I knew, too well, the kind of trouble they carried around on them.

Rosie lounged in one of the overstuffed chairs in the lobby of the Ocean Forest Hotel, and she was positioned at an angle, away from the front doors, so she didn't see me approaching. It gave me time to give her the once over as I came walking up.

She looked good, better even than I remembered, and that was saying a lot. It had been over a year since I'd last laid eyes on her, but it seemed more like a lifetime ago. It seemed more like a dream.

We'd been an item for a while, back up in Baltimore, before things turned all dark and crusty. I was a different guy back then, before Rosie got her hooks into me and turned me into something else, something I wasn't very proud of.

Just the sight of her took me back to another time and another place. From the first moment I saw her, she had seeped into my brain matter like molasses, and I knew no amount of soda water would ever wash her away.

She was eased back in the comfortable chair with her slender arms crossed in front of her, the thin beige dress draped smoothly over her figure. Her legs were crossed, and she was tapping the high heel of her shoe to the ground like she was nervous or anxious, maybe just impatient. Each time she did it the muscle of her calf shifted under her stocking, sending a series of delightful tingles through my brain. Those long legs of hers had always had that effect on me.

She was a raven-haired beauty with a striking face and the kind of deep brown eyes that could cause a guy to make some pretty stupid decisions. If the face didn't do it, with her high cheek bones, arching brows and pouting red lips, the figure was enough to close the deal.

Some girls have the kind of figure that can stop traffic. Rosie's could stop air traffic.

She turned her head and caught sight of me, locking those deep browns on mine and giving me the soft, sultry smile she'd used on me so many times before.

"Frankie McKeller," she said, all breathless and kitten like.

As she stood, she gave a half wiggle of her hips that freed the fabric of her skimpy dress from against her body, allowing it to fall freely down her figure, where it landed perfectly in place on her curves. It was a veteran move by a woman who knew what she was doing and left nothing to chance.

She stepped toward me and wrapped her arms around my neck, letting the rest of her go limp against my torso, turning her head to the side and pressing it into my chest. I could feel the heels of my feet melt away a little in my shoes.

"What are you doing here, Rosie?" I managed to choke out.

"I missed you, Frankie," she answered with a sigh.

"How did you find me?"

She looked up at me, and her eyes were all wide and innocent, like I'd insulted her in some way. "You act as if you aren't happy to see me."

"How did you find me?" I asked again.

"It just so happens I ran into your mother at the Cross Street Market not long ago. She's very proud of her son, the big time house detective at the Ocean Forest."

"So you figured you'd make that long trip down here just to come and say hi?"

She gasped with exasperation. "Really, Frankie. You act as though you aren't glad to see me."

"It's not that," I replied. "It's always a pleasure to *see* you, Rosie. It's the rest of the package I'm a little leery of."

"Oh, don't be like that, Hon. Can't a girl take a vacation and stop by to see an old friend? I thought a few days lying on the beach and working on my tan might do me some good." There was a twinkle in her eye when she said it, like she knew I was busy picturing her in a revealing bathing suit. It just so happens it was exactly what I was doing.

Rosie stepped back and looked around the hotel lobby, striking one of her patented poses and giving me another chance to check out the goods. "It looks like you're doing all right for yourself," she said, all flirty and girlie. "You've got quite a gig going here. It's a far cry from that dirty little office you used to have on Baltimore Street."

"Yeah, well, I still keep a dirty little office downstairs, but the perks are a little better."

"I hear you've carved a nice little niche for yourself down here. They say you've even solved a couple of big time cases."

"Don't believe everything you hear. My mother tends to exaggerate when it comes to her little boy."

She took my hand in both of her hands and squeezed it tight in her fingers. "Don't you ever think about me anymore, Frankie?"

I took a deep breath, trying to keep my head clear. "Sure I do, Rosie. I think about you all the time. I think about all the good times we had, and I think about how upset you used to get when the money got tight. I think about that night club owner you dumped me for too sometimes."

Rosie gave one of her signature giggles. "Oh, Frankie, don't be like that. It was such a long time ago. Blake never meant anything to me, you know that. We were just friends, is all."

"Yeah, I seem to remember walking into a little gin mill and seeing you two getting all friendly with each other."

She shot me one of those looks, lifting one eyebrow and fixing her eyes on mine. "In case you haven't noticed, I didn't spend twelve hours on a train to come down and see Blake."

"Why exactly did you come down?" I asked.

"Where are your manners, Frankie? You could at least offer to buy a girl a drink, for old time's sake."

I gave her another once over. It's not like the thought of soaking her in for a few hours didn't sound inviting. Like I said, she wasn't exactly hard on the eyes. As long as I kept my wits about me and steered clear of those little tricks I'd always fallen for, it might be fun to catch up. What did I have to lose?

She said she needed to powder her nose first, so I headed downstairs to the Brookgreen Room and bellied up to the bar. It was something I was known to do from time to time.

"What'll it be, McKeller?"

"Bourbon," I replied. "Make it a double." I shot it back hard and sat staring off at the bar back, my mind drifting to the old days, back to when Rosie and me were an item.

It was a time I didn't allow myself to think about very often, a time I had pushed back to some dark corner of my brain. I'd made some bad decisions back then, done some things I didn't know I was capable of. When Rosie showed up, out of the blue, she brought all those old memories with her, all the old craziness, all the old hurt that came with it.

In the end, I had been a real mess back then. The kind of mess all the king's horses and all the king's men wouldn't have bothered to take a broom to.

When she dumped me, it was quick and final and I was left holding my bloody heart in my hands. From there, things got dark. There was a lot of "woe is me" stuff. Late night phone calls to her apartment. I even showed up on her doorstep a couple of times.

For a tough guy I turned to mush pretty quick. She turned my back bone to Jello, and it was a long time before I could begin to gather my dignity back up. It was a long time before I could look at other women the same way. It made me wonder what in the hell I was doing sitting in a bar waiting for her to turn my life upside down again.

Rosie strolled into the room like she owned it and planted herself on the stool beside me. She gave me a wink and a smile and asked, "So, how about that drink you were going to buy me?"

Warning sirens were blaring in my skull. The thing to do was get as far away from Rosie as I could. Every last ounce of common sense I had was telling me to run.

I ordered up two boilermakers.

Chapter Two

Rolling over took about everything I had in me. Lifting my head was nothing short of torture. Somehow I managed to work the phone off its cradle and call down to the front desk.

"Curtis, what room is Rosie Carter in?"

"I don't have a Rosie Carter on the books," the desk clerk answered.

I thought for a second. "Did we have any young women check in alone yesterday?"

"You mean the brunette with the great gams?" he replied with a wolfish tinge to his voice.

"Yeah," I sighed. "That would be the one."

"Sally Young, she's in 309."

By the time I'd cleaned up, dressed and taken more than twice the recommended dosage of aspirin, I was feeling almost human again. I made my way to room 309 but got no answer at the door. I seemed to remember something about Rosie wanting to work on her tan so decided to take a stroll through the hotel lobby and out the back door, taking the long, dreaded walk across the back lawn toward the beach.

Before I could get there, somebody else had other plans. I was cut off in the lobby by a short fellow with wide shoulders and dark, serious eyes behind wire-framed glasses. His hair was greased and perfectly combed, parted down the middle.

"Are you McKeller?" he asked.

I wasn't in the mood for the mundane hotel duties I was paid to take care of, and I didn't much appreciate the tone of his voice. Rosie had squirreled her way into my head and was the only thing I had any interest in at the moment.

"I'm looking for Frank McKeller."

"You found him," I admitted.

"The name is Simmons. I understand you're in charge of security here at the hotel."

"I'm the house detective, if that's what you mean."

"Let's take a walk," he said, turning away and starting through the lobby like he expected me to follow. I stood my ground and watched him take a few steps before he realized I wasn't tagging along. He turned back and shot me a snarl.

"You waiting for an engraved invitation?"

"Maybe just a please and thank you."

He let out a sigh. "Sorry, didn't realize you were such a sensitive type. Would you please take a little walk with me?"

"When you put it like that, how could I refuse?"

We walked along in silence for a bit, through the lobby and out onto the back veranda, the one the locals called Peacock Alley. It was where the pretty people liked to get all dolled up and mingle. This time of day it was quiet, with just a few guests checking out the ocean.

I half noticed a guy sitting alone at a table off to the right. I only noticed him because he got up just as we came out and lowered the brim of his Fedora on his face, like he didn't want to be noticed, before slipping back inside. The guy was thin, medium height, average features, pinstriped conservative suit. Even though I'd only caught a glimpse of his face, I couldn't help but think there was something familiar about him. It wasn't so surprising, as I crossed paths with a lot of people in my job.

Simmons walked up to the railing and leaned his girth against it, glancing around at the few people gathered about. He didn't seem in any hurry to spark the conversation. I'd already put the skinny guy in the pinstriped suit out of my head and was busy scanning the beach for Rosie. I caught sight of a lone brunette on a beach blanket off in the distance.

"Nice view," he said.

"We here for the view, or were you planning a romantic walk on the beach too?" I asked.

"I represent some very important people."

"Well, I'm glad to hear that public school education is paying off for you."

"Very important people who are very much in the public eye," he explained.

"Is that so? Any chance you can get me Ginger Rogers' autograph?"

"Enough with the wisecracks."

"Look, Simmons, I'm a busy guy. Why don't you cut to the chase and tell me what you want?"

He hesitated a moment, giving me the hairy eyeball. "You ever hear of Arthur Wright?"

"Senator Arthur Wright, Republican out of North Carolina? I've heard of him. Right wing, American values, baseball, Mom and apple pie."

"That's the one."

"If you're trying to recruit my vote, I have to warn you, I'm not registered in North Carolina."

"Senator Wright is coming here this weekend. He's bringing a few friends."

"The more the merrier."

"They're planning on a little get together up on the tenth floor. There will be some very prominent people with some very recognizable faces in attendance."

"I'm guessing you're not here to invite me to the party."

"Your boss, Mr. Buntemeyer, assured me I could count on your complete cooperation."

"Yeah, he's good like that."

"This little get together isn't the kind of thing that's meant for public consumption. All parties involved are looking for discretion on the part of the hotel and its employees."

"Why the big hush hush?"

"Let's just say that when these parties get together they value their privacy. They like to keep to themselves, play a friendly game of cards—"

"That's what this is all about?" I asked. "Wright is throwing a high stakes poker game?"

I'd heard about the infamous poker games on the tenth floor of the Ocean Forest Hotel, but I hadn't witnessed one since joining the staff. They said they attracted the best of the best, the movers and shakers of South Carolina and beyond. They say if you have to ask what the ante is, you can't afford to sit in. It was a regular tradition at the Ocean Forest.

"We're hoping we can count on your cooperation as well as your discretion."

"What do I care if Wright and his cronies want to indulge in a friendly game of cards? I'm just glad to see those tax dollars are going to good use."

"As hotel security, we're going to need you to be on hand for anything we need. You know this place as well as anybody. You know the people who come and go."

"It's a hotel, Simmons. I don't know the people all that well."

"I'm going to count on you to help coordinate things," he explained.

I shrugged. "When is this little shindig?"

"The senator and his friends will be arriving Friday night."

"Nothing like a little advance warning, huh?"

"We're not going to require a lot on your part. Our people will handle most of the security issues. We just need you to be on the lookout and help keep it all under wraps. Only a handful of people will even know they're here."

That was fine by me. The last thing I wanted to do was babysit a bunch of bigwigs. I was still more interested in getting out to see Rosie. I couldn't help but feel like there were some things we needed to talk about.

I walked with Simmons back to the front desk, while he continued to stress the importance of keeping the senator's little get together under my hat. He kept telling me he was counting on my help, but I still wasn't sure exactly what he wanted from me. He told me the senator and his friends would be arriving by seven on Friday night. They would be leaving on Sunday morning. He wanted me to be on hand for the arrival in case he needed my assistance.

We said our short and sweet goodbyes and he was on his way. I took the opportunity to check with Curtis on the hotel's occupancy and goings on.

Forty percent full with no VIP's in house sounded like my plate was going to be relatively clean, and I was already thinking about setting aside a block of time for a quick nap in my office. I barely noticed when the big lug came strolling up to the desk.

"How's business?" the guy asked as he placed two paws on the counter top and leaned in toward the desk clerk.

The guy was thick and broad shouldered with a flat face that looked like it had taken its share of pelts over the years. He looked kind of like a gorilla stuffed in a navy blue suit.

"Look, Mack, maybe you can help me out."

"Of course, sir. How may I be of assistance?" Curtis asked.

"I'm looking for a girl, a real looker. You can't miss her, dark hair, dark eyes, a pair of getaway sticks to die for—"

"Does she have a sister?" I asked, butting into the conversation before Curtis could answer the man. I had a pretty good idea who he was looking for.

The guy chuckled. "Nah, not this one. She's a one of a kind, a real piece of work, if you know what I mean."

"I know the type."

"You seen anybody around this joint who fits the bill?"

"I would have noticed a broad like that hanging around."

The guy gave another chuckle but it was a forced attempt at friendliness.

"This brunette supposed to meet you here at the hotel?" I asked, ignoring the confused looks I was getting from Curtis.

"Nah, I was hoping to pop in and surprise her," he replied, and I thought I detected something sinister in his tone. "I thought she might be down, looking up an old friend."

"Someone who lives here in town?"

"Actually, a guy who works here at the Ocean Forest Hotel, a guy by the name of McKeller."

My back was up against a wall, and I had already dove in with both feet, covering for Rosie. I had about a split second to decide how many lies I could dig myself out from under.

"Well, that's a coincidence," I decided to go with. "My name's McKeller."

"Well," he said with a sigh and a grin. "How about that?"

"Yeah, small world, huh?"

"Ain't it, though?" His eyes were locked with mine like he was sizing me up, maybe trying to make me flinch. "You remember a girl from up north named Rosie Carter?"

"Rosie's not the kind of gal a guy forgets," I replied, matching his glare.

"No, I guess not. You seen her around lately?"

"I haven't heard from Rosie in over a year now, not since before I left Baltimore. We didn't exactly part ways on friendly terms, if you know what I mean."

He gave a nod. "She's been known to burn a few bridges."

"With Rosie, it's more like hurricane force destruction. She doesn't leave much standing in her wake," I pointed out.

"You might say that."

"Look, buddy," I tried. "I don't know what your deal with Rosie is, but I know Rosie. If you want my advice, whatever it is you're looking for from her, forget it. Cut your losses and consider yourself lucky."

"I wish it was that simple."

"Yeah, well, I wish I could help you out, but, like I said, Rosie and me aren't what you'd call pen pals these days."

"Too bad, I got a friend back home who wants me to deliver a message for him," he said, glancing around the hotel lobby. "Pretty swank set up you got here."

"We like it."

"Maybe I'll bed down here for a few nights, treat myself to a little relaxation." It sounded like a challenge.

"Yeah, that might be a problem. We're booked solid for the next few nights." I thought when I said it Curtis might swallow his tongue. The big guy didn't look too happy either.

The guy took another look around the empty lobby. "It don't look so busy."

I shrugged. "What can I say? We've got two busloads of dentists on their way down from Jersey. I don't have a single room to spare.

He gave a smile. "Dentists, huh? Ain't that just like my luck? A day late and a dollar short."

"Yeah, tough break."

"I'm guessing this ain't the only hotel in town. Maybe I'll find myself something real close by."

"It's a free country."

"That's what they tell me." He gave a half nod of his head. "Thanks for all the help, just the same. I'll be seeing you around."

"You know where to find me."

"That, I do," he said as he turned around and started for the front door.

He'd barely walked away when Curtis started in on me about turning away potential paying customers. "Mr. Buntemeyer would flip if he knew. Sixty percent of our rooms are empty."

"You're going to have to trust me on this one, Curtis. I've got a feeling he's not the kind of guest we need around here."

"I'm not so sure Mr. Buntemeyer would agree."

Rosie's little surprise visit was beginning to make more sense, even though I had no idea what was going on. A trip to the beach seemed in order.

Chapter Three

The beach and I aren't exactly chums. I'd had my issues with the Atlantic since taking some shrapnel to the leg on a beach a half a world away, but I was trying to put all that past me and get on with my life. I ignored the pounding waves in the background, her not so subtle taunts toward me, and limped through the sand toward a lone brunette on a beach blanket.

I still had that imaginary image in my head of Rosie in a bathing suit, but the real thing put that to shame. If the hot sun beating off the sand wasn't enough to take my breath away, the sight of Rosie sprawled out, wearing next to nothing, was the clincher. It was a lavender number that looked like it was sprayed on, and it might have been illegal to wear in public in more than a few states.

Catching my breath as best I could and ignoring the sweat running down my face, I squatted down next to her. She lifted her upper body on her elbows and crossed one of her perfect legs over the other, peering up over shaded spectacles. It was another Rosie pose, designed for maximum effect.

"How'd you sleep?" she purred.

"OK, Rosie, let's stop fooling around. Why are you really here?"

"Frankie, we talked about all this last night."

The mere mention of the night before got my head to pounding again. "Let's pretend last night is a little blurry to me. Why don't you spill it out, again."

Rosie laughed. "You always were a light weight."

I wasn't really, but Rosie had the unique ability to drink like a sailor, and she could always put me under the table. "Yeah, well, that aside, why are you here?"

"I came down for the sun."

"Rosie, I've known you a long time. You don't take vacations. There's no profit in it. What gives?"

She rolled those brown eyes like I was annoying her. "Frankie, when did you become so cynical?"

I was trying to keep my eyes aligned with hers and not let them wander down any farther. "All right, so you're on vacation. There's no law against that. Just so we understand each other."

"What we had was a long time ago. I'm not looking to take any strolls down memory lane and I'm not looking to jump start any old flings. It might look like I'm living the life of Riley down here but I don't own this place, I just work here. If you think you're going to waltz in here for a big score you're sadly mistaken."

"If this is how you treat your old friends, you're going to fall off a lot of Christmas card lists."

"Level with me, Rosie, why didn't you check in under your real name?"

Her eyes got wider. "I'm incognito."

"Hiding from all your adoring fans, are you?"

"Just looking for some privacy."

"All right, so that's how we're going to play it, huh?"

"Frankie, I think you're getting paranoid in your old age."

"Yeah, maybe I am. Maybe it was just paranoia when the big lug with the flat face and bad attitude came up and asked if I'd heard from you."

Rosie's face went pale and her jaw went slack.

"Do you want to tell me what you've gotten yourself into?"

Rosie was on her feet in a second. Gathering up her things, folding up her beach blanket.

"What's going on, Rosie?"

She stopped what she was doing long enough to shoot me a glare. "What did you tell him?"

"I told him if he had any brains he'd turn tail and get as far away from you as possible."

"Stop talking in circles, Frankie. What did you say to him?" She had reached over and grabbed me by the arm, squeezing tight through my sports coat.

"How about what he said to me?" I replied. "He knew who I was, and he knew we had a history. He knew you were coming here."

"Does he know I'm here now?"

"What have you got yourself into?"

She squeezed my arm harder. "Does he know I'm here?"

I hesitated for a moment before answering, giving her my best scolding parent look. "I told him we parted on bad terms, and I haven't seen you in better than a year."

Rosie let out a sigh of relief.

"I don't know whether he bought it or not. Something tells me he'll be back. He didn't seem like the type that gives up easy."

Rosie went back to gathering her things, scooping them up like she was in a hurry to get out of there.

"So, are you going to tell me what this is all about?"

She ignored me and went scurrying up the beach, trudging her way through the sand, back toward the hotel. It wasn't really working for me.

She hadn't made it five steps when I placed a hand on her bare shoulder and stopped her in her tracks. Rosie let out a huff and turned back toward me, looking up at me with those big browns.

"You're not going anywhere until you tell me what's going on."

She was giving me her puppy dog eyes. "Nothing is going on."

"Yeah, right, and I'm next in line for the throne of England."

"It's not what you think, Frankie."

"I think you're lying."

Right before me she seemed to melt into something else. Her features went all soft and vulnerable, her eyes wide and watery. "He hits me, Frankie."

"Who hits you?" I asked, picturing the gorilla in the blue suit putting his paws on her.

"Blake."

"The night club guy? The guy you told me meant nothing to you?"

"I don't know. I got caught up in all of it before I knew what was happening."

"You've been with that guy ever since we ..." I couldn't finish my sentence. Old memories came flooding back over me. I remembered what it had been like when she dumped me. I remembered seeing her in that bar with him, the dead carcass of our relationship not even stinking the joint up yet.

"He's a very important man. He has connections. The night club is just one of his business ventures. He has guys who work for him. They do things."

"What does that have to do with him putting his hands on you?"

"It was exciting at first. He had money and he would buy me things. He would take me to the nicest restaurants." She was tearing up pretty good.

"What does any of this have to do with me?"

"I started seeing a different side of him. Blake has a temper. He started getting angry with me. Nothing I did was good enough.

"The first time he hit me I left him. I walked right out and didn't speak to him for a week. He sent flowers and candy. He showed up on my doorstep with a fur coat. He apologized and promised it would never happen again.

"For a long time it didn't but then one day ..."

A single tear rolled down her cheek. "I don't know why I kept going back to him. I guess I'm just stupid like that. I really thought things would be different.

"Two months ago he gave me a black eye. I went to stay with my mother in Curtis Bay. I swore I'd never speak to him again. I told him to leave me alone, that we were done for good. He sent Ralphy to bring me back."

"Ralphy?"

"The guy with the flat face and bad attitude." She wiped her cheek with the back of her hand. "He's here to take me back. I didn't know where to turn, Frankie."

I took a moment, soaking it all in, trying to decide if she was on the level or simply handing me load of hogwash. I'd been played by Rosie before, and I knew from firsthand experience there weren't many lines she wasn't willing to cross to get what she wanted. It was part of her charm.

This time seemed different. There was something sincere and vulnerable in the way she stood looking up at me, her watering eyes squinting in the harsh sunlight. Her cheeks were flushed, the rest of her delicate face pale against her jet black hair. She was holding her beach things in tight against her body, like she was trying to shield herself from some unseen or unwanted advances.

"I shouldn't have come here, Frankie, I know. I didn't know who else I could turn to."

I knew right then and there I was a goner.

"We need to keep you under wraps," I said, before I had time to think. "He suspects you're here but he doesn't know for sure. We can hide you out in the hotel until we figure out what to do. That means you're going to have to lay low awhile."

"I can do that." Her entire demeanor seemed to perk up a few notches.

"You keep to yourself, take your meals in your room. No hanging out in the lobby or the bar or the restaurant and, especially, no more sun bathing on the beach."

"Whatever you say, Frankie."

"If we can keep you out of sight, maybe he'll figure you made a run for it and move on."

"He'll never stop looking for me. Blake wouldn't allow it."

"Yeah, well, maybe if he doesn't find you here he'll go look somewhere else. At least we can buy some time until we figure out someplace safe to put you."

"Frankie, I don't know how to thank you for this," she said, leaning in toward me and pressing herself into my chest. I instinctively wrapped my arms around her and held her soft body against mine, holding her like I had so many times before. My heart was racing and sweat was running down my brow. There was a tingling in the back of my neck and my mind was unable to lock onto anything other than the feel of her snuggled in against me. It felt natural. It felt familiar.

I was a goner all right.

Chapter Four

I walked Rosie back up to the hotel, stressing the importance of her staying out of sight. By the time we reached the elevator she was back to her old self, all flirty and girlish. Any signs of the scared young woman on the beach were completely gone.

"If you need anything, you call me. You don't have any contact with anybody else for the next few days."

"Sure, Frankie. Whatever you say," she replied like she was half listening.

"I'm serious, Rosie. The fewer people who know you're here the safer it is."

"I'll blend right in like I'm part of the woodwork."

At that moment the elevator arrived. It was manned by a young operator named Clifford. He was a skinny teenager with Ginger Snap hair and the kind of pale skin that burns from being too close to a light bulb. Clifford and I had been pals since before I'd started working at the hotel, and he was one of the few people I knew I could trust.

When he caught a glimpse of the hot number in the lavender swimsuit, as the doors opened, I saw him spring to attention like he'd spotted a Polar Bear in the lobby. I thought at first he was going to miss the floor but he brought the elevator to a sudden stop and pulled open the cage door like the thing was on fire.

"Going up?" he asked, a little too eagerly.

"Why, yes," Rosie answered in her friendliest tone. "Third floor, please."

Rosie stepped into the box and turned back toward me with a smile. Young Clifford stood slightly behind her, gawking at her like

25

she was made of strawberry ice cream. I could almost see him straining to keep his tongue in his mouth.

I pulled a five spot from my pocket and held it toward Clifford. "If anybody comes around asking about Miss Young, here," I said, holding the money for him to take, "you haven't seen her. You got that, Clifford?"

"Yes sir, Mr. McKeller," he answered while awkwardly closing the gate and reaching back for the elevator control lever. The entire time, he never took his eyes off the little barefoot brunette in the skimpy lavender bathing suit. So much so that he never noticed the fin I was holding out for him to snatch up.

Rosie shot me that smile and added a wink to it, like she was well aware of the stumbling young man fawning over her shoulder and like it was the most natural thing on earth. "Don't worry, Frankie. I'll keep to myself and nobody will even know I'm here."

"Yeah, I get it," I replied, sticking the five bucks back in my pocket. "You'll blend in like you're part of the woodwork."

I stood watching as the elevator jolted into action and began the slow ascent, up and away, my eyes locked on the various parts of Rosie as she rose out of sight. The image of her lingered in my head for a few moments after she was gone and I had to shake my head to let it go.

My next stop was the front desk where I made arrangements to have Rosie moved to a different room, just in case someone had spotted her coming and going from 309. From there I went down to my office and started making phone calls.

I still had connections in Baltimore and, although I wanted to trust Rosie, I figured I needed to check out her story as best I could. She was still Rosie, after all.

I remembered the Blake character from back when things had gone sour between me and Rosie. He was a pretty boy type who liked to throw money around and always wore expensive suits, tailor made. I remembered how I'd felt the first time I'd seen her with him, like I had no chance to compete.

Rosie was about the only one who ever called him Blake, and most people referred to him as Martin, his last name. I made some calls to some old friends and acquaintances, most of whom weren't so thrilled to hear from me.

The consensus was pretty much the same from everyone I talk-ed to. Martin was bad news. As far as I could gather he'd started out small time, running a little after-hours joint in Sowebo, which is what the locals called South West Baltimore City. He ran a little numbers racket on the side and business was good. He started in-vesting in other local businesses, neighborhood bars, a night club.

Nobody I talked to thought he was actually in the Mob, but most figured he had plenty of friends who were. Some said after he got his numbers racket going pretty good he turned it over to the mobsters, and in return they helped look after his business ventures. Either way, it sounded like he had connections.

When I met him he had the hottest night spot on Charles Street. They say his newest night club in Fells Point is even more popular.

Everyone I talked to said he traveled with an entourage. They also said he was seen around town a lot with beautiful brunette on his arm, one with a killer figure and long legs to die for. Maybe he wasn't mob, but it sounded like he liked to pretend he was. Either way he sounded dangerous and like the kind of guy who would have no trouble tracking down a helpless woman on the run.

As far as I could tell, Rosie's story checked out. As much of it as I could trace, at least.

I went back upstairs and saw to Rosie's move from the third floor to the ninth. I figured it would be better to keep her as far away from the other guests as possible. We still had close to a month before our season really kicked in so she'd be the only guest on the ninth floor for now. She complained about being so far up but I told her it was in her best interest.

When we switched her room, we conveniently left it off the books so that only myself, the desk clerk and Clifford, the elevator operator, knew she was still staying at the hotel. The fewer people who knew she was there, the better chance I had to keep it quiet. I even wrote it up in the log book like there was some kind of trouble with the plumbing in 918 so nobody would accidentally book another guest into the room. I figured I had most of the bases covered, and as long as Rosie cooperated we'd be just fine.

Once I had her settled in, I went about my regular hotel duties. Later that night I had dinner with her in her room. I brought up cheeseburgers from the Brookgreen Room, and we sat around, feasting, chuckling about old times.

We talked about all the good times we'd had together. Neither of us brought up any of the bad stuff. Neither of us mentioned the awkward circumstances of our initial meeting. Nobody said a word about the about the way it ended.

At one point, she placed her hand over mine and gave it a slight squeeze. "I always liked you, Frankie. You were always a real good egg."

A million memories flashed through my head when she said it. The bad ones I pushed away and wouldn't allow myself to think about.

"I always liked you too, Rosie. We had a lot of fun together."

"That we did," she said with a smile.

Chapter Five

The next morning came a little too soon for my liking. I awoke to a loud banging on my door. By the intensity and repetition, I figured it for my boss. It wasn't the first time Buntemeyer had begun my day like that.

I barely cracked the door open when Buntemeyer barreled his way into my room and began pacing back and forth.

"What do I pay you for, McKeller?"

"My cheerful disposition and the way I boost the morale of the other workers?" I tried.

"I pay you to be in charge of security around here. That means I expect my hotel to be secure under your watch. I don't expect my hotel to fall victim to acts of vandalism and destruction."

"I'm going to go out on a limb and say something happened."

"You're darn right something happened," Buntemeyer snapped back. "One of our rooms was broken into last night and torn to pieces."

"Torn to pieces?"

"Furniture was over turned, the mattress was slashed open. The place was wrecked. Do you have any idea what it's going to cost to put that back together and make it habitable again?"

"I can't be everywhere at once, boss. From time to time, things are going to happen."

"Did you even make your rounds last night? Did you see any suspicious characters lurking about?"

"Of course I did," I lied. "I didn't see anything out of the ordinary."

"Well someone went in there and trashed that room. It didn't happen by itself."

"It was probably just some kids being stupid."

"Kids being stupid? I want the perpetrator caught and brought to justice. I want someone to pay for ransacking my hotel room."

I let out a sigh. "I'll take a look and see what I can find but, I gotta be honest, I don't know how you expect me to find some random vandal?"

"You are the house detective, and I expect you to get to the bottom of this."

"All right, I'll go take a look. What room is it?"

"Room 309."

My heart stopped for a second. That was Rosie's old room, the one I moved her out of the day before.

"I'll get right on it, boss."

I ran a razor across my chin, threw some clothes on and took the elevator down to the third floor. Clifford was at his usual post.

"Don't they ever give you a day off, Clifford?" I asked as he took me down.

He chuckled. "Got to make that money, Mr. McKeller. Been putting in all the overtime they'll give me."

"Let me ask you something, Clifford. Did you see a guy last night, bulky fellow with a flat face?"

He didn't think for more than a couple of seconds. "Yeah, I had a guy like that in my elevator last night. Took him up to the third floor about nine o'clock."

"I kind of figured you might say that."

When I first got to the Ocean Forest, I remember thinking how huge the rooms seemed. Now that I had been around for a while, I no longer thought so. These days they seemed on the small side, cozy and comfortable but nothing large and lavish. This one looked even smaller, busted up and strewn with debris.

The room was trashed all right. Buntemeyer wasn't kidding about the expense to put it back together. It was going to be out of commission for a while.

Whoever did it left nothing in the room intact. All of the furniture had been tossed around, some of it busted up. Dresser drawers looked like they had been flung against the wall. The bed had been pulled apart and the mattress was sliced open. It looked like somebody was trying to send a serious message. I had a pretty good idea who that somebody was.

From there I went straight to Rosie's room to check up on her and make sure she was all right. She answered the door in a flimsy little nightgown that didn't leave a lot to the imagination. Her hair was tussled and unkempt and her eyes still sleepy and distant. She looked smaller and more frail than I was used to seeing, and it was all I could do not to throw my arms around her and hold her for all I was worth.

"What time is it?" she asked in a raspy morning voice.

"Early," I answered. "There's been an incident."

"An incident?" she smiled. "I like it when you talk all detectivey."

"Somebody broke into the room you were staying in and vandalized it, tore it to shreds."

Rosie gasped. "Ralphy?"

"That's my guess. Clifford says he took a guy up there last night who matches his description. I don't think it's safe for you here."

She walked over and sat on the edge of the unmade bed, the one she'd been cuddled up in moments before. I followed her in, closing the door and going over to sit next to her.

"How did he know?" she asked in a breathless whisper.

I shrugged. "People talk, a maid, a bellman, anybody could have tipped him off. They see a pretty girl coming and going. A guy comes along and asks a few questions. It wouldn't be difficult."

Rosie was staring up at me and her eyes were wide as saucers. "What do I do now?"

"I don't think you can stay here. He knows you're here."

The tears were welling up in her eyes. "Where am I going to go, Frankie?"

There was a knot in my gut the size of a fist. "I have some money. We can send you away, someplace he won't think to look."

"Where, Frankie? And what then? Do I just keep running for the rest of my life?"

"I don't know, Rosie. Maybe it will blow over after a while. Maybe Blake will move on, find another girl to sink his hooks into."

She leaned into me and hiked one of her tan bare legs over mine, snuggling herself into my side. I put my arms around her and held her in close, not knowing what to say or do.

She had her face against my chest and eased her chin higher until she was looking up at me with those big brown slices of heaven.

Staring back into them made me dizzy and the room began to spin around, but I couldn't look away. Her eyes held me locked, lost in some dream-like place I wanted to pack up and move to.

Rosie's lips parted slightly, like she was going to speak, but she never uttered a sound, and my eyes fell to her waiting lips, moist and inviting. I couldn't take it any longer.

I lowered my face to hers and pulled her in closer.

The kiss was like carnival music in my mouth. It was Christmas morning and the Fourth of July all rolled into one. Her hands were pulling at the back of my head pressing my face to hers, her head tilting off this way and that. I had my arms around her back, groping and exploring.

We fell back onto the bed, never losing the embrace, our lips locked, bodies clinging to each other. I was on top of her. Her hands were on either side of my face. My left hand was under her, the right holding her thigh, touching and kneading at the smooth soft skin of her leg.

The only sounds were breathless pants and moans, the occasional smack of lips embracing. My heart was racing, my breathing deep and frenzied, hers escaping in soft whimpers, each one sending me farther over the edge. Squeezing and touching her body, I moved my hand up and under the nightgown, over her hip and along her side, my fingers relishing the softness of her.

Through it all we continued to kiss, the slow, soft, furious and unrestrained kiss that felt like it began somewhere in my toes and merely manifested itself on her sweet, delicious lips. It was one, long, uninterrupted kiss that I thought might never end.

But it did end.

I felt her small hands pushing at my shoulders, and she tossed her head back, resting it on the bed and letting out a long-winded breath. I lowered my forehead onto her chest and began to take long steady gulps of air, trying to get my breathing under control.

"Wow," she sighed. "I forgot what a good kisser you are." Typical Rosie.

"You're not so bad yourself," I managed to pant, raising my head so I could look at her again.

"We can't do this, Frankie. Not now. There's too much going on."

"I don't know, seemed like just enough was going on to me."

Rosie reached up and placed one finger against my lips. "I want to, Frankie. I really do. It's just, with Blake hanging over my head, I don't think I can give myself to you completely."

"Right about now I'll take what I can get," I said through her finger.

"You know what I mean. It wouldn't be right. Not like this. I have to figure this mess out first."

"I get what you're saying, Rosie, but any chance we could figure that stuff out later?"

"You know how I feel about you, Frankie. I want to be with you again, but as long as he's out there ..."

"I don't see a lot of options there. It's not like he's just going to go away."

Rosie scooted herself up onto her elbows, lifting her torso and looking back at me. "You could make him go away, Frankie. You could make him go away forever."

The way she said it stopped me cold in my tracks for a second. I sat staring back into those hypnotic eyes, trying to wrap my brain around it. "What are you saying, Rosie? You want me to kill him?"

There was an awkward pause before she let out a nervous laugh. "No, of course not," she said like she wasn't so convinced. "Nothing like that. I meant you could go talk to him. Tell him we know he broke into the hotel room and trashed it. Tell him you put me on a train to New York or you booked me a flight, somewhere out West. Tell him anything, just convince him I left."

"Why would he believe me?"

"Why wouldn't he believe you? What am I, your crazy ex-girlfriend? Why would you want me around, especially if I brought trouble with me?"

"I don't know."

"You could do this, Frankie. I know you could. You're good at this stuff, I've seen you."

I stood up, looking down at Rosie, all sprawled out on the bed with her hair in tangles and her nightgown hiked up past her thighs. "Good at what stuff?"

She shrugged. "I don't know, stuff is all."

"Lying? Is that what you meant? Because I lied to your husband back in the day, I can lie to Ralphy, I can lie to Blake?"

Rosie was on her feet and at my side in an instant, trying to put her arms around me, but I kept backing away. "No, Baby, that's not what I meant. I just meant you're good at handling people and everything."

My juices were going pretty good. "I never felt good about that back then, you know that."

"Of course I know that, Frankie. I never liked it either. We did what we had to to be together."

"I always felt like a heel for doing it that way," I told her, admitting to it out loud for the first time. "It used to gnaw at my gut. I hated the way we did it."

Rosie folded her arms in front of her and gave me a look, not the flirty kind I was used to getting from her. "You think I'm proud of what we did? He was my husband, Frankie. I didn't like it either, but it was the only way we could be together."

I straightened my tie and returned the look she was giving me. "Yeah, that may be true, but I was the one taking his money at the same time."

Rosie didn't respond. She stood staring at me as I walked over to the door and let myself out.

Chapter Six

It's a funny thing about guilt. Sometimes you can convince yourself that you have nothing to feel guilty about, but once it's there it's a bitch to get rid of. Eventually it comes rolling back over you like waves in the ocean.

I had plenty of skeletons in my closet and had been dragging enough guilt around, over the years, to fill an oil tanker. The guilt I carried around over Oscar Carter was as big as any I was saddled with.

After I was wounded in the war, I spent nine months rehabilitating, learning to walk again. I'd never be able to do it without a limp, but I got to where I could get around pretty decent. I toyed with the idea of going back to work on the docks like I had before the Japs decided they didn't like the way Pearl Harbor was laid out, but it didn't appeal to me.

I got the crazy notion that I wanted to be a Private Eye, that I wanted a life full of adventure and intrigue. That didn't work out so much either.

I enrolled in the Staley School of Private Investigation, courtesy of Uncle Sam via the G. I. Bill. After six weeks of not so intense studies, I found a little office to rent downtown on Baltimore Street. What it lacked in size and comfort, it made up for in dirt and grime.

Times were lean in the early days. They weren't much better later on. After two months and five kinds of nothing, a guy came strolling into my office. My first potential client.

He was a likable bloke, easy going and personable. He didn't even care that I'd never had a real case before. He had a problem, and he wanted my help.

I'll never forget him. He was of medium height and stocky, a little on the overweight side, early forties with a receding hairline and a thick mustache. He wasn't rich but he held a steady job and made a decent living, well groomed and dressed nice in a conservative suit, pinstripes, usually. His name was Oscar Carter and I liked him from the get go.

It seems he had a wife. She was quite a bit younger and a real looker. Oscar was crazy about her.

They'd been married just under three years and Oscar started noticing that she was away from home more and more. She told him she was going to see her sister or visit a sick friend and Oscar never questioned her, not even when she started going to see sick friends more frequently and staying at her sister's till the wee hours of the morning.

By the time he came to me he just wanted to know. Like a lot of guys, he still couldn't make himself believe it, still held out hope he was wrong. It was my job to find out, once and for all.

I followed Rosie around for a week, from one little gin mill to another. She was the life of the party wherever she went and seemed to have a different guy in every bar she went to. There was always some stooge waiting to buy her a drink, wrap his arm around her, show her a good time.

She came and went like the breeze, but I never saw her leave with any of them. I didn't know what to report back to Oscar. All I'd ever seen her do was flirt and drink, maybe a quick peck every now and again, so I kept following her.

I told myself I was waiting to catch her for real, sneaking off to do the nasty with one of her boyfriends. The truth is, I liked following Rosie around. I was smitten.

Rosie hit me like a .45 slug to the chest the first time I saw her. She was like no woman I'd ever laid eyes on. She was sugar and spice and all the things I wanted to get my dirty little mitts on. Looking her in the eyes was enough to break my heart.

I don't know exactly when she made me, I never asked. I wasn't very good at the job back in those days, so it was probably pretty early on. On the seventh night of following her around from bar to bar, she walked over and sat beside me.

She said, "We seem to frequent the same haunts."

I stuttered and stumbled and said something like, "Yeah, I like to bounce around."

Rosie saw right through me. She looked me square in the eye and asked if I was working for Oscar. I couldn't lie. I didn't even try.

Lying to her husband came much easier for some reason.

We began seeing each other regular. The whole time I was reporting back to Oscar that his good little wife was visiting friends in Pigtown or at her sister's house in Lansdowne. He wasn't buying it. He was sure something was up so, he kept me on, determined to find out what was going on.

It got to where Rosie and I were seeing each other exclusively. She liked my company for some reason, and we became almost like a real couple. The whole time I was charging her husband thirty-five bucks a week plus expenses.

It never really sat right in my gut, what I was doing to Oscar. I tried to quit several times, but he begged and pleaded for me to stay on. He needed my help, and I was the only one he could trust. Besides, it wasn't like I didn't need the money, even when other clients and cases began to trickle in. Rosie was never what you would call a cheap date.

I was in over my head and didn't know up from down. All I knew was, when I was with Rosie it was all worth it. I couldn't get enough of her.

She was a good time—I'm not going to lie. I loved every minute with her. I loved walking into a joint with her on my arm and seeing the heads turn. I loved the craziness and the excitement of it all.

There was the physical part, of course. Amazing as it was, it isn't what I remember about being with her. What I remember was the way she made me feel. I remember getting lost in those big brown eyes. I remember when she laughed it was like being warmed by morning sunlight.

Oscar finally got fed up with my bogus reports and let me go. He never suspected what was really going on, but he got tired of paying good money to hear his wife was the perfect angel. He had to know something was fishy.

Money got tight and Rosie wasn't very happy about it. I was busting my ass trying to make a few bucks wherever I could, trying to see Rosie whenever I wasn't working.

One day she stopped calling.

I couldn't understand it.

I guess I kind of got my feelings hurt. I started hitting the bottle pretty good.

I tried calling her, but she didn't want to talk to me. If Oscar answered I'd hang up. If she answered, I'd try to speak with her, but she would end up hanging up.

I showed up on her doorstep, twice. Not some of my prouder moments. I remember trying to explain things to her, trying to ask her why I wasn't worth a thirty second phone call. She told me I was acting like a little girl.

Things get pretty dark and fuzzy from there. I proceeded to go on a four day bender.

One day I stumbled into a little gin mill on Calvert Street. Rosie was sitting at a table with Blake. I didn't know who he was at the time, and I didn't care. I waited until I saw her walking to the ladies room, and I made my move.

"Can we speak for a minute?" I asked as she came walking by.

"I don't think so," she answered and kept on walking. She didn't even slow down.

It was about as small as I ever felt.

I hit it pretty hard from there, drinking like I was on a mission. By two in the morning I was blind drunk and back in my office. The fifth of bourbon I'd put away made it seem like a good idea to try calling her again, to take one last stab at making her understand.

I don't know how many phone calls there were, I was too hammered to keep count. She answered a few times and told me to stop calling. Most of the time she let it ring.

Finally, Oscar picked up.

"That's enough, McKeller," he said. "My wife doesn't want to talk to you. It's over and if you show up here I'm going to call the cops."

Talk about your wake up calls. It was like coming out of a bad dream and realizing it wasn't a dream at all. There it was, pure and simple and from the horse's mouth.

"I'm sorry, Oscar," was all I could muster to say. In return I got a click on the other end.

So, there it is, my dirty little story. The one I've kept bottled up for all this time.

Rosie left a hole in me the size of Nebraska and I'd been trying to plug it with cheap bourbon and moonshine ever since. Seeing her again had opened it back up, and I was left with a sucking chest wound you could drive a Buick through.

Oscar left a scar on me too. His was the scar of shame and guilt. I'd done him wrong and played him in a way I didn't know I was capable of. My lust and desire for his wife turned me into the kind of person I didn't like very much, and seeing Rosie again reminded me of that too. It reminded me of how flawed I am and of the many times in my life I'd failed to measure up to being the man I wanted to be.

Chapter Seven

Despite the fact it was still early in the a.m., I headed down to my office for a couple of belts from the bottle I kept stashed in my filing cabinet. It was the only remedy I knew for the common Rosie.

The second was still burning in my throat when she appeared in my doorway. She had slipped into a white cotton dress that clung to her like it was wet and she had the top three front buttons undone. She wore it with flat sandals and bare legs.

Rosie stood leaning against the door jam, one knee cocked up in front of the other.

That guilt inside me was still eating at my innards and I needed to get it out. "Whatever came of Oscar?"

"What's the big deal with my husband? Why do you care?"

I shrugged. "I don't know. I just do."

She leaned her head against the doorway and let out a sigh, looking off to some distant spot behind me.

"It got to the point where I didn't want to be married anymore. I'd put it off for far too long. One day I came home and told him it was over, I wanted out. Oscar went crazy. He yelled and screamed, he cried and pleaded. He made you look pretty tame by comparison."

I ignored the comment.

"Oscar just lost it. He was calling me all the time, showing up with flowers and candy. He begged me for another chance, but I just couldn't do it. I just didn't feel it anymore.

"I didn't see him for a long time. Blake set me up with a place of my own. One day Oscar showed up at my door. I almost didn't recognize him. He told me hadn't been eating or sleeping in months and it looked it. He'd wasted away to about nothing. He confessed his undying love for me and told me we were destined to be together forever. He was half out of his mind.

"I felt sorry for him, I really did. I tried to explain that it was over, but he still didn't want to hear it, after all that time. He started showing up places, in my neighborhood, joints I would go with Blake. There were phone calls in the middle of the night, hang ups mostly, but I knew it was him. He would send me stuff, gifts and such. It got to be pretty creepy. It got to be where I was afraid to go anywhere.

"Finally, I went to Blake about it. He sent Ralphy to go have a talk with him. After that, I stopped seeing Oscar around. Even the phone calls stopped."

I took a moment, soaking in her story. Part of me took some solace in the fact I wasn't the only lunk-head who'd lost my cookies over Rosie. There was even a part me that was glad Oscar had gone so much farther over the deep end then I ever had. Most of me just felt guilty for the part I'd played in another man's misery.

Rosie lifted her head and looked at me, back in the moment. "Up there earlier, I didn't mean to insult you." she said.

I thought about Oscar. I thought about me back when it all went down. "You should have talked to me, Rosie."

"I was talking to you."

"Back then, when you dumped me. You cut me off cold turkey, and you wouldn't give me the time of day."

"You were acting crazy."

"One day you were the most important person in my life," I replied. "The next I wasn't worth answering a phone for."

"It was a long time ago."

"I thought we had something, Rosie."

Rosie did a little sashay thing, into the room, closing the office door behind her. She came up to the far side of the desk and leaned over it, palms on the desk, arms extended and turned in.

"It was pretty good for a while," she said, looking down at me in my chair.

"I thought so."

Her lips curled up into a smile. "You like to play the tough guy but you were always a softy at heart. You put up a good front, McKeller, but deep down inside you're just like the rest of us."

"Don't kid yourself. I'm pretty tough."

"Yeah, when you want to be but, underneath, you're just a big ole softy."

"Am not," was all I could come up with.

"That's what this is all about, isn't it? I broke your heart back then, didn't I?"

"I'm a big boy. I got over it."

She was looking at me like she could see right through me. "I don't think you did. I think you're still carrying that torch around for me."

"Don't flatter yourself."

"If it makes you feel any better, I always cared about you, Frankie. What we had was always special to me."

"It doesn't."

"I've always regretted the way it ended."

"Don't do this, Rosie."

"I'm serious. I think about you all the time, wondering what it would be like if we were still together. Why do you think I came down to see you?"

"I think you came down because you were in trouble, and you needed help. You figured me for an easy mark."

Rosie shook her head slowly, side to side. "I could have gone to anyone, Frankie. I came to see you."

She was leaned over the desk as far as she could go, her weight resting on her arms, an arch to her back that set all the soft curves of her on display. She was so close I could smell the flavor of her toothpaste.

"What kind of schmuck do you take me for?" I asked.

"I don't know, Frankie. Seeing you like this, after all this time, it stirs up feelings I didn't know I still had. It makes me wonder about things. It makes me wonder if there's still a chance for us."

It was classic Rosie. She was playing me, I was sure of it. She was telling me everything she thought I wanted to hear, and she expected me to turn to warm butter in her hands. I'd been down that road before, and I'd swallowed her load of hogwash more times than I could remember. Unfortunately for me, I was still that same schmuck that couldn't resist her.

"What are we going to do about our broken hearts?" she purred.

I stood from my chair and met her in the middle of the desk, placing my hand behind her neck and pulling her face into mine for another long, breathless kiss. We stayed like that for a while, kissing and tasting each other like it was the first time, like it was the last kiss we'd ever have.

I had simmered for about as long as I could simmer before I reached my boiling point. I swept my left arm across the desk, clearing it with one swipe. There was the sound of shattering glass and the shuffling sound of papers, the phone hitting the floor with a thud and a half dead ring. With my other hand I turned her around and laid her across the now clear surface, climbing up and hovering over her.

We were on top of the desk, her beneath me, both of us hanging half off the small space. Both her hands were working my tie loose, my hand unbuttoning the buttons down the front of her. The entire time we never stopped kissing.

My brain had ceased to function and my body went through the motions, completely out of my control. Clothes came off and were tossed aside, our bodies closing together into the familiar bond we had shared so many times before.

A little voice in the back of my head kept telling me it was a mistake but I refused to listen.

I could watch Rosie get dressed every day for the rest of my life and never get tired of it, the way she primps and pulls and gathers everything perfectly into place. Neither of us said a word as we dressed ourselves.

When she was decent again, she walked over and gave me a kiss on the cheek. "Do you feel better now?"

"Look, Rosie..." I started to say, but she cut me off.

"It's fine, Frankie. It was fun. It was like old times."

"Things got a little crazy," I added.

She shrugged those skinny shoulders. "As I remember, we never had any problems in that department."

My heart was still pumping hard, and I felt light headed and weak. Rosie looked soft and dreamy, fit snug into the thin white dress, her dark hair hanging free and slightly wild. She leaned herself against me and tucked her face into my chest. I had my arms around her and was holding her in close.

"What now?" she asked.

"I don't know."

"Maybe you're right, Frankie. I should go away, just disappear."

"No."

"It's better for everybody."

"No."

"Maybe I can go someplace they won't be able to find me."

"No, Rosie. You can't go like that. Not now."

"I can't stay here. It's only a matter of time before he finds me."

I tried to swallow away the lump in my throat, but it wasn't going anywhere. "I'll go see Ralphy. I'll talk to him. Maybe I can convince him you've already left, that you're back on the run."

Rosie looked up at me. "You don't have to do that, Frankie. It's not your problem."

"Yeah, it kind of is," I replied.

Chapter Eight

This was a bad idea. I knew it from the start. I didn't know the Ralphy character very well but I was reasonably sure he wasn't the kind of guy I could sit down and have a pow-wow with. I knew his background, and I didn't figure him for the friendly chit chat type.

I thought about taking my .45 along, just in case, but I thought better of it. The thing about taking a gun with you is you better be prepared to use it. I was hoping it wouldn't come to that.

Instead, I decided to go with my trusty blackjack. It was pretty basic as far as weapons go, a six inch leather pouch, half of it a handle, the business end filled with lead. I hoped it would be enough.

I made some calls around town and figured out he was staying at the Chesterfield Inn. He was even checked in under his real name.

He answered the door in his shirt sleeves, no tie, wide shoulders and beefy arms straining the fabric of his open shirt. Everything about him looked rough and meaty.

"Ain't this a pleasant surprise?" he asked with sarcasm.

"Can we talk a minute?"

Ralphy opened the door wider and motioned me an invite with a jerk of his head. I was wondering if it was a mistake, going in, not standing my ground in the hallway, but I went in anyway.

"It worked," I said after he'd shut the door behind me.

"Is that so? And just what might that be that worked so well?"

"Your little device to smoke Rosie out," I replied.

"My little device, huh?"

"It worked like a charm. Trashing the hotel room really put the scare in her, let her know you meant business. Only problem is, it worked a little too well. She skipped town."

"Is that right?"

"I put her on the train myself."

"And just where might she be heading?"

"The ticket says Buffalo but I wouldn't be surprised if she got off somewhere earlier, maybe hops on another one heading West."

"You ain't so bright, are you, McKeller?"

"I can see where you might think that." I shrugged. "I usually play to the crowd. I tend to dumb it down, depending on the company I'm in."

Ralphy chuckled. "This is what you and your little girlfriend came up with? Some trashed hotel room, and she's off on a train to who knows where?"

"That's the way it is, like or not."

"I don't like being screwed with."

"I'd think you'd be used to it."

Ralphy moved pretty good for a big ox. Before I knew what was happening, he lowered his shoulder and bull rushed me into the wall so hard it knocked the wind out of me. I was still trying to gasp in some air when he slugged me in the jaw.

The punch turned me sideways and Ralphy took hold of my shoulder, following through with my momentum, turning me completely around and slamming me face first into the wall. An instant later he had my arm twisted up behind me in a chicken wing hold. He applied pressure and a surge of pain ripped through my body, like he was taking my arm off. When I tried to struggle he simply lifted my wrist a quarter inch higher and the excruciating fire in my arm and shoulder brought me to a sudden stop.

He had me pinned against the wall, my right arm folded up behind me, my left hand pressing against the surface, searching for a way to brace myself against his attack. He had me right where he wanted me.

"It's a funny thing about bones," he said in a voice as calm as a Sunday school teacher's. "They're usually pretty strong but you twist them just right and you can snap'em like a twig." He applied a bit more leverage to illustrate his point.

My face was pressed into the wallpaper and I was grunting pretty good, still trying to fill my lungs with some oxygen.

"I don't know what kind of game you're playing here, McKeller. Maybe you think you're dealing with some two-bit, country bumpkin but we don't play it that way in the big city."

I let out another grunt.

"You don't know me very well, but I'm a pretty trusting guy. Once you break that trust and start lying to me, it makes it hard for me to trust you anymore." He gave my arm another little twist and I followed suit with a few more moans and grunts.

"You lied to me yesterday when you told me you hadn't seen Rosie in over a year." Another twist and more groveling by me.

"I'm guessing it was you who called my room last night and told me Rosie was in room 309 at the Ocean Forest. I wasted a lot of my valuable time going over there to find an empty room."

"Is that why you ripped the place to shreds?" I grunted back to him.

Another flick of my wrist that sent lightning bolts shooting through my body.

"What kind of amateur do you take me for? Why would I tear up an empty hotel room?"

"I don't know," I answered through clenched teeth. "Maybe you didn't like the decor.

"You two are playing some silly game, running me around. Rosie's in room 309, somebody trashed an empty hotel room, Rosie's on a train heading to Buffalo ..."

My right arm was wedged up behind me, farther than it was meant to go. My left was free but my blackjack was in the right side pocket of my sports coat. I eased my free hand down the wall and tried to squeeze it in between me and the hard surface.

"I don't like silly games," he snarled. He was pressed in behind me, his head in close to mine.

Arching my back to make room to get my hand past my gut put more pressure on my arm and shoulder, and I could feel tears of pain swelling in my eyes, but I forced myself to hold firm and continue on. I squeezed my left arm in between me and the wall, forcing it through.

"That girlfriend of yours is a piece of work. A real ball buster."

My left hand was out past my right side but there wasn't much room to work with. My fingertips barely reached the very edge of my jacket, and I couldn't get enough to grab hold.

"She's made a lot of enemies, McKeller."

When Ralphy gave my arm another painful twist, it shifted my body, and I was able catch the edge of my coat in my fingertips, barely enough to hold it. I began working my fingers, pulling the fabric toward me an inch at a time.

"She took something from my boss and he wants it back. If I have to snap your arm in two and break your shoulder bone to send her a message, so be it. That bitch is going to learn."

Once I had enough cloth in my fist, I pulled and groped at it, working the loose hanging side toward me, searching for where the pocket opened up.

"She done screwed with the wrong people this time."

Two fingers were all I could work into the pocket but it was enough to grab hold of the blackjack, and I was able to ease it out of my pocket. I struggled to position it into my palm, wrapping my fingers around it, holding it tight in my fist.

"I hope she was worth it, McKeller, when you're spending the rest of your life wiping your ass with your other arm."

I arched back again, trying to ignore the burning sensation it caused in my shoulder, forcing my left hand up, squeezing it between my body and the wall, up past my chest, until I had it positioned at my right shoulder.

"You just remember, it didn't have to go down like this. Mr. Martin just wants what's rightfully his."

Ralphy was pretty cocky by now. He was leaned in and over my shoulder, talking into my ear, wet angry words I was trying to block out. I knew I'd only get one shot at it. I also knew there was a pretty good chance my arm was going to get snapped in the process. I figured, odds were, that was going to happen either way.

"You might want to take a deep breath," he sneered. "This is going to hurt a lot."

He was leaned in against my ear, his face in close to my head. In one quick motion I brought the blackjack up over my shoulder and swung it down as hard as I could across his face. There wasn't much room but it was just enough and it caught him by surprise. He stumbled back half a step and the tension on my shoulder let up for a split second. I backed myself into him and put a foot to the wall, kicking myself back into him and sending us both toppling over, him on his back, me on top of him.

He'd lost his grip on my wrist and I rolled myself across him, turning myself about so I came up on my knees with him lying in front of me. He started to sit up.

My right arm was numb and useless but I still had the blackjack tight in the grip of my left hand. Before he could get his bearings, I swung my hand around with all the juice I could muster. I caught him in the left temple, and the lead filled blackjack made a dull thud sound when it connected. His eyes went dull and his body limp. I caught him just right.

I back peddled myself until I was up against the far wall and sat resting against it, massaging my right arm, catching my breath. Ralphy was passed out cold, taking deep even breaths, a purple bruise beginning to show on his temple.

I was reasonably sure my arm wasn't broken, but it was throbbing and weak, and it was minutes before I could move my fingers again. I figured it was going to be sore for a while, but I'd live.

Ralphy was beginning to stir, moaning and shifting about. I decided it wasn't such a good idea to be there when he came to. He might have a little payback in mind, and I wasn't so sure there was much chance of me getting lucky with him a second time around.

Chapter Nine

Things couldn't have gone much worse. I hadn't accomplished anything, unless you counted nearly getting my arm broke and pissing off the big guy. If anything, I had made a bigger mess out of everything and, chances were, I'd put Rosie and me in more danger.

I went straight to Rosie's room to give her a report on what happened. Of course, I got no answer. Why would I think for a second she'd heed my advice and lay low?

I tried the bar, the restaurant, the beach and the lobby. No sign of Rosie.

My shoulder was aching, my elbow ablaze with a steady burning sensation. Even my bum leg was giving me fits. With nothing else to do but wait, I hobbled over to one of the big comfy chairs in the lobby and plopped myself down. I leaned back into the soft cushion and lowered the brim of my fedora over my eyes, letting myself totally relax for what seemed the first time in ages.

My mind drifted. I thought about my encounter with big Ralphy, all the mistakes I'd made, how I'd let my guard down and nearly had my arm ripped off. I thought about Rosie, wondering where she was, what she was doing.

I used to do that a lot, back in the day. After she dumped me I made a regular habit of sitting at my desk with a bottle of rot gut and wondering what Rosie was doing, who she was with. I about drove myself crazy.

I was pretty much useless for the first couple of months. Sure, I could pull it together when I had to, when a paying client had a job for me, but the rest of the time I sat around in a funk, wondering why, feeling sorry for myself.

My case load was picking up some. It's not like I was busy but I was getting enough to get by on. Pretty much everything I was getting were infidelity cases, following some husband or wife to a sleazy motel. Nine out of ten times the client was right. Almost every time I'd go back and report their spouse was running around with somebody else, their suspicions confirmed.

In a sick way I almost enjoyed it. At least I wasn't the only sap who'd had it handed to him. I wasn't the only lunk-head wallowing in self-pity and despair. I was a member of a not-so-exclusive club.

I can't say how many times I picked up a phone and started to dial Rosie's number, how many letters I started but never finished, never sent.

If there was one good thing to come out of it, thanks to Rosie, I got pretty good at my job. It was all I had and I threw myself into it completely. I got to where I could follow anybody almost anywhere. I learned to be discreet and stealthy, how to blend into a room or sink into a shadow. If I was on your tail, chances are, you'd never know it. Not until your wife or husband handed you that manilla envelope with all the evidence they'd need to turn your life upside down.

The thing about surveillance work is it's a lonely job. It gives a guy plenty of time to beat himself up, to mull things over in his head. Sometimes I'd be sitting in a bar or standing across the street from some fleabag motel, and I'd catch myself talking out loud, talking to Rosie, telling her all the things I wanted to say but never got the chance. If that isn't the definition of pathetic, I don't know what is.

It got easier over time. Eventually I got to where I was thinking about her less and less. Before long, I could sit through a movie or hear or a song on the jukebox that didn't remind me of her. I even stopped having those one-sided conversations with her.

Maybe that's why I was so surprised when I heard myself say out loud, "Where in the hell are you. Rosie?"

Old habits die hard.

"Who is Rosie?" A voice tugged me back to reality.

I looked up to find Simmons staring down at me. I jumped up and snatched the hat off my head, slightly embarrassed he'd caught me having a private moment to myself.

"So, who's Rosie?" he asked again.

"My pet Cocker Spaniel, ran away from home a few days ago."

"Really? I would have figured you for a cat guy."

"Is there something you need?"

"Yeah, as a matter of fact, there is. If you're not too broken up about Rover, maybe you could give me the grand tour. I want to be familiar with the layout when the senator gets here."

"I'm not much of a tour guide."

He glanced back at the chair I was about to doze off in. "Yeah, I can see you're really busy. Maybe you could squeeze me into your schedule."

I shrugged. "I guess my pedicure can wait."

We went by the front desk and picked up the key for the Presidential Suite on the tenth floor, then hopped on the elevator. Clifford was unusually quiet and business like as he took us up.

"How long you been pulling security for Wright?"

"Couple a years," he replied without looking back at me.

"Before that?"

"You writing a book?"

"I'm just naturally curious," I said. "And I like to know who I'm dealing with."

Simmons took a deep breath and let it out. "NYPD, fifteen years."

I should have guessed. He had the look of a big city cop, the attitude too. He even had the smell of one, a mix of cigarettes, pastrami and cheap cologne. Replace the pastrami with bourbon, and he smelled a lot like me.

The Presidential Suite at the Ocean Forest was about as nice as things get. It took up most of the top floor in the center tower of the hotel. If you've never seen the Ocean Forest, it's a long sprawling hotel, stretched out over what would be about three city blocks, three floors high on the sides, ten stories jetting up in the center. The locals call her the Castle in the Sand. It fits.

The Suite opens up to a large, open living area, complete with a couple of plush sofas and matching chairs spread around some imported mahogany tables. The little set up probably cost more than I make in a year. There's a fully-stocked bar off to one side that seats more people than some dives I've hung out in. Back past the bar is an intimate little dining area that seats eighteen.

Off to the back side of the hotel are two glass-paned doors which open up to a terrace and a view of the Atlantic that few people ever get to experience. I'm not much for the ocean these days, but I have to admit, the view from up there is pretty spectacular, something off a picture postcard.

I almost forgot to mention the four bedrooms and three baths that are connected to the suite, in case you're looking for a little privacy, each one immaculate and luxurious. This was serious living and it cost some serious money to stay in.

Simmons didn't seem too impressed as he walked around, opening doors and getting familiar with the layout. I guess deluxe accommodations were just part of the deal when you travel with a senator.

"Stairs?" he asked.

"Back out in the hallway and to the right. They run down the south side of the building."

"How many more rooms on this floor?"

Rooms? This was a little more than your average hotel room. "Just one." I answered. "The Honeymoon Suite. It's set up a lot like this but not as deluxe, just two bedrooms."

Simmons nodded. "How many rooms below us?"

"Twenty. It's set up like the rest of the floors."

"Let's go take a look."

"There's not much to see, a hallway with a bunch of doors. Nobody's even staying on the ninth floor right now." There was no need to tell him about Rosie.

"Yeah, well, let's go take a look anyway."

We took the steps down to the ninth floor, Simmons inspecting every nook and cranny along the way. As I opened up the door that led into the far end of the hallway, I was surprised to see a man standing a few doors down, right outside of room 918, Rosie's room. He was standing and waiting like he'd just knocked.

"Nobody staying down here, huh?" Simmons said with a little edge to his voice.

I didn't recognize the guy. He was tall and lean, athletic looking and a few years younger than me. He had sandy blondish hair, cropped long, parted lazily to one side and he was dressed casual, tan slacks, white shirt, open collar.

"Can I help you with something?"

The kid looked up and smiled a million dollar smile. "No thanks," he said all chipper and friendly. "Just visiting a friend."

"Yeah, I think maybe you got the wrong room. This floor is unoccupied at the moment."

The guy looked at the door and then down the hall, like he was trying to get his bearings. "Oh, OK. My mistake." With that he turned and headed away, back toward the elevator.

There was something about his voice, his accent or lack thereof. It sounded familiar and reminded me of home.

Simmons monopolized my time for the next forty-five minutes, making me take him through about half of the hotel, poking and prodding, getting his lay of the land. He took his security assignment pretty seriously. When he'd had his fill, he dismissed me like I was one of his lackeys.

"You sure that's all you need?" I asked. "Maybe I could whip you up a sandwich or something."

The first thing I did was cruise by Rosie's room, but she still didn't answer. From there I went down to the front desk. Curtis was at his usual station.

"Curtis, do we have a young guy staying here, blondish hair, good looking?"

"Do you know the name?" Curtis asked.

I shook my head.

"Kind of tall, thin?"

"Yeah, that sounds about right. Northerner, maybe from Maryland or Pennsylvania?"

"Yeah," he checked in a couple of days ago," Curtis said, thumbing through the check-in log. "I haven't seen him around much, but he's here. There he is, Taylor Mills, room 418."

I turned the book toward me and gave it a read. He'd checked in the same day as Rosie. "Have you seen Miss Young around today, the brunette—"

"With the long legs?" He finished my sentence. "Did I ever. I just saw her go by not long ago in a bathing suit with a towel over her shoulder. She was heading downstairs."

I left a grinning Curtis at the front desk and headed downstairs. I had a pretty good idea where I'd find her. If you wanted to go to the beach, the back door is straight out the lobby. Downstairs held a variety of things at the Ocean Forest. There was the bar, the Brookgreen Room, plus a gift shop, a barber shop, a bowling alley and a large indoor pool.

The pool room opened up to a plate glass window on the ocean side of the building. There wasn't much to it unless you counted the long narrow concrete pond dug into the floor. It was 45 yards long and 25 wide, and they kept it filled with fresh saltwater piped in straight from the ocean. People swore by the healing properties of saltwater and it wasn't uncommon to find groups of old ladies sitting on the edge of the pool, soaking their bunions in the water.

Today it was empty except for a lone woman swimming laps in a tight fitting one piece bathing suit and a swim cap. The suit was blue, and I stood in the musky hot air, watching Rosie kick and paddle the length of the pool, dipping under the water and turning herself around, heading back to the other end.

She was poetry in the water, her body in complete synchronization, her arms working in time with her legs, gliding herself smoothly through the murky water, each part of her flexing and contracting. It was the breast stroke and her head lifted and fell with each stroke, perfect fluid movements propelling her the length of the pool. I didn't even know she could swim.

I stood watching in awe for a while, until she came to a stop at the near end, reaching her arms back over the edge and holding herself half in and half out of the water. She had her back to me and I didn't think she knew I was there.

"You can join me, you know?" she said without turning around. Of course she knew I was there. Rosie always knew.

"I'm not much of a swimmer."

"Maybe I could teach you sometime."

"I thought we agreed you were going to lay low?"

"I got bored. I needed to get out of the room for a while."

"That wasn't the agreement."

"Don't be such a fuddy-duddy, Frankie. A girl's allowed a little fun from time to time." She peeled the rubber swim cap from her head and her thick dark mane came rushing down over her bare shoulders, tumbling out in every direction. She turned and looked at me, giving me the full effect, a slight twinkle in her eye.

"Don't you want to know how it went with Ralphy?"

"I figured you'd get around to telling me."

"It didn't go so good."

"Oh well, we tried."

"I was lucky to get out of there with my arm in one piece."

Rosie turned herself around, supporting herself on her elbows, still hanging half in the water, kicking her feet slightly. "You look like you fared all right, no black eyes, no broken bones ..."

"He didn't buy it, Rosie. All I ended up doing was pissing him off. He'll be back looking for you."

"I guess we'll just have to think of something else." She said it like she didn't have a care in the world.

"It's going to get ugly."

"You worry too much, Frankie. Why don't you come in and take a dip with me?"

I ignored the invitation. "Do you have any friends in the hotel I should know about?"

"Just you."

"No young guys with blondish hair, maybe down from Maryland?"

Rosie giggled. "There's that Frankie paranoia I miss so much."

"Level with me, Rosie. You don't know a guy staying at the hotel?"

Her smile grew wider. "Are you jealous?"

"I'm concerned. You've been known to steer me in the wrong direction before."

"I am here by myself, Frankie. I am totally and completely yours."

Chapter Ten

Rosie said she was tired and wanted to get some sleep. She didn't invite me to join her. That was all right by me, my arm, shoulder and leg were all killing me, and a good night between the sheets sounded like just what I needed.

I swung by the kitchen for a ham and cheese on rye and took it up to my room. My plan was to eat and pass out, meet Rosie early the next day and figure out a plan. I wasn't two bites into my sandwich when the knock came to my door.

It was too calm and business like to be Buntemeyer, my boss, too firm and steady to be Rosie. I hadn't heard Ralphy's knock yet so I took my blackjack with me to answer, just in case.

Sheriff Talbert was the last person I expected to find on the other side.

Talbert was sheriff and disciplinarian for Myrtle Beach proper, the last word and strong arm over everything that went down in *his* town. He was a wiry fellow with a steel jaw and the disposition of a tugboat.

He also had never been a big fan of yours truly, so I figured he wasn't there for a social call.

"Hi, Sheriff. If you had called first, I would have popped up some popcorn."

"Always with the jokes, McKeller."

"Jokes? You've never had my popcorn."

"Do you want to tell me what you were doing at the Chesterfield Inn this afternoon?"

"I like to check out the competition, see who's hiring."

Talbert shot me a look. "You didn't happen to see a guy named

Henderson, did you, Ralph Henderson?"

"Why, did he file a complaint?"

"That would have been tough for him to do, what with the three bullet holes in his chest. I think his complaint days are over."

I could only imagine how white I turned.

"Do you have something to tell me, McKeller?"

My mind couldn't quite wrap itself around the news, and thoughts were zipping through my head like ricochet bullets. I was going to have to tell the good sheriff something, but I was on slippery ground. One slip of the tongue, and I could easily find myself the lead suspect in a murder case. There was Rosie to consider too. I had to keep her distanced from this thing until I could get some kind of handle on it.

"Yeah, I knew Ralphy. I went to see him this afternoon."

"See him about what?"

I shrugged. "We were both from Baltimore, had some mutual friends. He stopped in to see me at the hotel the other day, told me to stop by and catch up. I went over, shot the breeze with him for a little while and left. He was alive and breathing when I left him."

"You sure the breeze is all you shot?"

"Like I said, he was in one piece the last I saw him."

"Did you know this guy well?"

I thought for a second, picking my lies as carefully as I could. "Not really, we were both from Baltimore, like I said, we had some mutual friends. I don't know a lot about him but I do know he was kind of a shady character. He worked for some unsavory types up north. I'm guessing he made his share of enemies along the way."

"And you wouldn't happen to be one of them?"

"Sheriff, I barely knew the guy."

"You didn't take a swing at him with something, did you? A bell-hop reported seeing you leave, twenty minutes later room service delivered some ice to his room, said he was holding a towel to the side of his head when he answered the door. When we found him, besides the bullet holes, he had a pretty good whelp on his noggin, looked pretty fresh."

"I guess that proves he was still alive when I left him," I offered.

"It doesn't prove you didn't run home and get a gun, maybe go back for a return visit. I'm going to ask you again, did you take a swing at him?"

"Take a look at me, Sheriff? Did you see the size of that guy?"

Talbert was staring me down. "Something don't add up here, McKeller. I don't know what, but I know it seems every time there's trouble in this town, your head seems to pop up in the middle of it."

"I guess I'm just lucky like that."

"Well, Mr. Lucky, what do you say me and you take a little ride downtown? I have a few more questions that need answering." I always got a kick out of it when someone called downtown Myrtle Beach downtown. It was about a three block cluster of buildings surrounded by beach homes, empty lots and sand, not exactly downtown Baltimore.

"Sure, you know me, Sheriff, always willing to cooperate with law enforcement."

"Yeah," he said with a snarl.

The next few hours weren't much fun. Talbert questioned me from every angle he could think of, but I didn't have a lot to give him. What little I knew I had to keep to myself to keep Rosie out of the picture. I wasn't sure it was the smart play, but until I could get away and talk to Rosie, it was all I had.

I got the feeling Talbert was chomping at the bit to lock me up, and the fact Ralphy was seen after I was spotted leaving was the only thing keeping me out of the hoosegow.

The entire time he was questioning me, I was running my encounter over in my head. Something was gnawing at me, something Ralphy had said. At the time, I'd been more concerned about getting to my blackjack and had tuned him out for the most part, concentrating more on what I had to do than what he was saying.

It was coming back to me now, thanks to the sheriff's intense line of questions. Ralphy had said something about Rosie taking something from Martin, about getting it back. It didn't jive with Rosie's story about being on the run from an abusive boyfriend, but it added up. Rosie had played me again. She'd played Martin too and had taken something from him, something important enough to send his strong arm to get it back.

It was well after midnight by the time Sheriff Talbert decided he wasn't going to get anything else out of me. "You make sure you stay real close to home. Don't go wandering off anywhere, this ain't over yet," he told me.

"Whatever you need, Sheriff."

"And just so we're clear," he said with a grunt. "This is an official homicide investigation, in case you get any bright ideas about poking your nose where it doesn't belong."

"Sheriff, you ought to know me better than that. I like to keep to myself and mind my own business."

"Yeah, you're a regular hermit."

Deputy Dale dropped me off at the hotel, and I went straight up to Rosie's room. Again, I got no answer at the door. I stopped by the front desk where Curtis reported he hadn't seen her since she'd headed back up from her swim. He was reasonably sure he would have noticed if she'd come walking by.

Not being able to talk to Rosie was making me crazy, a lot like it used to in the old days. This time there was more than my broken heart on the line. This time it was my neck, and the fact she conveniently disappeared from sight about the time Ralphy showed up dead got me to thinking. I didn't like the way things were adding up, and it made me wonder just how far this game of hers went. It got me wondering about the guy with the shaggy blonde hair, too.

I thought about making a visit up to 418, but on the off chance he wasn't somehow connected to Rosie, I thought better of it. Buntemeyer, my boss, frowns upon his employees disturbing guests after midnight for no good reason.

Instead, I decided a drink might be in order, so I headed down to the Brookgreen Room for a nightcap.

The bar was a quiet. There was a young couple at one end, cozied up together and whispering in each other's ears, nursing a couple of glasses of wine. There were three guys sitting at a table, keeping to themselves, and an elderly couple at another table with coffee drinks.

I took a seat and ordered up a bourbon with a water chaser. A guy has to stay hydrated, after all.

My thoughts were drifting back to Rosie, like usual. This time it wasn't the hum drum melancholy of how she'd broken my heart or left me cold. This time it was more wondering just how far she was willing to take things to get what she wanted.

Was it possible that my sweet little conniving Rosie was capable of much worse than I'd ever thought possible? Was she willing to cross the line between lying, cheating and using men to actually killing one? Could it even be possible that the girl I thought I knew so well had that kind of ice in her veins?

One of the guys from the table behind me came over and took the empty bar stool beside me. I barely glanced over, still lost in my thoughts about Rosie.

You would think I'd be better at this stuff after all this time on the job. You'd think I'd learn to pay closer attention to my surroundings, but I tend to get lazy. I didn't even notice it was Blake Martin sitting next to me.

"Can I buy you a drink?" he asked, "You look like you've had a rough day."

Martin looked about like I remembered. He was tall and slightly stocky, dark hair, darker eyes, a thin mustache on his upper lip. His expression was friendly and serious at the same time, a knowing look in his eyes. He was wearing a blue pinstriped suit with a gold tie. It looked brand new and perfectly tailored.

"You got here quick. The body isn't even cold yet."

"Yeah, that's ... unfortunate. The truth is, I was already on my way. Ralphy called and said he found her, so I headed straight down. I found out about Ralphy when I got into town."

"Maybe you got here a little earlier. Maybe you didn't like the job he was doing and decided to teach him a little lesson."

Martin laughed. "That wouldn't be very good business on my part."

"Well, I don't know exactly how you do business."

"We've never been properly introduced. My name is Blake, Blake Martin. You're Rosie's ex, McKeller, right?" He held out his hand for me to shake. I opted for the rest of my bourbon instead.

"I remember you."

"Yeah, I seem to remember you too. I remember seeing you around sometimes when I was out with Rosie in the old days. I recall you'd just show up where we were sometimes, sit alone at the bar drinking, watching us from across the room."

I might have forgotten to mention that part, the way I'd show up at our old haunts, hoping to run into her, hoping she might decide to give me the time of day. All I ever saw was her hanging all over

Martin. I was pretty pathetic for a while.

"Back then," he said, "I offered to take care of it for her, send one of my boys to have a little talk with you, get you to leave her alone. She felt sorry for you and asked me not to, said you were harmless. I guess it all worked out."

He was rubbing my nose in it.

"Is there something you wanted?" I ordered another bourbon neat.

"Let me get that." Martin offered.

"I can pay my own way, thanks."

"Yeah, I hear you're doing pretty good for yourself, babysitting a bunch of society types in this fancy hotel, went out and got yourself a real job. Good for you."

"It puts bacon on the table."

"Yeah, I bet it does, but, you know, a girl like Rosie expects to find a little more than bacon on the table. She has what you'd call expensive tastes. I should know."

"Is that a tinge of jealousy I detect?" I asked.

Martin laughed. "No, not at all. I think it's cute that you two have rekindled your old flame. Best of luck to you. You're going to need it with that one."

"Is that why you came down, to pass out congratulations and wish us all the best?"

Martin laughed again. "We both know why I'm down here, McKeller. I was hoping we could be civil about this."

"I didn't figure civil for your strong suit."

"It's not always my end game, but it could save everyone involved a lot of grief if you agreed to cooperate."

"Look, Martin, why don't you quit jerking my chain and tell me what it is you want?"

This one was more of a snicker. "Like you don't know? Like you and Rosie aren't in on this together?"

"Let's pretend I'm a little slow," I said. "Why don't you go ahead and spell it out for me?"

"In that case, I'll be real clear so you're sure to understand," he replied, enunciating every syllable. "I want what she took from me. She can keep the money, we'll call it a finder's fee, but I want the books back and I'm not paying another dime. If you two think you're going to bleed another red cent out of me, you're sadly mistaken."

"Books, huh? I wouldn't have guessed you for much of a reader."

"Funny guy, I want my books back."

"And if we don't hand over the books?"

"Well, let's just say that would be a very bad mistake on your part."

"What are you going to do, give her another black eye?"

The smirk was back. "You know Rosie. She's a little high strung. Sometimes you have to put her in her place."

I felt my entire body clench and fought back the urge to sock him in the jaw.

"To answer your question," he continued. "If I don't get those books back, she's going to wish all I gave her was a black eye. You too for that matter."

I could only sit there, gritting my teeth.

"We'll call Ralphy a casualty of war and leave it at that. You were a soldier, McKeller, you know how that goes. I don't know which one of you plugged him and, honestly, I don't care. I just want the books back."

"I can see you're all broken up about Ralphy."

"Ralphy knew the score. There wasn't much to like about him, but he was good at his job. I'll have him replaced before breakfast. In the meantime, you go back to your little girlfriend and tell her where we stand. You tell her I want those books back in my hands by tomorrow night."

I shot back my bourbon and shrugged. "I'll pass on the message, but you know how Rosie can be sometimes. She doesn't much like being told what to do."

Martin's grin faded. "Don't play games with me, McKeller. You don't know who you're dealing with. I pick guys like you from between my teeth after lunch. Just pass it on, and I'll meet you back here tomorrow evening, say around six-ish?"

"What assurances do we have that you'll hold up your end?"

The slick smile was back. "You don't have any. You're just going to have to rely on my good nature."

I stood up and slipped my fedora on. "Good nature, huh? Seems like a stretch to me."

"Look, Rosie and me have a history too. She is what she is, but we had some laughs for a while. For old time's sake, I'm willing to forget this whole matter, just so long as I get my property back. Once I get that, you and Rosie are free to go on your merry way with my blessing."

"You don't really come off as the forgiving type."

"Oh, there's no forgiving involved. You end up with Rosie. You'll get yours in the end. It always works out that way with Rosie."

I shrugged. "OK, then. Guess I'll see you in the funny papers."

I was making my way out of the bar when he called out to me, "Six o'clock, McKeller. Don't keep me waiting. My patience only stretches so thin."

Chapter Eleven

The nagging question was, what the hell was going on?

Rosie's story didn't exactly wash, and I was getting a clearer picture of what had actually brought her down to Myrtle Beach. It wasn't about running away from an abusive boyfriend, and it certainly wasn't about coming down to see me.

She'd taken something from Martin, books of some kind, and he wanted them back pretty bad. Once again, Rosie had managed to drag me into the middle of her mess, and I'd been all too willing to let her. That's how it had always been with me and Rosie.

From the Brookgreen Room, I made my way back to Rosie's, taking the long way around and making sure I wasn't followed by one of Martin's goons. Again, I got no answer at the door.

I took the stairs down to the fourth floor and parked myself at the end of the corridor, the far end, away from the elevator, and waited. I was half sitting on the window ledge and chain smoking cigarettes, putting out the butts on the sill and collecting a nice little pile. Buntemeyer would have flipped if he caught me, but I was beyond caring.

I was running scenarios through my head, trying to piece things together from what I got from Martin and the lies and bullshit Rosie had handed me. Part of me wanted to find some kind of truth in what she'd told me, but the other part of me, the part with a working brain, knew she'd played me again to get whatever it was she was after.

It was almost two in the morning when the door to 418 opened and Rosie stepped out, turning away and heading toward the elevator. She hadn't even bothered to check the hallway, so she didn't spot me down at the far end.

She was wearing a long pink nightgown, silky and shimmery, with

65

a matching robe pulled over it, fluffy high heeled slippers on her feet. Her hair was down long and straight, flowing over her shoulders.

When I saw her step out into the hallway I felt something drop inside my chest, my suspicions confirmed. It was like someone was prodding an old wound with a stick, a wound I thought had scabbed over ages ago.

I put out my latest butt and went after her, taking my time at a leisurely stride.

Rosie was waiting at the elevator when I came up behind her. "Out for an evening stroll?" I asked.

She turned around quick, her eyes wide and surprised. "Frankie? Hi."

"Hi." I smiled back.

"This hotel is so big and confusing. I get lost sometimes."

"Yeah, I bet you do."

"I wanted to get some air so—"

"Cut the crap, Rosie. Who's your friend in 418?"

"I don't know what you're talking about," she tried.

"Just how stupid do you think I am? Level with me, Rosie, who is this Taylor Mills guy, and what is he doing here?"

"If you already know who he is, why are you asking?"

"I know his name and his room number, and I know he's down from Maryland. I also know he checked in on the same day as you, and I know he was looking for you on the ninth floor earlier. That, and I know you just left his room at two in the morning after I've been trying to get a hold of you all night. Want to fill me in on the rest?"

"It's not what you think."

"I think you're lying again."

"Why would you automatically assume I'm lying?"

"Because words are coming out of your mouth. What gives?"

"He's a friend, Frankie, that's all."

"Great, another *friend*. Where do you find time to be so friendly?"

"It's not what it looks like."

"It looks like you're up to your old tricks."

"I met Taylor up in Baltimore. He was someone I could talk to when things went sour between Blake and me. We're just friends, Frankie, but he took a liking to me. He wanted to be more than just friends. I never tried to lead him on ..."

"No, of course not. Not you."

"I mentioned that I was coming down to see you. He must have followed me down. I swear I didn't know he was coming."

"Do you have a system for keeping up with all the bullshit you spill out, or do you just kind of wing it and hope it all falls into place?"

Rosie let out a huff and turned back to the elevator.

"Let's pretend for a second that I believe even part of your story," I said to the back of her head. "How does this all fit in with Blake Martin and his missing books?"

That got her attention. She whipped back around with a question mark in her eyes.

"Yeah, I just had a drink in the bar with your old pal, Blake. His story doesn't exactly match up with yours."

"He's lying, Frankie."

"Rosie, stop playing me like I'm that gullible chump you used to toy with up in Baltimore. You're in way over your head on this one, and I'm about ready to walk away from the whole deal. You either come clean with me, or I'll have a bellman up to your room in twenty minutes to collect your luggage and put you out in the streets."

She let out a breath. "OK, I took his stupid books. He deserved it after what he did to me."

"Rosie," I said with a sigh, shaking my head. "How about Ralphy? Did he deserve what he got too?"

"Ralphy?" she asked, all innocent and shy, like she had no idea what I was talking about.

"Are you going to pretend you didn't know Ralphy was gunned down in his hotel room earlier?"

Rosie gasped, covering her mouth with her palm. "Oh my gosh. Frankie, you *didn't ...*"

"Of course I didn't," I shot back. "You know damn well I didn't, and if I didn't, who in the hell did? Just how many enemies do you figure Ralphy had in Myrtle Beach?"

"What are you saying?"

"I'm saying it's pretty convenient for you that Ralphy went and got himself dead."

"You think I—"

"Stop playing me for the sap, Rosie. I'm not falling for the damsel in distress routine any more. What exactly is going on here?"

"I swear to you, Frankie. I don't know anything about Ralphy. The last I heard of him is that you went to see him."

"So you didn't go pay him a little visit afterward?"

"No, of course not."

"What about lover boy?" I asked, motioning my head back toward 418.

"No, it's not like that, and he would never—"

"Well somebody sure as hell did, and I'm not going to be the one to take the fall for it," I snapped back.

"Do they suspect you, Frankie?"

"Let's just say the sheriff was mighty interested in why I was seen leaving his hotel room earlier today."

"I'm sorry, Frankie. I never meant to get you involved in all this."

"Of course you did, Rosie. That's what you do. You stir up the pot and pull me into the middle of it, just like always."

"I promise, Frankie. I never meant to put you in harm's way."

"What's your game plan here, Rosie? What is it that you're after?"

She hesitated. "I want what I've got coming to me. I want what I deserve, and I want Blake Martin to pay through the nose."

"You're playing with fire, Rosie. A man is dead. That's murder one."

"I didn't kill anybody. I swear." She said it with passion. I wanted to believe her.

"Things are out of hand. It's time to pull in the reins and cut your losses," I tried.

Her eyes went narrow, her jaw taunt. I could see the fire behind her eyes. "Do you know what it's like to be somebody's punching bag? Do you know what that feels like?"

It was my turn to hesitate. "Yeah, I guess I've been on that end of it a few times."

"He's going to pay for what he did to me, one way or the other."

"He said you took some money."

"Yeah, I went into his safe and I took two grand and his precious little books."

"Two grand is a pretty nice chunk of change. Why don't you take the money and walk away. He says he just wants the books back."

"Two grand is just a down payment on what he owes me."

"Where does pretty boy fit in?" I asked, motioning back to where she had come from.

She shrugged. "He's a friend, that's all. I went to his room to talk to him, try to convince him he should go home."

"How much does he know?"

"The bare minimum. He knows about me and Blake. He knows how he treated me. I think he wants to protect me from him. He's really a sweet guy."

"What about Ralphy and the books? Does he know about all that?"

She shook her head. "I'd like to keep it that way." Rosie glanced down to the floor and back up at me, her eyes all wide and innocent. "I know I've hurt a lot of people over the years, including you. I don't want to do that anymore, Frankie. I don't want to drag any more innocent people into my mess. I don't want anyone else getting hurt. I just want what's owed me."

I took a deep breath and let it out slow. I figured there was about a one percent chance she was telling the truth, but what can I say? I've always been a sucker for long shots, especially where Rosie was concerned.

"I think maybe I need to take a look at these books, see exactly why Martin wants them back so bad."

Rosie bit her lip. "Yeah ..."

"Is there a problem?"

"Well ..."

"You do have them, right?"

"Yes, of course, kind of ..."

"What does that mean?"

"I couldn't take a chance on getting caught with them on me. I knew he'd send Ralphy after me."

"Where are the books, Rosie?"

"They're on their way."

"On their way?"

"I mailed them to myself, here at the Ocean Forest Hotel. I mailed them right before I got on the train."

"It could be days before they find their way down here."

She smiled. "In the meantime, they are safe and sound, in the hands of the U.S. Postal Service."

"Wish we were safe in the hands of the U.S. Postal Service. Martin gave us until six tomorrow night to come up with them."

"We'll just have to stall him."

"Just stall him, huh? Easy as that?"

Chapter Twelve

I know what you're thinking. There's one born every minute, and I must have come along right on schedule. It's not like I didn't suspect she was pulling the wool over my eyes. I knew, chances were, it was the whole damn sheep, but there was that little part of me that wanted to believe Rosie. There was that little piece of me that wanted to think this time was the real deal, and she was coming clean. I never claimed to be the brightest guy to come down the pike.

It was late and we were both exhausted. I didn't want to think why Rosie might be so tired.

With Blake Martin on the prowl I figured staying in either of our rooms wasn't the safest way to go, so I got us a cozy little number up on the eighth floor, an unregistered room that would make it hard to track us down. Rosie insisted on two beds.

Sleep didn't come easy. I spent most of the night tossing and turning, my mind packed full of nagging questions.

Somebody put three slugs into Ralphy, and there was a good chance that somebody was sleeping four feet away from me. If Rosie was nursing a guilty conscience, you couldn't tell by the way she slept. She was like a rock, never moving, quiet as a church mouse, her steady breaths a distant whisper in the room.

I caught myself staring in her direction more than once. She gave new meaning to the term doll face, her soft delicate features like porcelain in the moonlight. Everything about her seemed angelic and peaceful, the opposite of the craziness and turmoil she'd unleashed around her.

I was having trouble wrapping my head around the possibility Rosie might have snuffed out Ralphy, something in my gut refusing to believe it. My mind kept drifting back to Pretty Boy in 418, the sight of her leaving his room at two in the morning. What exactly had gone on behind that closed door? How involved was he in this mess? How involved was he with Rosie, enough to pull the trigger on her number one threat?

I'm not going to lie, there was a part of me that was fuming with jealousy and wanted Pretty Boy to be at the bottom of it. That was the part of me that was chomping at the bit for the chance to prove it and have him put away, get him out of the picture for good.

It made sense. If what Rosie had told me was even partially true, and he'd followed her down with a puppy dog crush, why wouldn't he go the whole nine yards? If he was so hell bent on protecting her, why not eliminate her biggest problem?

She was Rosie, after all, and I knew, first hand, the way she could seep into a guy's brain and cause him to make some stupid choices. The question was whether this Taylor guy had it bad enough to make the ultimate stupid choice.

Rosie was still sleeping the sleep of the just when I slipped out of the room in the morning. Maybe it was the sleep of the just-the-way-it-is. Either way, I swung by my room for a quick shave and a whore bath before making my way down to the lobby. Buntemeyer, my boss, was waiting to greet me at the front desk.

"Where in the hell have you been?"

"Friday mornings are my Bridge Club meetings," I replied. "Where do you think I've been?"

"I was banging on your door for half an hour."

"It's not even nine-thirty in the morning, boss. Maybe we need to have a little talk about privacy."

"Senator Wright's security team has been here since seven. They want to go over the arrangements with you."

"Do you mind if I grab a cup of java first, maybe a scrambled egg and a piece of toast?"

"There's no time for lollygagging, McKeller. We have a big day ahead of us."

I took a deep breath and let it out slow. "Great," I sighed. It was going to be one of those days.

There would be no eggs in my immediate future, not so much as a sip of coffee. Simmons saw to that. I spent the next few hours briefing his people, familiarizing them with the layout of the hotel, going over the senator's itinerary.

Senator Wright and his party were due to arrive at two that afternoon with a small reception slated for out on the back veranda from three to five. From there it was dinner served in his suite for him and his guests, followed by the infamous poker game they were all coming down for.

His security team was more like a force and they were sprinkled all over the hotel. Spread out as they were, it was hard to get an accurate count, but there must have been close to a dozen in all, with more to arrive with the senator. It made me wonder how many guys it took to guard the president.

By one in the afternoon things had settled down enough to where I figured I could slip away long enough to grab some quick grub. My stomach had been growling reminders at me for hours.

I decided to forgo the formalities of the dining room and headed for the kitchen to get it straight from the source. I was half way through the lobby when Sheriff Talbert cut me off.

"You heading somewhere in particular?" he asked me. He had Deputy Dale at his side.

"Thought I'd grab a bite. You guys are welcome to join me," I said, nodding a hello to Dale.

"I could eat," Dale offered.

The sheriff turned and gave him a sharp look. "We ain't here on no social call."

"Aw shucks, Sheriff, and here I thought maybe you just missed my company."

Talbert's attention turned back to me. "You see, I have a little problem, McKeller."

"Anything I can help with?"

"Yeah, maybe you can. Maybe you can tell me why I have a dead body at the Chesterfield Inn, and I can't seem to find a single connection to this guy and anybody in this town? Anybody except you, that is."

"I really wouldn't call what I had a connection, Sheriff. I barely knew the guy."

"That seems to be a far sight more than anybody else in Myrtle Beach."

"I met the guy exactly two times."

"That's about two more than anybody else I've talked to. Not to mention, I have reason to believe that second time didn't end so friendly. Maybe there's a third time you're a little reluctant to mention. Maybe that third time ended with the big guy getting plugged."

"Yeah, and maybe he wasn't happy with his accommodations at the Chesterfield and decided to plug himself three times, but we both know that's not very likely either."

"You're awfully glib for someone at the top of a murder suspect list."

"We both know if you had anything on me I'd be rotting away in a jail cell right now. The fact is, I was seen leaving back when he was still breathing. That makes it pretty hard to pin this one anywhere near my direction. I'm guessing you've got nothing else, so you figure you'll shake my branches and see what kind of fruit falls out. The problem is, Sheriff, I've got nothing to give you."

Talbert's face got even more tense than usual. "Just because I can't place you at the murder scene doesn't mean I can't take you in for some more routine questioning. Sometimes that routine questioning can go on for a mighty long time, days in fact."

He had my attention, and I thought better of pushing any harder. The sheriff's jail cell was the last place I wanted to be cooling my heels for the next few days.

Talbert could see he had me against a wall, and he allowed himself a slight smile when he said, "Now, I know you're very busy these days, what with the senator coming in and all."

I was surprised he knew about Wright. I thought the senator's trip was on a need-to-know basis. "You know about that, huh?"

"There ain't no secrets in Myrtle Beach, McKeller. This is a small town. There's things people know and things people are bound to find out about in time."

"Well, if that's the case, you can just sit back and wait to hear who killed Ralphy, right?"

"Or maybe I can just squeeze the right little bird 'til he starts chirping."

"Just make sure you got the right bird," I added.

"Speaking of birds, you want to tell me about one staying here at the hotel, a pretty little brunette down from Baltimore?"

"I'm impressed. You've got your ear to the ground."

"We're not quite as backwards as you city slickers seem to think we are. You want to tell me about her?"

I nodded for a second, trying to figure out how much I could spill without incriminating Rosie or myself. "She's an old flame from back home, a girl I used to run around with back in the day. She thought she'd look me up for old time's sake."

"She got a name?"

"Rosie Carter."

It was Talbert's turn to nod. "That's funny because there's no Rosie Carter registered at the hotel. I checked."

"You're nothing if not thorough."

"What gives?"

"She's been staying with me, off the books. It's not the kind of thing a nice respectable girl likes to advertise."

"It's a little hard for me to picture you with a nice respectable girl."

"Ouch, that stings."

"This Rosie ever go by the name Sally Young?"

The good sheriff was pulling out all the stops, and I had to hide my surprise at how much he knew. "Why do you ask?"

"It's just that we found a slip of paper by Ralph Henderson's phone with the number 309 scratched on it. Turns out 309 at the Chester-field is empty, but there was a girl by the name of Sally Young here at the Ocean Forest in 309 the other night. Looks like she checked out rather suddenly. I asked around and people say she was a pretty brunette from up north. One of my deputies responded to a call here the other night about room 309 getting vandalized, too."

"You're really doing your homework on this one," I said, my head scrambling to come up with explanations.

"Us country bumpkins aren't always as slow as we're made out to be."

"All right, look, I'll level with you. Rosie made the trip down here to get away from an ex-boyfriend, one who likes to put his hands on women."

"This boyfriend wouldn't be named Ralph Henderson would it?"

I shook my head. "No, it wasn't Ralphy. I decided it would be safer to hole her up in the hotel in case he comes looking for her."

"Do you see my dilemma here, McKeller? You're from Baltimore,

Henderson was from Baltimore and your little girlfriend is from Baltimore. Kind of a coincidence isn't it?"

"There's a lot of people from Baltimore, Sheriff."

"Not so many down here, but that doesn't make us any less smart."

"Trust me, Sheriff, I wouldn't underestimate you." I wasn't lying.

"Maybe I should have a little talk with this Rosie."

"She's not around at the moment. She went into town to do a little shopping. I expect her back this evening."

"I guess I'll have to come back this evening."

"Just so you know, it's not what you think. Rosie didn't have anything to do with Ralphy's death. I guarantee it."

"Well, if you guarantee it, that's good enough for me. I'll just forget about the whole thing."

I didn't have an answer.

"On second thought," Talbert said, all cocky and feisty. "You tell this Rosie to make herself available this evening. I have a few questions I'd like to ask her."

"I'll be sure to let her know."

"You do that," he replied.

Chapter Thirteen

Food didn't seem like such a priority anymore, and I high tailed it up to the eighth floor where Rosie and I had spent the night. She was gone.

From there I went by her room on the ninth floor, but she wasn't there either. I figured maybe it was time to pay a visit to room 418.

Pretty Boy answered after about three minutes of knocking.

"Yeah?" he asked, peeking out from the cracked open door.

"Room Service," I said kicking the door open and waltzing into the room.

"Hey, what's the big idea?"

"I'll ask the questions. Where's Rosie?" I glanced around the room. The bed was unmade, slacks and shirts were strewn over the dresser top. There was no sign of anyone else in the room.

"Rosie who?" the guy asked.

"Rosie the one you followed down from Baltimore, the one who might very well get you implicated in a murder."

"I don't know what you're talking about." He stood up straight, bowing up to me. His hair was as shaggy and unkempt as before, his shirt untucked. He was wearing white slacks and white socks, no shoes.

"Look, kid, I got no time for games. Where is she?"

He shifted his shoulders back and stuck out his chest. "I'm not a kid."

I took my forefinger and poked him in his inflated chest, hard. "You don't know who you're messing with, punk. I need to talk to Rosie, pronto."

As I said it, I went to poke him with my finger a second time but he deflected my arm with his and shifted to the side. In a blur of motion, he gave me a Karate chop to the neck that bent me over and a split second later he brought his knee up into my gut, knocking the wind out of me. His moves were lightning fast and packed more wallop than I'd expected.

Stunned and breathless, I dropped to my knees, gasping for air I couldn't pull in. He was hovering over me in some sort of Judo stance, ready to pounce on me again.

"You want some more, mister?" he grunted.

The bathroom door opened and Rosie came rushing to my side. "Stop, Taylor, it's all right. It's just Frankie, the guy I told you about."

"Yeah, well, he needs to learn some manners."

I was still trying to catch my breath, wheezing pretty good, slumped over on the floor.

"Taylor is a Karate instructor," Rosie said, leaning over me and holding me around the shoulders.

I managed to grunt out a breathless, "Yeah."

The two of them got me to my feet and walked me over to the bed, where they sat me down on the edge. I was just starting to get my breath back. My dignity, however, was long gone.

"I didn't mean to hurt you bad, Mister. I just kind of react sometimes. I don't much like people putting their hands on me," Taylor explained.

"I'll try to remember that."

"What's this all about, Frankie?" Rosie asked.

I looked around the room. "What's *this* all about?"

"I've already told you. Taylor is my friend."

I glanced at Taylor. He wasn't offering anything else. "I just had a little chat with the local sheriff. He knows about you, Rosie. He suspects there's a connection to you and Ralphy."

"What did you tell him?"

"I told him as little as I could get away with without ending up in the slammer."

"Rosie didn't kill anybody," the kid said. "She was with me, taking a long walk on the beach. I can vouch for her whereabouts the whole time."

"That's all very sweet, but what makes you think you're not going to be a suspect in all this?"

That caught Pretty Boy off guard, and his face turned a little pale.

He stood there with a dumbfounded look on his mug.

"This ain't some game, kids. This is murder and, like it or not, we're all smack dab in the middle of it. Sheriff Talbert isn't just going to fade away."

"We didn't kill anybody," Rosie offered.

"Well, somebody killed him, and they're not going to stop until they find the murderer."

Rosie was nibbling on her bottom lip, all nervous like.

"First thing, Rosie, you have to forget about this Blake Martin nonsense. There's too much going on to be playing games with the likes of Martin. You've got too many balls in the air. Just give him back his books."

"I can't do that, Frankie."

"We need that money," the kid added.

There it was. *We.*

I looked over at Rosie. She couldn't look me back in the eye. I shifted my gaze to Taylor Mills. His eyes were all wide and star struck, milky whites floating in their sockets.

I recognized the look. I'd worn it myself not so long ago.

"So, that's the way it is, huh?"

Nobody answered me.

"This is your big plan? You're going to extort money from Blake Martin and run off with Jujitsu boy?"

"Hey!" Mills snapped.

"It's not like that, Frankie. Taylor is my friend. He's been a big help through everything that's happened."

"A man is dead, Rosie, and the most likely suspects are all in this room. It's time to cut your losses and play the smart hand."

"What about Blake? Why isn't he a suspect? How do we know he didn't get down here and find Ralphy still alive? How do we know he didn't kill him?"

"And why would he do that?"

"He has a temper, Frankie. You don't know what he's like. I've seen how he gets. I've seen it first hand."

"Rosie, you're juggling rattle snakes here. You're going to end up getting bit. I think it's time to go to the sheriff and come clean with everything you know. If Martin is responsible he'll find out."

"We can't do that," the kid interjected.

"Yeah, and why is that?"

"We just can't is all. It's not an option."

I couldn't help wonder why it wasn't an option. It made me wonder if Pretty Boy had more to hide than he was telling or if he was just love sick for Rosie.

"You two do what you want, but I'm out. I'm done sticking my neck on the line. I'm telling Talbert everything I know. He can sort it out from there."

Soft and girlie Rosie was back, and she snuggled herself in next to me. "Please, Frankie, you can't do that. Not just yet. I need time to get my hands on those books."

"You don't even know when they're getting here."

"That's why I have to buy more time. Once I have those books, I'll have protection against him. Without those books I'll never get out from under Blake Martin."

Her eyes were all misty and wide, her cheeks pink with blush. Those ruby reds were moist and open, pleading their case in a perfect O that made me ache to kiss them.

It made me wonder if she could see that same lost and longing look on my face that I'd seen on the kid. It made me wonder just how strong the hold was she had on me.

"One day," I said. "One day, then I'm going to the sheriff with the whole ball of wax."

"One day is all I need," she replied with a smile. Squeezing my arm in her hands. "In the meantime, we need to stall Blake. We need to buy a little time."

Against my better judgment, I said, "I might have a way to do that. He's not going to like it much but it might buy you a little time."

Rosie's smile grew bigger. "You're really something, Frankie. The absolute best."

I was thinking I was something, right about then, but the best didn't seem like the word for it.

Chapter Fourteen

It was just about two o'clock and I knew they'd be looking for me downstairs. The entire lobby was a flurry of activity by the time I got there. Even Buntemeyer had donned his best blue suit for the occasion, complete with a red silk handkerchief in the breast pocket. He was beaming with pride, awaiting the arrival of his esteemed guest.

He was busy inspecting the property and his employees when I came walking up.

"Is that what you plan on wearing?" he asked, running his eyes down my drab gray wool suit.

"My prom dress is at the cleaners."

He didn't care much for that one. "Straighten that tie, McKeller."

The security team was spread around the lobby, each of them in matching dark gray suits, all of them trying to blend in around the edges of the room, looking into the main area, arms crossed. There wasn't a hint of a smile to be found in the lot of them.

Simmons came rushing through the front door, announcing, "OK, people, the senator has arrived. Everybody look alive!"

Even if I hadn't known Wright from the newspapers, I would have known which one the senator was. He was the calm in the center of the storm, the smiling, handshaking sturdiness in the middle of a circle of constant motion and energy. With bodyguards at arm's length and all around him, he moved through the lobby, gripping palms, kissing cheeks and making quick spurts of small talk with various people he breezed by.

He spent a few extra moments with Buntemeyer, no doubt complimenting him on his fine establishment, before he made his way toward me, Simmons leading the way.

"Senator, this is Frank McKeller, head of hotel security," Simmons said.

Senator Wright reached out and shook my hand firmly, flashing me the million dollar smile that earned him votes at every whistle stop he made.

"Nice to meet you, Frank. I'm looking forward to you working very closely with my people."

"Yes sir."

"Beautiful hotel you have here. I've stayed here many times, and I always look forward to my visits to the Ocean Forest."

He was a young sixty with a healthy tan and just enough gray in his hair to convey authority and wisdom. Tall and an athletic trim, he was the picture of proper breeding and down home Southern charm, long, lean arms, thin elegant fingers free of jewelry. With the soft easy smile of a career politician and a voice like rich sausage gravy running down the side of a homemade biscuit, he was exactly what Central Casting would dial up to play a distinguished Southern senator.

Before I could come up with some kind of a response, he had moved on to the next person, making sure to personally greet everyone in his wake, winning over each and every contact he made. He was a political machine in a gray flannel suit.

Simmons had cozied up next to me and we both stood watching as Wright continued to make his rounds. If there had been any babies there the senator would have been kissing them.

"This is where he's at his best," Simmons said with admiration in his voice. "This is when he's truly in his element."

"And when he's not in his element?"

"Senator Wright is a great man. He's doing a lot of good things for this country."

"So I hear."

"There's no telling how far he can go, maybe all the way to the White House."

"Is that the reason for the small army you have surrounding him?" I asked.

"He is a very important man with more than his share of enemies. His guests have a right to expect security as well. "

"That first day, you told me you wanted to keep this little shindig under wraps. It doesn't look like you're trying real hard to hide his visit."

"There's no reason to hide this part. This is where the senator shines."

"So, what part are you trying to hide?"

Simmons gave me a look, the kind of look you give a guy when you're trying to decide about him, whether he'd kidding or just stupid. "Our job is to protect the senator from outside forces, that's a given. Senator Wright is a man of big visions and ideals. He's also a man of large appetites. Sometimes our job is to protect the senator from himself too."

"That's where *I* fit in. You need me to run rumor control in the hotel, keep the senator's antics quiet."

"I'm sure the senator's not the first high profile guest you've had who's looking for a little low profile fun."

"I guess that depends on what kind of fun we're talking about."

"Just your run of the mill, old fashioned fun between consenting adults. Nobody's going to get hurt or anything."

I caught Simmons glancing across the lobby toward the elevator and my eyes followed his. Two men in dark suits were escorting a cluster of women toward the elevator, coming from the other direction like they'd been brought in through the side door.

The women were all young and pretty, blondes, brunettes and redheads, six of them in all. They were dressed to the nines, slinky evening gowns that molded to their trim little figures, lipstick and high heels, perfect hair and bright shiny smiles. If they were working girls they were the cream of the crop, the best money could buy. If they weren't, they were the kind of party girls who were always ready for a good time. You could see it in everything about them.

"I think I get the picture," I said to Simmons before I wandered away, off toward the back veranda where the senator's reception was just beginning.

The senator's guests were beginning to arrive behind him, all of them men, all of them traveling stag. A few of them looked familiar, one I thought I recognized from the movies. All of them looked like money.

I weaved my way through the crowd and found myself standing within earshot of the senator. One of the hotel's waitresses was standing in front of him, offering a tray of champagne glasses for him to pick from.

She was relatively new to the hotel, but I'd seen her around of late. I couldn't recall her name but she was a cute little blonde with a face like a daisy and a figure like an hourglass, one of those pretty young things that conjured up images of sparkles and sunshine. Her smile could melt candle wax, and her voice was like salt water taffy. She couldn't have been more than seventeen, and I suspected she was probably still courting her high school beau.

"What a delightful creature you are," the senator said with a leer as he plucked a glass from her tray. "And what is your name?"

"Rachel Rae Miller," she answered, "but my friends call me Rae Rae."

"Well, then I'm going to call you Rae Rae too, because I can tell we're going to be very good friends."

Little Rae Rae blushed and giggled.

"You must be sure to stop by my little get together later this evening, after you get off work."

"Oh, I couldn't," Rachel replied. "We aren't allowed—"

"Nonsense, my dear. I am a United States Senator. There are no rules or regulations my authority does not override. Consider it your patriotic duty."

Little Rae Rae giggled again.

My first impressions of the esteemed senator had taken a sudden turn to the left.

Buntemeyer came up behind me and he gave me an uncharacteristic nudge. "Things are going splendidly, don't you think?"

It was rare that my boss ever asked for my opinion. "Just peachy," I answered.

"I want you to be on hand for whatever the senator and his people require, McKeller. This function is extremely important to the reputation of this hotel. I don't want anything to go wrong. I expect you to be on top of things."

"You can count on me, Boss," I replied, trying to throw in a dash of sincerity for effect.

"By the way," he began, "the sheriff was here earlier asking about a young woman who was staying here, a woman by the name of Young?"

"Yeah, I talked to him."

Buntemeyer gave me one of his looks. "What's this all about?"

I shrugged. "It's nothing. I have it under control."

His eyebrows furled and his look turned stern. "McKeller," he said like my last name was two words. "I don't want any shenanigans in this hotel during the senator's stay. Whatever the sheriff's interest in this young woman, you see to it there's no issues that could embarrass the hotel."

"Don't worry, boss, I've got it."

"You had better."

"In fact," I offered. "I'm going to go look into that right now."

Buntemeyer huffed. "The reception is just getting started."

"I'll be back before they go up to dinner," I said.

"I expect you to be on hand for whatever the senator's people need of you."

I glanced back at Wright. He was still laying it on pretty thick for little starstruck Rae Rae. "I don't think anything's going to happen before tonight. Nobody will even miss me."

"McKeller ..."

I turned and made my way back through the hotel. The whole way I was wondering who this Mick Keller guy was.

Chapter Fifteen

I only had a few hours to work with. By six o'clock the senator's dinner would be in full swing. Blake Martin would be around by then too, looking to collect those books that we couldn't exactly get our hands on. The sheriff would be back by that time looking for some face time with Rosie as well.

You always have to have a plan, even if you're not quite sure what it is. Mine was vague at best, but I was hoping it would buy me some time all the way around. I didn't figure it would make me any new friends, but it was all I had.

In the meantime, there was the little matter of the murder of Ralphy Henderson. My problem was that I'd spent so much time trying to keep Rosie and myself out of the rifle sights that I'd neglected the best way to keep us from harm's way. That was to find out who actually pulled the trigger on Ralphy.

There was something that still bothered me from earlier in the day. When I'd tried to convince Rosie to give up on Martin's books and come clean with what she knows, it had been Taylor Mills who seemed so hell bent against it. It made me wonder if he had something to hide, and it made me wonder if I couldn't place him at the scene of the crime.

I didn't figure I had much to go on, but I had to start somewhere. The Chesterfield Inn seemed like as good a place as any.

Only a couple of years old, the Chesterfield was located on Ocean Drive, right smack dab in the heart of Myrtle Beach, the perfect location for those who wanted easy access to the beach and downtown goings on. It was three stories of brick, long and rectangular, with a raised basement foundation and a line of extended windows built into the side of the roof. Its colonial style made it stand out from the rest of the storefronts, shops and beach houses which surrounded it. While it wasn't as deluxe as the Ocean Forest Hotel, it was a quaint and cozy spot that attracted a solid clientele.

The lobby was quiet, one guy napping in a wicker chair, another guy reading the newspaper. The clerk at the front desk didn't pay me any attention as I casually strolled by like I belonged there. It was just as well, I had no interest in speaking to him. He would have been the first person the sheriff talked to.

Working in a hotel myself, I knew the people who knew the real goings on in a hotel this size, and they weren't the ones who checked them in and out.

Ralphy had been staying on the fifth floor, so I went there first. I didn't bother going by his room, there wouldn't be anything there to find, nothing the sheriff hadn't already found, anyway. I wasn't looking for physical evidence.

After I wandered the hallway for a few minutes, a door opened and a maid came out, rolling her maid's cart out into the hallway. She was an elderly woman, stocky, with silver hair and a light complexion. She paid me no notice as she wheeled her cart past me.

"That's really something, huh?" I asked as she went by.

"What's that, Darlin'?" She was all South Carolina with a full twangy accent, firm and friendly.

"I was just saying, that's really something, huh? A guy actually getting killed here?"

The woman crossed herself and gave a worrisome look to the heavens. "So sad," she said.

"I guess that sort of thing doesn't happen here much."

"Of course not," she replied, a look of shock overtaking her face. "This is a fine and family friendly hotel. We've never had anything like that happen before."

"Did you know the guy?"

"I never met the gentleman, but I heard he was a Yankee from up North. You know how they can be."

"Yes ma'am, I sure do," I replied, adding a touch of twang to my own voice.

"I don't like to speak ill of the dead, but Harold told me he wasn't the nicest of fellows, said he was downright rude, in fact."

"Harold?"

"Harold works room service. He served him his meals and said he was none too friendly. He said he was always in a big rush, like those Yankees tend to be."

"Is that so?"

"I'm not saying he got what he deserved, I would never wish that on any of God's creatures, but we do reap what we sow."

"How true."

"Harold said something was not right about that fellow, said it right from the start. Did you know that, just before that poor man was killed, Harold delivered an icepack to his room? Harold said he had a big ole welt on the side of his head, like he'd been in a fight. One of the other maids said she heard some commotion coming from there just before."

"You don't say."

"I wouldn't wish it on anyone, but we do reap what we sow."

"Did you ever see anyone coming or going from the room?"

"I have been off for a few days. My sister had come for a visit from Sumter. We hadn't seen each other in so long. We had such a nice visit."

"That's nice."

"My sister is six years younger than me, married a carpenter in Sumter. They're doing very well for themselves. He has his own business and everything."

"You must be proud. Do you know if Harold ever saw anyone else coming or going from the room."

"Yes, we are very proud, the entire family is."

"And Harold?"

"Why, silly, Harold doesn't even know my sister."

"I meant did he ever see anybody coming or going?"

The woman glanced around the hall, making sure we were alone. "I don't like to speak out of school, and I certainly would never advocate gossip, but Harold said he took breakfast up to that fellow that very morning, said there was another fellow in the room. Harold said they rushed him out of there before he could hardly drop off the food proper. Harold said he didn't even offer a tip."

"That's just not right."

"Sometimes that's just how those Yankees are," she confided. "Not all of them, mind you. Some of them are right nice people."

"I'm sure they are. This guy Harold saw, was he another Northerner, kind of young, bushy blonde hair?"

"Said he was a Northerner all right, dressed in a proper suit and all. He didn't say anything about bushy hair but he said he looked kind of mean and dirty, like some people are. Harold said he's staying at the hotel, he'd delivered to his room as well."

"Did Harold tell the police about him?"

"The police? You mean the sheriff?" She glanced around the hall again. "I told him he needed to tell somebody but ... well, Harold is an older gentleman of color, and he doesn't like to get involved in such things. He'd much rather keep to himself and stay away from all the hoopla. I can't say as I blame him."

"Is Harold working today?"

The lady gave me a strange look, like I'd somehow crossed a line. "Why do you ask?"

"I thought maybe I'd order up some service, maybe make up for that tip he didn't get earlier. This Harold sounds like a good egg."

"That is very nice of you. I'm sure he would appreciate that. He is working, as a matter of fact."

I thanked her for her time and offered up a quarter, a tip for her.

"What's that for?"

I shrugged. "For when you clean my room."

"That's very sweet of you. What room are you in?"

"605," I replied.

"605? I thought that nice couple from Georgia was in 605."

"Did I say 605? I meant to say 606."

She didn't seem too concerned and went about her business, quarter in hand. I headed downstairs.

I didn't know the layout of the Chesterfield Inn, as I'd never been in the meat of the hotel, but I figured it couldn't be much different than the Ocean Forest. There were some things all hotels have in common.

First off, I found the restaurant, from there the kitchen. I figured Room Service couldn't be far. Nobody paid me any attention as I made my way through the kitchen. The cooks were busy getting ready for the dinner rush, and it's been my experience if you walk briskly and act like you know where you're going, people will usually let you be.

Just past the kitchen area was a small hallway. There was a cramped office to the left, a packed storage room to the right. The next door on the right led to another storage room but this one sported a little desk in the center with not much more than a telephone on top of it.

A lanky black man sat slouched in a chair, waiting for the phone to ring. He looked lost in his thoughts, maybe drifting off a tad. He was dressed in black pants and a white waiter's jacket, black bow tie, his short graying hair trimmed neatly over his ears.

"Harold?"

He jumped to his feet like I'd caught him doing something wrong. "Yes Sir, can I help you with something?"

"No, you're fine. I didn't mean to disturb you."

"No Sir, not at all. You ain't disturbing me. What can I do for you?"

"I was talking to the cleaning lady, she told me I should talk to you."

"Oh yeah, which one is that?"

I'd never thought to get her name. I should have; it was an amateur move and knowing it might give me more credibility. "Older lady, heavy set, gray hair ... Her sister lives in Sumter?"

"Oh, Betsy, sure. Good woman, that Betsy, real nice lady."

"She said you might know something about that guy who got killed."

His friendly demeanor changed and he looked around nervously. "Are you some kind of law man?"

"No sir, I'm not."

"I ain't got nothing to say. I don't know nothing."

"Betsy said you saw another man in his room when you dropped off his breakfast," I tried.

"That Miss Betsy's a real nice lady but she talks too dang much, and she don't know what she's talking about half the time."

I pulled out a five spot and let him get a good look at it. "Anything you tell me stays between us. I just want a little information is all."

"I don't know nothing. I didn't see nobody."

"Look, Harold, I wouldn't want this to get around but I was in that room that day. When you delivered that ice for the welt on the side of his head, I'm the one that put it there. The thing is, somebody saw me leaving, and I'm the prime suspect in this case, but I didn't kill anybody. I could use a little help."

He paused and looked me over, his stance softening. "You Mc-Keller?"

"Yeah."

"My friend, Marty, he's a bellman, he seen you leaving. His wife works housekeeping at the Ocean Forest, so he knew who you were. Says he's seen you around when he goes to pick her up from work. Says you're a right nice fella. He didn't mean to get you in no trouble. He told the sheriff that fella was alive after you left."

I nodded one time, not sure how to answer.

"They say you found the killer of that girl up in Atlantic Beach some time ago. Not many white folks would have gone to the trouble."

"She was a friend of a friend."

"That's what I hear. They say you're all right."

"I'm in a bit of a jam here."

"You gonna go back to the sheriff with what I say?"

"Not if I don't have to. I don't want to go down for a murder I didn't commit, but I promise I'll try to keep your name out of it as best I can."

"All right. I guess that's fair enough."

"This guy you saw that morning, was he a young guy, blonde hair, could use a good haircut?" I was half hoping old Betsy might have got her facts crossed.

"No Sir, this guy didn't look nothing like that. He wasn't no young fella, maybe a few years older than you. He was a thick guy, broad shoulders, dark hair, kind of dirty looking, if you know what I mean. He was one of those fellas that when you see him you want to put your hand on your wallet."

"A thug, huh?"

"The big guy what got himself killed, he was a thug. This fella was just kind of slimy, dirty like an old road, eyes like a buzzard. He had a scar too, under his left eye, shaped like a sideways V."

When he said that something jolted inside of me. I used know a guy who fit that description but he was a long way from Myrtle Beach, and he had no connection to any of this.

"What else can you tell me about him?"

"He was just mean is all, you could tell by looking at him, the way he looked back, the way he snarled when he talked. He was wearing a dark suit, brown maybe."

"Did you hear what they were talking about?"

"Whatever it was, they didn't want me to hear. They ushered me in and out of there just as quick as they could. I got the idea they was talking business, private business."

"Betsy said he was staying here."

"Yes Sir he was, but he ain't no more. He done checked out right after that fella got hisself killed, ain't seen him since. I figure if he the one who done it, he's far from the beach by now."

"They would have a record at the front desk, the name he was checked in under, wouldn't they?"

"Oh, I could tell you his name. He had to sign for his meals."

Harold walked over to a stack of cardboard boxes. He took the top off one and rifled through papers. "When they sign for the meals, they get it billed to their rooms. I turn them into the accounting lady in the office and she sees I get my tip off of it. I keep the carbon so I can double check it with my paycheck. They some nice people in the accounting office, but sometimes they make mistakes with the money. I keep the carbons so I can make sure they get my money right."

When he said carbon, he wasn't kidding. It looked like the guest check consisted of two pieces of paper with a piece of carbon paper in between. The idea was the guest gets one copy, and the hotel gets the other. If Harold hadn't been such a keen businessman, the carbon probably would have gone in the trash.

I held the thin blue carbon paper in my fingers, raising it to the light so I could read it clearly. He'd had a turkey sandwich and a cup of coffee. It had cost seventy-five cents and he'd left no tip. The signature was sloppy and difficult to read. If I didn't already know the name I might not have been able to make it out. It was a name I wasn't really expecting to see, even after hearing about the V shaped scar, but there it was scratched into the blue crinkled paper—the name Marcus Fletcher.

Chapter Sixteen

Old Harold couldn't have gotten it any more right if he'd known Fletcher for as long as I have. His description was point on, from his vulture-like eyes, to the way you wanted to wash your hands after you looked at him. He'd only met him briefly, but Harold was a good judge of character.

I met Fletcher up in Baltimore just after I'd graduated from the Staley School of Private Investigation. He was recruiting, looking for dumb punks who were willing to do his leg work.

Fletcher and I shared a common profession at one time, at least on paper. He ran an outfit he called Fletcher Investigations and he advertised his services in every two-bit rag in Baltimore. He hired me to do some skip trace work for him just out of school.

That's where you track down dead beats who skip out on their bail bondsmen, the guys who put up the money to bail them out of jail. When they don't show up for their trials, the bondsman can be out a pretty penny, unless they can find someone to hunt them down and turn them in. That's where guys like Fletcher come in, guys like me. You can make some decent money at it if you're not getting your dough from a middle man, and if you don't mind losing a few teeth every now and again.

I only worked one job for Fletcher. He hired me to track down a guy who was out on a Breaking and Entering charge. He guaranteed it was a piece of cake, a gravy job. The guy was a nonviolent offender, and he assured me it was easy money. He even knew where he was. He just needed me to go bring him in.

Twenty-three stitches and three broken ribs later, I brought him in on the third try. After the first two ended up with me in the Emergency Ward, I hired a hot little number I knew to get him blind drunk. Once he was all but passed out, I went by and collected him, took him downtown and poured him into the Central Lockup at the police headquarters building at Gaither Place.

If Fletcher had paid me what he owed me, I would have lost thirty bucks on the deal. As it was, I was out a lot more. He stiffed me good, and I never saw a cent. Once I set up my own office, he had the nerve to stop by sometimes, trying to farm out more work to me.

Our paths crossed plenty of times, and the longer I was in the business the more I'd hear about him. I was as low budget as they come, but he was something lower, something that had nothing to do with budgets.

Fletcher had a reputation as a guy who would do anything for a buck. There weren't a lot of lines he wouldn't cross, the kind of guy who would sell out his grandmother for bus fare. If you wanted to catch your husband cheating you came to me. If you wanted somebody to frame him in a two bit hotel with a couple of hookers, so you could make out in the divorce settlement, you went to Fletcher.

He was the bottom of the barrel, the scum that grows on scum. Stories of his exploits were legendary in Baltimore and most of us wondered how he kept his license.

All this time later and here he was in Myrtle Beach, my new backyard. It didn't make any sense. Martin had his own people; he wouldn't bother with the likes of Fletcher. Why rent out a dirtball when you can buy them up by the dozen and get better quality? There was no connection to Rosie. She was too smart to hook up with his kind of scumbag, especially when she could bat her eyes and have truckloads of guys falling over each other to do her bidding. That left Taylor Mills. He was the one I didn't know anything about. He was the wild card, and if there was a connection to Fletcher it had to be him.

As I was leaving the Chesterfield Inn, coming out of the kitchen and down the hallway toward the lobby, my mind was crammed full of nagging questions. I was barely paying attention to anything around me when something poked me in the brain and made me take a second look.

Up ahead, in the lobby, I caught sight of a guy, thin, in a brown, conservative suit with his fedora pulled low on his face. It was the same guy I'd spotted on the veranda of the Ocean Forest, the one who struck me as familiar but I couldn't place.

He was heading my way, a good distance away, but he stopped suddenly and changed directions, heading off into the lobby, like he'd seen me and decided to avoid me. I picked up my pace, almost jogging, or at least the closest thing my bum leg allowed. I made a dash for the lobby, but by the time I got there the guy was gone. I scoured the area, checking the adjoining hallways, the elevator, even the stairway. There was no sign of him. Maybe it was all in my head. Maybe he was just some guy I'd seen around town. I couldn't be sure but I couldn't shake the thought that there was something oddly familiar about him, maybe the way he walked.

I didn't have much time to dwell on it, as I needed to get back to the Ocean Forest for the senator's big dinner and what not. As far as detective work goes, I'd only managed to turn up more questions.

The senator's reception had broken up by the time I got back, the guests headed back to their rooms to freshen up before dinner. Simmons thought it would be a good idea if I made my rounds just to make sure everything was business as usual.

Things couldn't have been quieter. It was like the whole hotel was busy primping for the night or already out on the town. I'd made my rounds through the hallways and wound up back in the lobby when Sheriff Talbert and Deputy Dale came strolling in.

"Where is she?" was the first thing Talbert said.

"She's not here," I answered.

"I got half a mind to run you in."

"On what charge?"

"Obstructing justice, felony assault, suspicion of murder, maybe public littering, what's the difference? By the time the lawyers sort it out you'll be very acquainted with our facilities."

"I might have something else for you, Sheriff."

"This isn't some kind of game, McKeller. I'm not here to barter. I want to talk to the girl."

"Suppose I told you Ralphy's boss and a couple of his thugs are in the hotel?"

The sheriff's look hardened.

"I told you Ralphy was a shady character. He works for a guy named Martin. Martin's got his fingers in a lot of pies. He shows up in Myrtle Beach the same day Ralphy gets himself snuffed out. Co-incidence?"

"I'm listening."

"Look, you're the expert, Sheriff. I'm just a lowly house dick, but it might be an angle you'd want to look into."

"Why do I feel like you're giving me the business, McKeller?"

"What I'm giving you is a lead. Big city cops use them to crack cases."

Deputy Dale put a hand up to hide the smirk on his face.

"If you want to waste your time by dragging me downtown, be my guest. Things are pretty hectic at work these days and, quite frankly, I could use the rest. A long nap in a jail cell sounds better than babysitting the senator and his pals, but we both know you're barking up the wrong tree."

"You're sure Henderson was working for this Martin fella?"

"I'm sure. I don't know if Martin will own up to it, but Ralphy was one of his goons."

"And just where can I find this Martin character."

"He'll be in the Brookgreen Room at six tonight."

Talbert looked at his watch. It was quarter 'til. "How is it you're so privy to this Martin's schedule?"

"I'm the hotel detective," I offered up. "It's my business to know what's going on in my hotel. He'll be there all right."

"I still want to talk to the girl."

"Understood."

"I don't know what's going on with you, McKeller, but I get the feeling you're holding back. There's more here then you're letting on. If I were you I'd be real careful about the games you play. This is a murder investigation."

"Sheriff, you ought to know me better than that. I'm just a conscientious citizen trying to do my part, help out where I can."

"After I talk to Martin, I'm going to want to see the girl."

"We'll make it happen. In the meantime, you might want to watch yourself with Martin and his goons. They're sure to be packing heat."

The sheriff and Deputy Dale gave each other a look.

"I'm just saying, these guys aren't Sunday school teachers. Watch your back."

"We'll take care of that," the sheriff replied with a cocky grin.

"Don't you worry none about us."

"Oh, I'm not worried. I just want to make sure you go in with your eyes open."

"When we're done questioning Martin and his boys, we're going to want to see you and the girl."

I nodded.

Without another word, Sheriff Talbert and Deputy Dale walked off, toward the Brookgreen Room and their meeting with Blake Martin and his thugs.

I didn't expect the sheriff would get a lot out of Martin. He wasn't the type to run his mouth, and he wouldn't be intimidated by the local law, but I figured he'd have his hands full for a few hours. If nothing else, I'd bought a little extra time for Rosie and me. I didn't expect Martin would be too happy about it.

Chapter Seventeen

Freckle faced Clifford was manning the elevator when I stepped in. He was his usual jovial self.

"Howdy, Mr. McKeller."

"Clifford," I replied with a nod.

"Up to your room?"

"No, I'm still on the clock. Take me up to ten."

"Heading to the big party, huh? I hear they're having quite the shindig up there."

"Yeah, if you go for that sort of thing."

We got up to the fifth floor before Clifford brought us to a stop, yielding to the light signaling someone had called for the elevator. He was all business as he opened up the brass gates for our impending fellow rider.

I almost didn't recognize her when she stepped aboard. Little Rachel Rae Miller cleaned up nice. The sparkles and sunshine was all grown up, replaced with fire and brimstone sex appeal, heavy on the fire.

She was dolled up in a silver sparkled gown that melted to her figure like it was handcrafted to her. Her face was a soft and flawless flow of womanly features, thin cheeks, angular brows, bright blue eyes peeking out from behind the lipstick, rouge and powder. Her hair was down long, shimmering and luxurious, the right side tucked in behind her ear. There was an air about her she didn't have earlier, a confidence in the way she moved and stood, the way she gave a slight smile when she looked me in the eye and half nodded a greeting. She no longer looked like Daddy's little girl, but now the kind of girl who could mess with the heads of a lot of daddies.

"Going up?" Clifford asked, practically drooling over the young girl.

Rachel smiled her self-assured smile at him. "Tenth floor, please."

He had us going again in no time flat.

"Heading to the party?" I asked.

Rachel hesitated for a moment before answering. "Why, yes, I am, as a matter of fact. Senator Wright invited me." She looked for a second like she thought I might chastise her. "I know we aren't supposed to fraternize with the guests but ... he is a United States Senator, after all."

"He is that," I agreed. "I'm not going to rat you out. Just watch your back. He's a red-blooded American man too."

The little Rae Rae was back for a moment. I could see her again in the blush that reminded me there was a young girl hiding under all that womanly charm and make up. "I can take care of myself, Mr. McKeller."

"Men like Wright are used to getting what they want. I'm just saying, be careful and don't dig yourself a hole so deep you can't climb out if you want."

"I know what I'm doing. I'm not a little girl."

I gave her a quick once over, slender lines and curves packed into the tight fitting dress. "No, I guess you're not at that."

Clifford let us off at the tenth floor and we walked up to the door of the suite, guarded by two of the senator's security men. They waved us by without any questions.

Inside, the party was just getting rolling, the senator's entourage scattered about in small clusters, all of them with drinks in hand. Rae Rae made a beeline for the bar at the far side of the room, and I wandered off to the side, surveying the set up. I ended up over by the window, next to a guy in a tweed jacket. I was barely paying him any attention, but he decided to strike up a conversation just the same.

"The cream of the crop," he said all eloquent and dignified. "The crème de la crème. The very epitome of the elite and powerful. Never will you find a better collection of derelicts and renegades."

"Not a big fan, Mr. James?" I knew who he was.

"Ah, a literary man."

"I've been known to crack one of your books every so often."

Stuart James was, at one time, considered to be one of the finest

American novelists of his generation. His first six books shot to the top of the best seller list where they dug in and stayed. It had been quite a while since I'd heard his name mentioned.

He was a paunchy fellow with receding brown hair and rounded features. He wore his clothes a bit oversized and wrinkled, haphazardly thrown together, the tweed jacket and open-collared shirt not quite matching his checkered trousers.

Most everything about him seemed sloppy and indifferent, and I could tell he'd been hitting the sauce pretty hard, despite the fact he wasn't slurring his words or teetering in his stance.

"Just so long as you purchased said books and didn't borrow them from friends."

"No, you got your nickel from me."

"Much appreciated," he replied, toasting his glass toward me.

"Working on the next one?" I asked, making conversation while I scanned the crowd.

"Alas, I am afraid not. I am in the service of Satan these days, selling my soul to the devil. I have seen fit to prostitute my talents out to the demon Hollywood, writing the mind-numbing drivel of the silver screen."

"I hear there's good money in screenwriting."

"Whores of every level are usually well compensated, don't you find?"

"If I meet any I'll ask them."

"You shouldn't have to look far. This room will suffice quite nicely, and I'm not speaking of those lovely things in the evening gowns either."

"If you feel that way, why are you here?"

"An excellent question and one I have pondered myself for some time. I can only guess that it stems from some inner flaw, some genetic defect passed on by a distant relative. Well, that and the free booze."

"It's a long way to travel for free booze."

"Any excuse to escape the ungodly stench which is Hollywood, where the streets are stained with the blood of a thousand virgins."

"They should consider using that in the travel brochures."

Stuart James chuckled. "I call 'em like I see 'em."

I was glancing around the party. Over by the bar, Senator Wright had found Rachel, and the two were standing close together, in what seemed a very private conversation. "How do you see this one?"

"The same old same old," James said whimsically. "Another grand evening of decadence and debauchery, the very worst that money can buy. By the end of the night I expect the esteemed Senator Wright will have lined his pockets with graft in the form of poker winnings, as he always seems to win. I expect he'll be tasting the fruits of that young lovely by the time it's all said and done as well."

James pointed to a heavy-set man in a three piece suit. He was puffing on a fat cigar and sipping from a brandy snifter. "That particular oaf happens to be Luis Middleton of Middleton Steel. He'll be the big loser of the evening, conveniently losing a small fortune to the senator."

"Not a very lucky guy, huh?"

"Not unlucky enough, I'm afraid. Word is there's to be a bridge built in North Carolina, Beaufort Channel or some such. It's a big contract, and Middleton wants it bad. Since the decrease in military spending, at the end of the war, the big steel companies are reeling, fighting over every nickel they can land. The Beaufort Channel Bridge would be a huge boost to Middleton's fortunes.

"The Honorable Senator Wright heads the committee which decides on who gets the contract, and Middleton has had his nose up the senator's rear end since we got here. Rumor has it the contract is going to Wright's third cousin once removed, and Middleton is wasting his time."

"Tough luck for him."

"He's not about to give up so easy. He has the rest of the weekend to sway the senator's vote, or so he thinks."

"That's how it works, huh?"

"Take that one there," Stuart said nodding his head in the direction of a thin, middle-aged man in a tuxedo. It was the one I recognized from the movies but couldn't recall his name.

He was fit and trim, well groomed and distinguished. His hair was black but graying, slicked back and perfectly combed, a thin Errol Flynn mustache on his lip. His eyes were sunken with thick lines of age around them and he looked like he was somewhere between aging gracefully and desperately clinging to the good looks of his youth.

"Jonathon Masden, one time star of the screen and matinee idol, loved by millions, worshiped by women the world over. Ten years ago he was biggest box office draw in Hollywood. These days he can't buy his way into a walk-on part in a B picture.

"Wine, women and a taste for the fast life spelled his demise. They say he's lost three fortunes over the span of his career, blowing through money faster than they can print it. These days he is a leach on the buttocks of high society, clinging on to whomever will have him and sucking hard for all he's worth. I would venture to say he hasn't enough money in his pockets for bus fare into town."

"How does a guy like that end up here?"

James looked at me like I'd spit in the punch bowl. "He used to be Jonathon Masden, my dear fellow. Some might say he still is. That, in these circles, is a form of currency in itself. He uses his former stature to keep himself surrounded by the rich and affluent, hanging on for dear life by his fingernails."

"That's tough."

"Take my advice, don't lend him any money."

"I'll keep that in mind."

"Over there," he said, pointing to a book-wormy fellow with thick glasses and a button up collar. The guy was ghastly thin with a long boney face and bulging eyes. He was slumped over in a chair, nursing a Collins glass and looking around the room suspiciously.

"Thomas Gladding. Gladding's father was said to be one of the five richest men on the planet. He owned everything from railroads to newspapers and most everything in between. Young Thomas was a mere fifteen years old when the old man kicked the bucket, leaving his massive fortune to his lone descendent. As a result, young Thomas is now one of the most desired party guests in the country, despite the fact he's a miserable bore.

"He is the ultimate capitalist. He's taken his considerable inheritance and turned it into an empire, even larger than his father's. He specializes in acquiring assets, usually under the umbrella of his Skyline Industries. You name it, he buys it. His specialty seems to be buying up struggling companies and incorporating them into his vast portfolio. They say he can make a dime on a nickel.

"Nobody can quite figure him out. He's a strange bird, Gladding. Some say he's a closet pervert, others think he's mentally defective.

Suspicious and paranoid, with the personality of an eggshell, he slinks his way from one society event to another, never quite joining in, but always off in some corner, overseeing the festivities with nary a smile.

"Which do you figure he is?"

Stuart James raised his eyebrows like he wasn't catching my meaning.

"Is he the perv or the defective?"

"I suspect he's a little of both, a borderline schizoid who feels like his worth is measured by the power and influence of the people he surrounds himself with. He's been handed the world on a silver platter, but it's just not enough unless he's rubbing elbows with the power brokers of the world, buying up whatever he can get his grubby fingers on.

"As it is, nobody can stand to even speak to him for more than a couple of minutes. Being seated next to him at a dinner party brings on thoughts of suicide, but his bank wad makes him a must have at these kinds of affairs."

"So, how do you fit in with this crowd?"

"Oh, I'm the worst of the lot. I'm the incredibly talented and successful artist who squanders his talents in pursuit of quick cash and instant gratification. I'm the one in the room who's smart enough to recognize the others for what they are, but too stupid and lazy to separate myself from the herd. No, I'm the weak and deficient link in the chain, the one who has become addicted to the very thing I despise. I'm the most pathetic sell out in the bunch but, in my defense, my good nature and sparkling personality make me the life of the party."

"Yeah, I can see that."

"How about you? Now that I've spilled the family secrets, who might you be?"

"McKeller. I work security at the hotel."

"Ah, I feel more secure already."

"Yeah, I'm one of the babysitters here."

"That, McKeller, is a tall order with this bunch."

"So, how do these things usually go?"

"Your first babysitting job, huh?"

"Something like that."

"Well, let's see ... first off, we will all over indulge in wine and spirits for a while, washing away any inkling of common sense and good taste."

"Looks like everyone has a good start on that."

"We are professionals, McKeller. This is round one. A few drinks are required to take the edge off, bring one's inhibitions down to workable level. Much talk will be done, deals proposed that will never be followed up on. Women will be groped and surely an argument or two will break out but all in the spirit of good fun.

"Once we're all properly soused, dinner will be served. At this time, this group of proper and refined persons will be reduced to a pack of half-crazed gluttons, gorging themselves on some of the finest cuisine your fair state has to offer. It won't be a pretty sight. I, myself, plan to eat my own weight in beef."

"Nice."

"From there it will be cognac and cigars, the room becoming a murky cloud of loud talking and pompous imbeciles, each trying to one up the next. No doubt more women will be groped at this point.

"Once the plates have been cleared we will settle down around the table for a long game of shove-your-money-toward-the-senator, by way of poker. During this phase of the festivities, more alcohol will be consumed and more deals will be proposed, none of which will ever come to fruition. This will go on for the better part of the evening, until the senator has been properly funded.

"Once the fine senator from North Carolina has been thoroughly greased, the poker game will dissolve into melee of drunken disorder and utter stupidity. Dirty stories will be told and more women will be groped.

"The breakdown will be complete, and the worst components of our society will be on full display, all of us reduced to the most primitive of savages, any semblance of civilized behavior out the window. There is a very good chance women will be groped.

"This is the point where the weaker of the pack begin to get weeded out. Drunks will be carried off on luggage carts, back to their rooms to sleep it off.

"I will, most certainly, be among the last standing. This is out of necessity. You see, this is when the pairing off begins, the spoils of battle, so to speak. The senator will have first dibs, of course, the rest of us left to fight amongst ourselves for what's left."

I couldn't help but smirk. "I can see why you're such a good writer. That's some imagination you have there."

James snickered back. "So, you're under the impression I'm inventing all of this?"

"Embellishing, at the very least."

Stuart James let out a loud belly laugh. "You just keep thinking that, my friend."

"So, you're telling me all this money and power came all this way to rub elbows with their fellow fat cats and get lucky with the ladies?"

"The ladies, if you can call them that, are a mere sidebar to the festivities, the icing on the cake, so to speak. The real lure here is power, pure and simple, and the esteemed Senator Wright holds the majority."

"Seems like that Middleton Steel fellow and that Gladding chap have their fair share. Even you, the bestselling author, and the washed up movie star have more than the average Joe."

"You, obviously, don't understand the perverse allure of power and money, McKeller. Merely having it is never enough. It's more addictive than any drug. Once you've had a taste you can't help but crave more. There are no lengths one wouldn't go to keep one's self bathed in the luster it provides. As they say, once you've been there, there's no going back."

"Makes me kind of glad I never had any."

"Consider it a blessing, my friend. You have no idea."

"Well, as fascinating as you make it all sound, I'm going to have to take my leave. I have some other business I need to take care of."

"I hope I haven't scared you off."

"Not at all. I'll be back before the carnage is in full swing."

James smiled. "Carnage," he said. "Good word."

Chapter Eighteen

Hobnobbing with the status quo had given me a case of the willies, and I was ready for some fresh air and a cigarette. Stuart James had been an interesting enough fellow, despite his dark and cynical take on his world, but I was ready to get back to my own kind. There was the little matter of Rosie and the murdered guy to deal with as well.

I'd bought myself a little time where Martin was concerned, but I knew he'd be back sniffing around before long. The sheriff wouldn't be far behind him, and I needed to figure some things out before then.

As par for the course, I had no idea how to go about any of this.

I moseyed down to the lobby, opting for the stairs and the long quiet walk down, giving myself some time to piece things together in my head. By the time I reached the lobby, the pieces were just as scattered and fuzzy as ever, so I made my way out to Peacock Alley, the back veranda of the Ocean Forest.

It was a quiet night, only a few stray couples out, enjoying the evening ocean breeze, watching the moonlight twinkle off the waves of the Atlantic.

She was calm tonight, her surface almost as smooth as glass. Her usual crashing waves were replaced with the gentle hiss of the water easing itself up onto the sand. It was almost like she was napping, maybe just waiting and watching. I got the feeling she had a special eye on me, my old nemesis, waiting and watching my every movement, getting some perverse amusement out of the fact I was, once again, backed into a corner without the common sense to see my way out. She was funny like that.

I lit up a smoke and took a long drag, letting it out in a slow even breath, never taking my eyes off her. "I hope you're getting a kick out of all this," I said to her under my breath.

Movement behind me broke my attention away, and I turned in time to see Rosie come strolling out the doorway, silhouetted by the lobby lights behind her. It made me forget all about that other gal.

She had red shoes I couldn't believe, lipstick red with a strap across the front of her ankle, the back heel so high it made it look like she was walking on her tippy toes. I wondered how she managed it, keeping her balance, perched up on a heel not more the diameter of a kid's lead pencil.

Balance she did though, moving toward me with the slow fluid grace of a ballerina, one sultry step at a time, like she'd been born in those red shoes, her eyes locked on me the whole way.

Rosie looked like she was ready for a night on the town. Her dress matched the shoes, sex scandal red and fitted to her figure like it was there to hold everything perfectly in place. It was cut high enough on her calves to catch a glimpse of paradise and low enough down the front to make a fellow think he was getting a peek at something he wasn't supposed to.

Her hair was down long and straight, parted to one side and partially covering the side of her face, a face that didn't need to be covered. She looked like she'd stepped out of a glamor magazine, maybe a movie. She was a dream, a mirage, a hallucination I'd been having since the day I first saw her, and I thought about pinching myself to see if she was real, but there was a part of me that didn't want to know. Another part of me tried to tell me it was all smoke and mirrors, and that underneath the facade was the same Rosie who'd been scratching at my craw since the first time we'd met. I didn't want to hear it.

"You got another one of those, Hon?" she asked, motioning to the cigarette in my hand.

I fumbled the pack out of my pocket and fought one out of the cellophane, holding it up by the business end and offering it up to her.

Rosie made a move with her eyes that told me it was all on me, that she couldn't be bothered to reach out and take it on her own so I followed suit. I reached up and placed it between her ruby reds and snatched the Zippo out of my pocket as quick as I could, meeting her smoke with a flame and illuminating that perfect face in brilliant light.

"Thanks," she said, letting it dangle from her lips, barely taking any in.

I was still holding my lighter open, the flame going strong, my eyes soaking in the sight of her.

"I think you got it." Her eyes glanced to the lighter, still going in my hand, and then back to me. I clicked it shut and stuffed it back in my pocket.

"You look nice," I said.

"Thanks," she replied, like it was foregone conclusion.

"Going out?"

"I thought maybe I'd go see some of Myrtle Beach. I was hoping someone might volunteer to escort me."

"Do you think that's a good idea?"

Rosie shrugged. "I saw Blake leaving the hotel with a couple of officers. I figured the coast might be clear for a while."

"That would be Sheriff Talbert and his deputy. They had a few questions for Martin and his boys."

"How did you manage that one?"

"What makes you think I had anything to do with it?"

There was a slight smile on the edge of her lips and a twinkle in her eye. It was that look that I'd fallen for so many times before, the kind of look that makes a guy want to see more.

"You're too modest, Frankie."

"You know, the sheriff wants to have a word with you too, after he's done with Martin."

"I have nothing to hide."

"It's a good thing. I don't know where you'd hide it in that dress."

"Why, Frankie McKeller, I do believe you're flirting with me."

I tried not to blush. "Where's Karate Boy tonight?"

"It's not my turn to watch him. Back in his room, I suppose. Would you prefer I go ask him to take me out?"

"Level with me, Rosie. What's the deal with you and him?"

Rosie turned away and propped her arms on the railing of the veranda, tossing her cigarette aside and looking out into the night. "I don't know, Frankie. I was in a bad way and I needed somebody. He was there for me when everything happened with Blake.

"I never meant to lead him on. He was a friend I could count on, at first. It got to be where he wanted more. What can I say? Men just seem to get obsessed with me."

"Imagine that," I replied, glancing down the open back of her dress.

"As I recall, you did too, at one time."

"As I recall, you did a little more than bat your eyelashes at me."

She turned back at me with that look still in her eyes. "He doesn't mean anything to me, Frankie. He was someone I could turn to."

"What about now?"

She shrugged again. "How do you tell someone you don't need them anymore? How do you tell them there's someone else without hurting their feelings?"

My thoughts shot back, for a split second, to the time when she dumped me. "I wouldn't know."

Rosie let out a sigh like she was bored with the conversation. "Let's get out of here, Frankie. I don't want to think about any of this for now. I want to go out and laugh and hear music. Let's just get away from it all for a few hours, me and you."

"I have to work. There's a thing upstairs I need to check in on."

She made a pout and her eyes got all wide and innocent. "Just for a little while?"

I looked at her good and long, a million reasons for saying no swirling through my brain. "I might know a place. Just for a little while."

In the back of my head I thought I heard a little voice go off. It sounded like it said, "The Devil's got you now."

Chapter Nineteen

I don't know what kind of joint Rosie expected me to take her to, but it's a pretty fair guess she wasn't expecting a place like Mack's Dive. Mack's was a little juke joint located north of the Ocean Forest Hotel and Myrtle Beach proper. It was nestled in the middle of an area called Atlantic Beach but most of the locals referred to it as the Black Pearl.

It got its name from the simple fact that it was a scaled down resort area that catered to people of the darker persuasion. You weren't likely to find many of the local white folks hanging around on any given night but, from my first visit there, I'd took a shine to the place and had even managed to make a few friends there. It was one of the few places in town where I felt almost comfortable.

A lot of heads turned when I came walking in with Rosie on my arm. Tabby's was one of them.

Tabby was a cute little cocktail server, a main stay at Mack's and somebody I'd grown to consider a good friend. She was about as pretty as they come with skin like milk chocolate and a smile made of pure sunshine. She had a figure that could rival Rosie's and she always kept it packed in a tight fitting dress, bare legs, open-toed sandals.

There had been about a minute, some time back, when I thought Tabby and I might end up as more than just friends, but it hadn't been in the cards and, since then, we'd settled into a comfortable and casual friendship. I'd even helped her out awhile back when one of her childhood friends turned up dead, and I knew she'd always be someone I could count on in a pinch.

Her brother Russel was behind the bar and was hunched over it, wiping it down with a rag as we sat down in front of him. Russel was a big guy, downright affable once you got to know him, and he'd ended up warming up to me after getting to know me.

"How's things, McKeller?"

"Peachy keen, Russel. Yourself?"

"I can't complain. Nobody pays no mind anyway."

I made the introductions to Rosie and Russel took her dainty hand in his oversized mitt, giving it the gentlest of shakes. "It's a pleasure to make your acquaintance, ma'am."

"Likewise," she replied. "You got any hooch back there?"

"I reckon we just might." He smiled back.

Typical Rosie, blending herself into any place or situation.

Tabby had sauntered her way over to us as her brother went about pouring us a couple of belts of the local moonshine with ice water chasers.

"How's everything at the Big Digs these days?" she asked, using her nickname for the Ocean Forest Hotel.

"You know how it is," I replied. "Living the dream, basking in the sunshine, another day in paradise."

Her eyes were locked on Rosie, the two women sharing a silent greeting, maybe sizing each other up just a bit. It could have been my imagination.

"Rosie, Tabby. Tabby, Rosie."

"Any friend of Frankie's," Tabby said with a smile, shaking Rosie's hand. She almost never called me Frankie.

"It's a pleasure to meet you, Tabby."

"What brings you two up this way?"

"Rosie's an old friend, visiting down from Baltimore. I thought I'd bring her out and show her the sights."

"I don't suppose there's a whole lot of sights to see up this way, not compared to a big city like Baltimore, but welcome, just the same."

Rosie glanced around the half-empty barroom, surveying the faded paint on the walls, the mix of unmatched tables and chairs scattered about the room. "I like it," she said with a smile. "It has a homey, comfortable feel to it."

"That's one way to put it," Tabby replied.

Tabby and Russel got back to work, and Rosie and me sat cozied up together at the bar. We talked about old times, mutual friends, places we used to frequent back home. You'd never know we were mixed up in a murder, a case of blackmail with a gangster, maybe more. We were a couple of kids without a care in the world. It felt comfortable, like a home cooked meal or a perfectly broken in pair of leathers.

I was leaned in close to her, my face next hers, taking in the sweet scent of her, listening to her go on about this and that. I caught sight of Tabby crossing the room, and I watched her walk by, catching her looking back at me for a quick glance, turning away when she spotted me looking back. As she passed by the front door, I caught sight of something else, something that captured my attention and seemed out of place.

From outside the doorway stepped a man. He was medium height and thin, dressed conservatively in a gray pressed suit, pinstripes, and fedora. Two things stood out about him. For one, he was Caucasian, like me, the only other one I'd seen in this part of town. The other thing was the nagging sensation that I'd seen him before, like he was somehow familiar.

Rosie noticed my attentions had wandered and she turned her head to see what I was looking at.

It took me a second to figure out where I knew him from, or didn't, as the case may be. It was the same guy I'd seen on the veranda of the Ocean Forest and again at the Chesterfield Inn, the one I couldn't place but knew I'd seen before.

When he realized I was staring back at him, he pulled his fedora down low on his face and took a step to the side, out of my line of vision. I instinctively stood and started for the door, but Rosie grabbed hold of my arm and held me back, weaving her arms around mine.

"Where do you think you're going?"

"That guy ..."

"What guy?"

"The one outside the door. He was watching us."

I started for the door again, but Rosie tightened her grip and held me in place.

"What are you talking about, Frankie?"

"That guy, there's something about him, like I know him from somewhere."

"I didn't see any guy."

"He was right there in the doorway. You looked right at him."

"I didn't see anybody."

"I'll be right back," I said, making another move toward the door. Rosie held me firm again, pulling me back toward her, like she didn't want to let me go.

"I think you're seeing things, Frankie. There's nobody there."

I looked down at her arms wrapped around mine. It seemed like she was working pretty hard at keeping me from going out front.

"Is there any particular reason you don't want me to go take a look?"

Rosie released her grip and held her hands up in a surrender motion. "I don't know what you're talking about. I think you're getting paranoid again."

I ignored the remark and headed out the front door as quick as I could. The street wasn't very crowded, a few stray people walking this way and that, two old men on a bench across the street. I looked up and down, scanning the store fronts but there was no sign of a thin white man in a conservative suit.

I paced down to the alleyway alongside the bar but it was empty but for a couple of overflowing garbage cans, a stack of lumber leaned up against the building. Standing there, waiting, I looked around, searching for movement, anything to clue me in on which way he'd gone.

In return I got nothing but stillness, the muffled sound of voices coming from the bar, the distant blends of music from nearby radios mixing with the jukebox at Mack's. I'd come up empty, took too long to get outside to see which way he went.

What was it about the guy? There was something familiar about him. I'd noticed it the first time I'd seen him but I couldn't place my finger on it, like I knew him from somewhere long ago. It was like getting a song stuck in your head but not remembering exactly how the words go.

After a few minutes of nothing, I turned back and headed back into the bar. Rosie was waiting with a smile and a couple of fresh shots of moonshine.

"Well?" she asked.

I shook my head. "He's gone."

Rosie let out a giggle. "Maybe he was never there. Maybe your mind is playing tricks on you."

"He was there all right. You had to see him, thin guy, nice suit, gray hat sitting low on his head."

"There was nobody there when I looked up," she said, handing me a shot glass and toasting hers against it. I shot mine back hard, ignoring the burn in my throat, wondering how she'd missed him, why she'd been so adamant about keeping from going after him.

Rosie's smile got bigger. "That's better," she purred. "What do you say we sit here and tie one on instead of running around and chasing down invisible men in pinstriped suits."

"Yeah, I guess you're right," I said, settling back into my bar stool and ordering up two more. Rosie nestled in beside me, leaning herself against my arm. She was warm and cozy against me, soft feminine flesh pressed tight on my side, everything about her pretty and delicate, raw and fiery. It was almost enough to distract my thoughts.

"So, you figure I was just seeing things, huh?"

"Sure, Frankie, it happens, a guy looks up and thinks he sees something that isn't there."

"Yeah, I guess it does, sometimes."

"Sure it does. It's no big deal."

"Yeah, no big deal," I agreed. "Except for one little thing."

"What's that?"

"The way you didn't see him, but knew he was wearing a pinstriped suit."

Rosie gave me a confused look.

"I never mentioned anything about pinstripes," I said.

"I don't get what you're saying."

"I'm saying you're lying, Rosie. You're lying again, and you've probably lied to me about most everything you've told me so far, the way you've lied to me since the day we met."

"That's some way to talk," she tried.

"Yeah, ain't it though? You've been giving me the run around since you showed up on my doorstep. How did you know the invisible man was wearing a pinstriped suit?"

"You must have mentioned it."

"I didn't. I said he was in a suit with a gray hat."

"You're confusing me, Frankie. I don't know exactly what you said."

"You know a guy named Marcus Fletcher, from back home?"

"I never heard of him."

"You sure? I've got reason to believe he's in Myrtle Beach, and he was somehow connected to Ralph Henderson."

"I wouldn't know."

"Maybe Taylor Mills might know who he is."

"Maybe you should ask him yourself. I don't happen to know everyone Taylor knows and doesn't know."

"Maybe I will."

"Is that who you think you saw in the doorway, this Fletcher guy?"

"No, it wasn't Fletcher. This guy was thin, dressed immaculately. When he spotted me looking at him, he ducked behind the building, like he didn't want me to see him."

"Maybe it was just some random guy."

"Yeah, maybe it was just some random guy I've seen three times now, each time he's managed to skate away. The thing is, there's something about him, like I know him from somewhere."

She gave a nervous shrug. "I wouldn't know about that either."

"You don't know about much, do you? Except that one guy is dead and another guy is after you for some books he wants back, and he's willing to go to great lengths to get them. Other than that, a lot of people from Baltimore keep popping up, all of them connected to you somehow."

"You're talking crazy, Frankie."

"Am I? It's all fun and games until somebody gets strapped into the electric chair. I don't think you quite realize what you've got yourself wrapped up in here."

"Frankie, you have to believe me. I don't know any Fletcher, and I don't know anything about a guy in a pinstriped suit you think was watching us."

I finished my drink and slammed the empty glass down on the bar top. "Drink up, we're heading back."

"I thought we were having a night out together?"

I looked her over. She was perched up on her stool with her legs crossed, her top knee peeking out from under the hem of her red dress. It was a long path of smooth curvaceous skin that led down to her skinny ankles, her feet tucked into those scarlet heels. Her face was flushed and dazzling, painted up in lipstick and rouge, framed by her dark mane of flowing black hair. Those deep brown eyes were wide and bright, all her girlish energy glowing in them and focused on me.

As perfect as she was, she no longer seemed to have stepped out of a magazine. Now she seemed to be from somewhere else, somewhere entirely different.

"I don't think I'm so crazy about the company anymore."

"That's a fine way to be," she scoffed.

"Finish your drink."

It was a cold ride back to the hotel, and it had nothing to do with temperature. Rosie never said a word, sitting beside me in the '46 Studebaker Coupe the hotel allowed me use of. She sat stiff and rigid, blankly staring forward, stewing in her own juices and ignoring me like I wasn't there.

I spent most of the ride glancing over at her bare thighs, the hem of her dress riding up high when she sat down in the low sitting car. Hey, I may of had a beef with her, but I'm still made of flesh and blood, after all.

I pulled into the side lot off the right wing of the hotel and Rosie was out of the car before I had the engine shut off. By the time I got out she had a twenty-pace lead on me, and she was heading to the front stairs, taking brisk and steady steps. Even in those heels on the gravel and dirt parking lot, I had a tough time catching up to her, with my bum leg and all. She was just making her way up the steps when I caught her.

"Wait up, Rosie."

She stopped abruptly and crossed her arms in front of her. I continued up a few more steps until I was looking down at her. Her face was pinched with anger, her eyes squinting.

"What do you expect from me? How am I supposed to react when all you feed me is bullshit and lies?"

Rosie didn't answer.

"Do you want to tell me who the guy in the suit was?"

Still nothing.

"You keep telling me you want my help, but you won't give me all the facts. Every time I turn around I find something else you haven't told me about."

"I've told you everything," she replied with a scowl.

"Yeah, after I had it half figured out myself. You didn't tell me about Ralphy at first. You didn't tell me about Martin and his books. You didn't tell me about Taylor Mills until I found out about him. How do you expect me to believe anything you say?"

"You just have to trust me, Frankie." She said it all soft and frail.

"You make it tough for a guy to do that."

"Look, I just want what's coming to me. Once those books come I'll get my money from Blake, and I'll be out of your hair for good."

"There's still the little matter of the dead guy."

"I didn't kill anybody, you know that."

"Maybe I do and maybe I don't. You've got to admit, it doesn't look good. Either way, you're smack dab in the middle of it, and that's not going to change."

"It won't come back on me. It can't."

"Glad you're so confident."

"Frankie, I thought we were on the same team here. Why do you want to fight me on this stuff? We both want the same thing."

"I'm not a hundred percent sure what team you're on, Rosie."

"That's a fine way to be with an old friend."

"We've been a lot of things over the years, Darling. I'm not sure friends was ever one of them."

Chapter Twenty

Rosie and I parted ways for the evening. She said she was heading up to her room for the night and I had no choice but to take her at her word. It was time for me to get back to work.

I was greeted by a sea of gray as I stepped off the elevator, the hallway lined with members of the senator's security detail. They were spaced out every few feet, a dozen or so men keeping watch over the empty corridor and protecting the area leading up to Wright's suite. A small army would have had a tough time fighting their way to the senator's door. I merely walked up and was let in by one of Simmons' lieutenants who recognized me from earlier.

The room smelled of cigar smoke and stale booze. The tables were littered with empty glasses and overflowing ashtrays, and it looked like the maid service had been turned away. There were playing cards strewn across the surface of the dining room table like they'd been tossed aside by their players hours ago.

Simmons was nowhere to be found, and only a few of the crew from earlier was still in place, and even they looked a little worse for wear. Stuart James was propped up on a stool by the bar, and it looked like it was taking everything he had to keep himself there. He was swaying slightly and staring off at the far wall with a blank look on his face.

The wormy Gladding fellow came back into the room right after me and took the same spot he'd been in when I left. It looked like he might be nursing the same half-full Collins glass. There was no one seated near him and, after the conversation I'd had with James earlier, I had a fairly good idea why.

Missing from the proceedings were Jonathon Masden, the former movie star, and Luis Middleton, the Steel tycoon. I was a little surprised, as I hadn't figured either to fall to the wayside before the party was over.

There was no sign of the senator or of little Rachel Rae Miller, but the other young lovelies were scattered about the room, champagne glasses in hand, giggling and flirting with the various men they had coupled up with. I wandered over to Stuart James.

"How was the party?"

He looked up at me with a confused look, cocking his head to one side and looking me over like he was trying to figure out who I was.

"McKeller," I said, trying to help boost his memory.

"Right." He smiled. "The house dick ..."

"Yeah. How did it go?"

"Go?" he slurred. "Don't you mean how's it going? This party is just hitting its stride, young man."

I looked about the room. The drunken messes who had earlier been the dignified and upper crust crowd seemed to have dwindled down to a ragtag collection of lushes and misfits, just like James had predicted. They didn't seem to be hitting any kind of stride but, instead, seemed close to hitting the proverbial wall.

"How was the poker game?"

"Shock of all shocks, the esteemed senator was the big winner of the evening."

"Where is the honorable Senator Wright?"

Stuart James looked around the room, surveying what was left of the crowd. "Isn't he here? Seems like I just saw him a minute ago."

"Maybe he stepped out for some fresh air."

"Oh, I'm sure he stepped out for some fresh something," he replied with mischievous grin.

"How'd you fare?"

"Well, I'm probably down more than I can afford to lose, but when you factor in the booze and chow, I about broke even for the night."

"Eat your weight in beef, like you wanted?"

"Let's just say I gave it the old college try. The cows in these parts will be whispering my name in fear for years to come."

"Glad to hear it. Did I miss anything good?"

He cocked his head to the other side, thinking it over. "It was the usual array of drunken debauchery and ego stroking."

While we were talking, Luis Middleton and Jonathon Masden re-entered the room, side by side, through the front door. They were engrossed in conversation, Masden looking uneasy and uncomfortable. The Steel tycoon looked like he might be giving the former matinee idol a first rate lecture of some kind. Stuart James noticed their entrance and nodded in their direction.

"Back for round two," he said with a slur.

"They're looking pretty chummy."

"Hardly."

"Is that so?"

"You should have seen it earlier. It wasn't pretty."

"What happened?" I asked, looking over to the movie star who had separated from Middleton and was seated on a sofa, brooding over his drink.

"It seems the former star of the silver screen tried to wager using his personal note in lieu of cash. Some of the others decided his personal note was not worth the paper it was printed on."

"They called him out, huh?"

"It was brutal. It seems that certain members of our party have been accepting said notes for some time and have yet to collect on any of them. They decided cash would be necessary if Mr. Masden was to join in on the game."

"Ouch."

"I thought he might break down and cry at first. He started rambling on about a big score he was about to come into, but the others laughed it off. He is not exactly Hollywood royalty these days. I can't imagine who might hire him.

"To his credit, he held his head high, relegated to a spectator, as the rest of us indulged in one of the higher stakes games I have ever had the misfortune to be a part of. I, myself, used the strategy of folding early on most hands. I'm afraid I don't have a steel mill or a railroad resupplying my pockets."

"Sounds like a hoot."

"A hoot it was, my friend. A hoot it was."

There was a loud scream that caused us all to stop and look back toward one of the closed bedroom doors, a woman's voice, hysterical and curdling. When it resounded a second time, I rushed over to the closed door and tried the knob but it was locked from the inside.

Before I could reach into my pocket for my master key, I was pushed aside by one of the senator's security team who had come bursting into the room. One held me back while two others lowered their shoulders and slammed themselves into the door, battering ram style.

The door broke open and they disappeared into the room. I filed in behind them.

Senator Wright was sprawled across the bed, face up. He was half undressed, in a sleeveless under shirt, his shoes and socks off, trousers undone. His eyes were closed and there was a gash on his left temple, blood trickling down the side of his face. The phone was lying on the floor, on its side, the receiver off the cradle.

In the far corner, huddled against the wall and crouching low, was Rachel Rae Miller. Her hair was tussled and her eyes were wide and wet, tears streaming down her face, smudged with makeup. A splotch of red marked her right cheek, the size of a man's hand, and a small cut at the top of her high cheekbone, like she'd caught the edge of a ring. Her gown was half torn off, the right shoulder strap broken and the dress ripped down the side. She was holding it up and in front of her, doing her best to keep herself covered.

The security men were at the senator's side in an instant, checking his pulse, attempting to revive him. I went straight to Rachel who jumped to her feet and flung herself against me, curling up into my chest and holding tight to what was left of her sparkly gown. I wrapped my arms around her and tried to calm her down.

"It's OK, you're all right now."

"He ... attacked me. I tried to stop him but he got violent."

"It's all right, Rachel. It's all over."

"He ... he slapped me. He ripped my dress off. He went crazy."

"You're all right now. Everything's OK."

"I want this room cleared!" I hadn't seen Simmons come in, but he was standing in the middle of the room with his hands on his hips, barking orders. "I want everybody out of here. The girl stays, but everybody else is to be escorted out."

His men began to respond immediately, a handful to the doorway, pushing back the on-looking guests, two of them toward me and Rachel. The senator was stirring on the bed, coming back to his senses.

"I'm going to need you to exit the area, sir," one of the security team said, grabbing me by the shoulder and pulling me away from Rachel. I held her in tighter, refusing to let go.

"I'm not going anywhere," I said.

"I'm sorry, sir, but we need to secure this area. You are going to have to exit with the others."

"I'm staying put," I replied, raising my voice loud enough for Simmons to pick up on what was happening. "This is my hotel and this is one of my employees. I'm not leaving this room until I'm convinced she's all right."

Simmons was at my side in an instant. "It's all right, McKeller. My people can take it from here."

"I don't think so, Simmons. I'm security in this hotel. and this girl is my responsibility. If she stays, I stay."

He gave me the kind of hard look only a seasoned cop can give. "All right, let's get these other people out of here. I want this area cleared. McKeller and the girl can stay."

The security thugs bypassed me and headed out into the main area, clearing the guests and sending them back to their rooms. The senator was sitting upright on the bed now, holding a towel to his forehead.

"What happened?" he asked.

Simmons was on him like an obedient puppy. "I'm going to have to ask that you remain silent, Senator. We need to get these people out of here."

"I just want to know what happened."

"Please, Senator. I respectfully request that you don't say another word until we get everyone out. Anything you say could be potentially incriminating."

"Incriminating?" He looked confused and off kilter. When he caught sight of me holding Rachel in my arms, her dress ripped, makeup smeared with tears, his face went white with shock. "Did I do that?"

"Please, Senator," Simmons said forcefully. "I'm going to need you to remain quiet until we can get this thing contained."

"But—"

"Senator Wright! Please, let us do our job."

Wright seemed to slump over in the bed, the energy drained out of him. His eyes never left the young girl in my arms.

Simmons came back over to me and Rachel. "One of my men is going to escort the both of you to one of the adjoining bedrooms," he said. "The girl can get cleaned up in there."

"The girl has a name," I pointed out.

Simmons turned to Rachel. "Miss Miller, one of my men is going to escort you and Mr. McKeller into one of the adjoining bedrooms. You can change and get yourself together in there. I will be in to speak with you in a few minutes."

"I'd kind of like to hear what the senator has to say," I offered up.

"That's impossible. The senator will not be making any kind of statement until me and my men can ascertain just what happened here."

"It's pretty obvious what happened."

"McKeller, this is my jurisdiction. This is a United States Senator and we are going to follow protocol until we can establish just what went down in this room. You can accompany Miss Miller into the next room, or I can have you removed. It's your call. As far as I'm concerned, you are here as a courtesy to Miss Miller and to the hotel. What's it going to be?"

"I guess we'll be going to the other room."

"Good choice."

We were taken out of the room and into the next bedroom. The main area of the suite was empty except for men in gray suits keeping guard over the room. The bodyguard opened the door to the bedroom and closed it behind us once we were in.

"Are you all right?" I asked Rachel, once we were alone.

She nodded back.

"Go on into the bathroom and get yourself cleaned up. I'll be out here."

She nodded again and stood looking back at me with watering eyes, strands of blonde hair hanging haphazardly in her face. Her right arm was reached across her chest, holding the tattered remains of her dress against her, her left hand clenched at the top of it, holding it up and barely covering her all but exposed front.

"Mr. McKeller ... I can't thank you enough—"

"Forget it." I cut her off. "Go get yourself cleaned up."

She gave another nod and disappeared into the bathroom, closing the door behind her. I sat down on the edge of the bed and tapped out a Lucky Strike, the last one in my pack. I crumpled up the empty and tossed it to the floor, pulled out my lighter and lit up my smoke.

"This is a hell of a mess," I said to myself, taking in a long drag.

When she reemerged she had an embroidered Ocean Forest Hotel robe tied around her, and her hair pulled back in a ponytail. Her face was fresh and cleaned, the makeup washed away and her pale cheeks flushed with color, her eyes red and watery. There was still the pink imprint of a hand on her cheek, and the small ring-sized cut had stopped bleeding. She walked over, barefoot, and sat down next to me on the bed.

"You got another one of those?" she asked.

"Last one." I held the cigarette out, and she took it, placing in her lips and taking a deep drag of what was left. She held it in a second, then tilted her head back and blew a cloud of smoke into the air, handing me back the dying butt.

"Why would he do that?" she asked.

I shrugged. "Why don't you tell me everything that happened?"

Rachel wrapped her arms around her own shoulders and gave herself a squeeze. "I don't know," she said all distant and dreamy. "We were having fun. There were all those powerful men there and Senator Wright was paying me so much attention. He kept refilling my champagne, and it made me feel all light headed and silly.

"After dinner, I was sitting on his lap while they played cards. He said I brought him luck. He kept winning too. I've never seen so much money"

She paused and took a breath. Letting it out slow.

"After the card game the men were smoking cigars, drinking brandy and scotch. I didn't know people could drink so much. All of them were loud and laughing and telling stories ... they made me blush, some of them.

"I was having such a grand time, and the champagne got my head to spinning. Senator Wright asked me to go into the bedroom with him."

Rachel stopped and looked up at me, her eyes all wide and scared. "I wasn't going to go, honest Mister. I told him I was a good girl and I didn't do stuff like that.

"He told me there was something he wanted to show me. It was so stupid of me. I know I shouldn't have, but he's a United States Senator. I thought I could trust him.

"Once we were in the room, he was all over me. He had his arms around me, and he was kissing my face and my neck. I tried to push him away, but the more I tried the rougher he got. He pushed me down on the bed, and he was on top of me. His hands were everywhere.

"I tried to make him stop. I begged and pleaded. I fought back as best I could, but he was too strong. He told me to lie still, and to stop being such a child. He told me there were hundreds of girls who would kill to be in my position.

"That's when I kind of lost it. I started kicking and screaming, beating on his chest with my fists. He slapped me hard across the face. It stunned me for a second. I didn't know what was happening. He reached down and grabbed my dress by the front and pulled it so hard it ripped apart.

"I was half naked on the bed and he was groping and feeling me. His face was buried in my chest, sloppy wet kisses all over my skin. It made my flesh crawl.

"There was a telephone on the nightstand. It seemed so far away. I stretched out as far as I could, reaching for it, but I couldn't quite get to it. He put his hands up under my dress, pulling at my panties. It shifted me up the bed and I grabbed the phone. I swung it at him as hard as I could. I wanted to kill him.

"The senator went limp on top of me. I thought, for a second, I had killed him. I pushed him off and jumped up, pulling my dress back up around me. I started screaming. That's when the door burst open."

We both sat quiet for a long few moments.

"You're all right now," I said. "It's over."

"Am I going to get in trouble?" she asked. "I mean, I slugged a U.S. Senator."

"You did the right thing. You did what you had to do."

"I shouldn't have gone in there with him."

"Bad judgment on your part doesn't give him the right to do what he did, senator or not. You're not in any trouble."

"What happens now?"

"I don't know but, whatever it is, you'll get through it OK."

"You're not going to leave me with them, are you? I don't want to be alone with those men. They work for him."

"Don't you worry. I'm not going anywhere."

"Thank you, Mr. McKeller."

There was a light knock on the door and Simmons let himself in without waiting to be invited. He walked over to the foot of the bed and stood looking down at us, his fedora pushed back on his head.

"Are you all right, ma'am? Do you need a doctor or anything?"

"No, I'm fine, just a little shaken up. I could use a cigarette, if you've got an extra."

Simmons patted one out and handed it to her, lighting it for her after she placed it in her mouth. She was a cool cucumber, for a kid. After everything she'd been through, her hands weren't even shaking.

"Thanks."

"I'm going to need you to tell me exactly what happened."

Little Rachel Rae went through her story again, verbatim, word for word to what she told me. When she was finished she sat waiting, puffing on her smoke. Simmons took a minute to digest it all.

"I'm sure you can understand, this is a very sensitive situation. The senator is a very important man."

"That makes it all right, what he did to me?"

"Miss Miller, as of yet, we haven't established that anyone did anything to anyone. We are still investigating this matter and we have to proceed very carefully. The senator is a very high profile man and there are integrity issues to consider."

"So, what, you're saying I'm lying?"

"I didn't say that. I said we are investigating the matter and we intend to get to the bottom of this."

"Did you see what he did to my dress?"

"Did you see the number you did on the senator's head?"

"I was protecting myself. He tried to rape me."

"Now, let's not go throwing words like that around. You were at a party. You were drinking. Maybe you misinterpreted the senator's advances."

"Did I misinterpret it when he slapped me across the face and ripped my clothes off?"

"Just what were you doing alone in the bedroom with a man you barely knew?"

"I told you! He said he wanted to show me something."

I'd had about enough of this game. I stood up and made a move toward Simmons. "What do you say you and me step outside for a little pow-wow."

Simmons looked at Rachel, then back at me. "Yeah, sure."

When we were alone in the suite, I said, "What's the big idea running rough shod over that kid in there?"

"I'm just doing my job, McKeller."

"And what exactly is your job? Are you looking to get to the bottom of this or are you more interested in protecting the senator's reputation?"

Simmons didn't answer.

"Yeah, that's what I thought. Maybe it's time to bring in some outside help. A crime has been committed, and I say we let the local law enforcement sort this out."

"That's not going to happen."

"Yeah? Why not?"

"Because that's a United States Senator in there, not some farm boy who got a little too fresh with his best girl. As far as I'm concerned, this is a matter of national security."

"National security? What, do you figure that kid in there for a Commie spy?"

"We are investigating all possibilities at this time."

"Are you investigating the possibility that the good senator tied half a load on and tried to rape a young girl?"

"We are investigating all possibilities at this time."

"You guys kill me. You think you can just sweep this under the carpet? What's to prevent me from calling up the sheriff? I'm guessing he'd be pretty interested in what went down here tonight."

"I can't let you do that. As I stated, this is now a matter of national security. Any attempt, on your part, to impede with this investigation, in any way, would be seen as a breach in national security. That's federal prison time, no judge, no jury. I pick up a phone and you disappear into the system."

"Just like that?"

"Just like that," he repeated with a half nod of his head.

"That's some rules you guys play by."

"Don't kid yourself, McKeller. This is no game. I need to know I can count on your complete cooperation and your utmost discretion while we conduct our investigation. That goes for the girl too. I can't have any of this leaking out until we get to the bottom of this."

Neither of us had noticed Rachel standing in the doorway.

"I just want what's right," she said. "He shouldn't have done that to me."

Simmons turned to her. "If it's proven the senator did anything inappropriate, proper actions will be taken. In the meantime, I need you to keep this under your hat until we can figure this out."

"Who do you think I'm going to run off and tell? You think I want this in the papers?"

"Ma'am, at this point in the investigation, it's in everyone's best interest that this be kept quiet, for all parties involved. You should get some sleep. We'll talk more in the morning."

"I need to get my things," she replied, turning back into the bedroom and toward the bathroom.

"What about the senator? Did you get a statement from him?" I asked after she was gone.

Simmons hesitated, like he was considering how much information he wanted to give me. "The senator doesn't remember much. He remembers taking the girl into the bedroom. The next thing he remembers is waking up on the bed with a cut on his head."

"I think they call that a black-out drunk. It doesn't excuse his actions."

"We are investigating all possibilities at this time."

"Yeah, I heard that."

"I'm ready," Rachel said, back in the doorway. She was still wearing the robe and was holding her dress and shoes.

"Where do you stay?"

"I have a place in the bullpen." The bullpen was a three-story building down the street from the hotel that served as a sort of dormitory for the workers of the Ocean Forest, those who needed it.

"We'll get you a room at the hotel for tonight. "I'll run over and get some clothes for you in the morning."

"Thanks."

I called down to the front desk to find a room I could stash her in. Curtis told me 712 was open so I took her down on the elevator. Clifford was manning the controls, as usual. I could tell he wanted to ask why his pretty young coworker was with me in a bathrobe but, to his credit, he kept his curiosity in check. He did, however, make an observation about the party earlier.

"Must have been some shindig," he said. People have been coming and going like crazy, the last couple of hours."

"Yeah, it was something," I replied. Rachel didn't say a word.

I delivered her to room 712, letting her in with my master key. She thanked me again, and I promised to pick up some clothes and drop them off, first thing in the morning.

"Maybe I should hold onto that dress," I suggested.

"My dress? Why?"

"Wright ripped it when he attacked you. It's evidence. If it were to fall into the wrong hands and conveniently disappear, it would be one less strike against the senator. It would be your word against his. Maybe I should hold onto it for safe keeping."

"I paid a week's salary for that dress, and every man I meet wants to get me out of it," she said with a smile.

"I'll see you get it back."

Rachel handed me the dress. "You want the shoes too? They match."

"That's all right. I don't think they'd fit me, anyway."

"You're a pretty swell guy, Mr. McKeller."

"Yeah, well, you just don't know me very well."

"Maybe I wouldn't mind getting to know you better."

"Maybe you should get some sleep. It's been a long day."

"A girl could get kind of scared in this big hotel room, all by herself."

"Goodnight, Rachel."

"My friends call me Rae Rae."

"Goodnight, Rachel." I said again, turning away and heading back toward the elevator.

Chapter Twenty-One

It was late by the time I finished with Rachel. I was dead tired and my bum leg was killing me. There was nothing else to be done that night, so I made my way back to my room and turned in. I think I was asleep before my head hit the pillow.

I woke up early the next day, something I'm not in the habit of doing. After cleaning up, shaving and throwing on a suit, I swung by the kitchen for a cup of java and a few slices of toast, then headed over to the bullpen.

The bullpen was only a few blocks down the road, so I hoofed it. There wasn't anything fancy about it, especially when compared to the Ocean Forest Hotel. It was a three story, no frills structure, square and bland, whitewash paint broken up by the occasional window.

It had been put up to house the hotel staff, cooks, bellhops, maid service. It was a nice little perk for working at the hotel, free room and board, and more than half the employees took advantage of it. Pretty much all of the single staff, and it was notorious for the wild after work parties management wasn't invited to attend.

Early in the morning, it was quiet and peaceful, the inhabitants sleeping off last night's binge or resting up for the upcoming work day. The first floor was reserved for the male workers, the second floor catering to the females. The third floor was strictly for the black staff members, but they bent the rules to allow the occasional Mexican or Asian, and there was a separate entrance for them around back.

The place was set up like a college dorm, and there was a small sign-in desk located in the front lobby area, if you could call it that. Maybe they originally kept someone stationed at it, monitoring the comings and goings of the employees, making sure there wasn't any funny business going on. These days it sat empty, and nobody noticed when I walked by and made my way up to the second floor.

I had found Rachel's last name penciled in on the line of mailboxes out front, along with the name Seymour, for room 2E. It was halfway down the hall, on the right. I knocked and waited.

There was stirring on the other side of the door, the creaking of bed springs. The sound of footsteps across the floor was followed with the door being unlatched and opened up a few inches, a girl's face peeking out the crack. Her's was plain, angular and pale, uncombed hair and bloodshot eyes like she just woke up. I recognized her from the wait staff but couldn't remember her first name. She looked familiar but like there was something different about her I wasn't used to seeing.

"Miss Seymour?"

She squinted her eyes tight like she was confused. "Mr. McKeller? What are you doing here? I'm not scheduled 'til the lunch shift." Her voice was high pitched and scratchy, rich and full, at the same time. There wasn't a hint of Southern in it.

"No, you're fine. That's not why I'm here. Rachel's back at the hotel and she needs a change of clothes. She asked me to run by and pick them up for her."

"Rachel?"

"Your roommate?"

"Oh, yeah, Blondie," she said with a grin, opening up the door to let me in. "I almost forgot she's staying here. I see her more at work than I do here."

I stepped into the room. The Seymour girl was in a long, oversized, flannel nightgown, buttoned up tight at the neck and dropping straight down to the floor. It covered every inch of her and made her look lanky and narrow, not a hint of curves distinguishable under the thick fabric.

She was on the small side and thin. Her face was pleasant and well-proportioned with a slightly pointed jaw and dark eyes set around a slender nose, her mouth a narrow slit of pale thin lips. Her hair was cropped short, mousy brown and sticking out on the sides. There was something about her, a perky daintiness that made her seem soft and natural.

The room was cramped and sparsely furnished, two single beds, a bureau, an ironing board opened up in the center of it. One bed was made, the other turned up and disheveled like the Seymour girl had just climbed out of it. There were woman's clothes strewn about, over the made up bed and ironing board, some of them I recognized as the standard issue uniform of the restaurant wait staff.

"She doesn't sleep here?"

"Nope, not a night since she moved in."

"Where does she stay?"

"I couldn't tell you. I barely know her. She moved some stuff in here two weeks ago, when she was hired, but I haven't seen much of her since, just at work, and we don't talk a lot."

I knew Rachel was new to the hotel but didn't realize she was that new. "She got a boyfriend or something?"

The girl shrugged thin shoulders under wrinkled flannel. "Beats me." She hesitated. "I'm not one to talk but ... she's not the friendliest person I ever met. Keeps to herself, even at work. I used to try to strike up conversations with her but I got tired of the cold shoulder. She's kind of stuck up, if you know what I mean."

"I know the type."

"What are you going to do, right?

"It sounds like you don't much like working with her."

The Seymour girl shrugged. "I don't mind. I make more money when I work with her."

"How's that?"

"Well, she's not exactly the hardest working girl at the hotel. She's always willing to give up a shift and, when she does work, she gives up tables left and right. If she doesn't want to make the money, I'm too happy to take them."

"Don't you guys work for tips?"

"Duh. Yeah."

"So, how does she make money if she's always giving away her tables?"

"What do I care? Like I said, if she doesn't want the money ..."

She had wandered over to the dresser and pulled open the second drawer, fishing through clothes with both hands. "What kind of clothes does she want, work?"

"No, she's got the day off. Just something casual to beat around in."

Seymour went about selecting articles of clothing and folding them in a pile on the made up bed. It was a pair of slacks, a pullover sweater, some feminine underthings placed on top. "I don't know what she needs but this ought to do. She doesn't have a lot here to pick from."

"I'm sure it will be fine."

"Like I said, I don't know her real well."

"Rachel doesn't have many friends at the hotel?"

"Not female friends, anyway. She's one of those girls who turns on the charm when a man walks into the room, but when she's around other women, well, let's just say, she doesn't have much use for us."

"I see."

"It's not that uncommon. You, being a man, probably don't see it, but a lot of girls are like that. They're all cute and flirty when the men folk are around, but when it's just us girls they get all catty. It's just the way some women are. They don't like sharing the attention."

"I guess I have a lot to learn when it comes to women."

The Seymour girl giggled. "You and every other man I ever met. Don't feel bad. I don't really get it either. With her looks, it's not like she has anything to worry about. Men don't even see me when I'm in the same room with her."

"I doubt that's true."

She giggled again. "It's no big deal, just the way it is. I'm used to it," she said, handing me the pile of clothes with a pair of flat shoes placed on top.

"For the record," I said, nodding my thanks. "I think you're a very pretty girl."

She laughed again. "Is that so? Let me ask you something, Mr. McKeller. We've been working together for well over a year now. What's my first name?"

I went blank. She couldn't have tortured it out of me. All I could do was stand there with a dumb look on my mug.

"That's what I thought. Rachel's been here two weeks and she's got you running errands for her. You men are all the same."

She crossed the room and opened the door, making it clear our little visit was over. I filed past with my tail between my legs, stopping just past the doorway and turning around to look back in at her.

"So, you going to tell me your first name?"

Her dark eyes smiled back at me, mirroring the slight smirk on her lips. "You're the big time detective. You figure it out."

With that, she closed the door in my face and I stood there for a few seconds, trying to figure out what had just happened. I couldn't help but feel like I'd missed something.

From there, I headed back to the hotel, pondering my conversation with the Seymour girl the whole way. I went up to Rachel's room and knocked on the door. She answered in no time.

"I thought maybe you forgot about me," she said with a smile.

I held out the pile of clothes, and Rachel opened the door wider, inviting me in.

She was still wearing the bathrobe. It was tied around her small waist and pulled slightly open at the top of her chest, thin rounded calves flowing past the hemline, down to bare feet with painted red toes.

"Set them down anywhere," she said as I stepped into the room.

"Your roommate says Hi," I said, sitting the pile down on the unmade bed.

""My roommate?" she asked with a surprised tone to her voice. "Oh yes, how is Alice?"

"Alice," I repeated. "Alice is fine."

"I hope she's not worried or anything."

"No, not at all."

"She's a sweetheart and a good friend."

"Yeah, I got that impression. Has Simmons been by yet?"

"No, he called earlier. He said he'd be by in a while."

"You'll be here when he does, won't you?" She had that doe look in her eyes.

I nodded. "Yeah, sure. Why don't you get changed?"

Rachel scooped up the pile of clothes and disappeared into the bathroom, announcing, "I won't be but a minute."

I called out after her, "Are you hungry? I could have room service send something up."

"Yes, I am," she answered back. "Some scrambled eggs and coffee would be heavenly."

I sat down and lifted the receiver of the phone to my ear, dialing down to the front desk. Waiting for an answer on the other end, I noticed a book lying on the nightstand. It was a thick novel with a bookmark stuck three quarters of the way through it. It was called *The Last of the Best* and I'd read it before. It was by Stuart James.

"Have you been anywhere this morning?" I asked in a loud voice she could hear through the bathroom door.

"Just where do you think I could go, dressed in a bathrobe?"

"Just asking," I replied.

"The Ocean Forest Hotel, front desk. How may I help you?" a voice said on the phone. At the same moment, there was a knock at the door.

"Never mind," I said, hanging up the phone and heading for the door.

It was Simmons, and he looked like he hadn't slept in days. His tie was loose around his neck, his sports coat crumpled, the pants just as wrinkled. He had the sour look on his face of a man whose life was not going smoothly.

"Where's the girl?"

"Bathroom. Changing," I answered as he came walking in.

He blew out a breath of frustration and stood standing in the center of the room with his hands on his hips.

"How was your night?" I asked.

"How do you think it was?"

The bathroom door opened, and little Rachel stepped out. The pile of clothes I'd carried back from the bullpen looked much better stuffed with her. She had her blonde hair pulled back tight and tied up.

"How are you feeling today, Miss Miller?"

"I feel like a woman who was violated," she shot back.

Simmons cleared his throat. "I can't apologize enough on behalf of the senator for any misunderstanding which might have occurred during the events of last evening."

"Misunderstanding? That bastard attacked me."

I was a spectator at this point and just stood back and watched. I figured I could always step in if Rachel needed.

"First off, I need to know if you have discussed the situation with anyone."

"No, just McKeller. I haven't seen anybody and I haven't left this room since last night."

I glanced over to the Stuart James' book on the nightstand but decided to keep my mouth shut.

"I understand that you're upset, Miss Miller, but the fact is that all parties involved had been drinking heavily."

"What does that have to do with anything?"

"I'm just saying, in a state of intoxication, it's easy for a young woman to become confused, to misinterpret the actions of a given individual. I'm not saying the senator was right, by any means, in the way he behaved, but we don't need to exaggerate the details of what happened."

"I'm not exaggerating anything. That son of a bitch punched me in the face. He ripped my clothes off and tried to rape me."

"Now, Miss Miller, let's try to talk about this rationally. The senator is very sorry for the way you mistook his motives, and he is very anxious to resolve this issue as quickly and quietly as possible."

"What is that supposed to mean?"

"It means the senator realizes that you have suffered a certain amount of distress and inconvenience, and he believes you are entitled to a certain amount of compensation."

Rachel hesitated. "What do you mean by compensation?"

Simmons reached into his pocket and produced a slip of paper. He handed it to Rachel and said, "As I told you, the senator is very anxious to resolve this matter and put it behind him. He realizes you've been put through an ordeal, and he wishes to reach out and help to compensate you for any pain and suffering he may have accidentally inflicted on you."

Rachel opened up the slip of paper and stared down at it. After a few seconds she let out a full blown laugh. "You're trying to buy my silence?"

"The senator is merely trying to make sure you are compensated for any hardship you may feel you were put through."

Little Rachel Rae crumpled the piece of paper and tossed it aside. "You tell the senator that I'm not the kind of girl who can be bought off so easily. If I was, it would take a lot more than that. You tell him I was sitting there when he was scooping up all that money in the poker game last night."

Simmons looked over to me, an uneasy look on his face, then back at Rachel. "I will go back to the senator and relay your displeasure with his offer."

"You do that," she scoffed. "While you're at it, tell him he can stick it where the sun don't shine."

"Yes, ma'am," Simmons replied, turning and letting himself out of the room.

Once he was gone, I said, "What was that?"

"What was what?"

"Is that what this all about, money?"

"I didn't ask for any money. They offered. In case you didn't notice, I turned it down."

"You made it pretty clear it wasn't enough," I pointed out.

"What am I supposed to do? How do you think this thing is going to end, McKeller? Do you think I'm going to file charges and the senator is going to jail? They would never let that happen.

"I'm a waitress at a hotel. What do you want from me? If they want to throw a bunch of money in my lap, why shouldn't I at least consider it? I deserve it after what that bastard did to me. Nobody else is going to look out for me. Why shouldn't I get all I can out of this?"

"Look, I'm not judging," I replied. "You've got to do what you've got to do. Just make sure you're doing it for the right reasons. These things have a tendency to turn around and bite you in the ass sometimes."

"What would you have me do? Should I call the cops, file a report? Maybe I should take my story to the papers and try to ruin his career. What good would that do? In the end I'll be some tramp who put herself in a bad position and got what she deserved. Why shouldn't I get a payday out of all this? I didn't do anything wrong."

"Just be careful," I said, picking up my fedora and making a move toward the door.

"Where are you going? Aren't you going to be here when he comes back?"

"I've got things I need to do."

"You can't leave me, McKeller. I need you here."

"I've got a feeling you're going to be fine." I had my hand on the door knob, ready to leave.

"You're just going to up and leave me all alone up here?"

"You'll be all right. If you get lonely, you can always kick back and curl up with a good book."

Rachel didn't respond, just stood there looking back at me as I let myself out.

Things had become kind of hairy where Rachel and the senator were concerned and I wasn't sure what to think about it all. Maybe she wasn't the sweet and innocent kid I thought I'd met the night before, but that didn't give anybody the right to manhandle her. I wanted to give her the benefit of the doubt. She was still a young girl who'd been through a harrowing ordeal, even if she wasn't quite what she seemed.

Besides, I had other things to worry about.

Chapter Twenty-Two

I swung by my room to take a minute to myself and get my thoughts together. I wanted to make a few phone calls too.

The Marcus Fletcher angle had been bothering me since I heard he was in town, and I thought maybe I should try to track him down. Myrtle Beach was a small town, after all, and there were only so many places he could be holding up if he was still around.

I spent the next hour calling every little motel and flea bag motor lodge I could think of. Nobody had anyone named Fletcher registered and nobody I talked to recalled seeing a guy with a sideways V scar on his face.

On my fifteenth try, I got lucky. It was a little Mom and Pop hotel on the outskirts of town called the Sea Shade Inn. The Sea Shade was one of those places that did just enough business during the summer months to keep their doors open the rest of the year. It was the kind of place you stayed if you were looking to save a buck and didn't mind a certain lack of convenience and comfort. It might be the kind of place you'd stay if you were looking to lay low for a while.

"No, we ain't got nobody by the name of Fletcher," the guy on the phone said.

"This guy might be registered under a different name."

"Why would he do that?"

"He's funny like that. This guy has a scar under his eye, looks kind of like a sideways V."

There was a pause on the other end. "Why did you say you were looking for him?"

"He's an old Army buddy. I'm just trying to look him up."

"Yeah, well, we have a policy at the Sea Shade about not giving out

138

personal information about our guests. I really couldn't say, one way or the other."

"He wouldn't mind. He's an old buddy of mine. We fought together in the Pacific."

"Just the same, we have a policy."

"Sure, I understand. Thanks for your help."

"No problem, Mister."

It wasn't much, but it sounded like there might be some meat to it. I'd barely got the receiver back on its cradle when there was a light knock on the door. I opened it up to find Rosie waiting on the other side.

"Where in the hell have you been?" she asked, pushing her way past and letting herself in.

I shut the door behind her. "Working."

"Working? What kind of lame excuse is that? I expected you to come knocking at my door, first thing." She was in a lavender dress with white cuffs and trim, slim at the waist, puffy down the bottom, tight in all the right places up top.

"I had a long night. Hotel stuff."

"What's this?" Rosie went straight over to the nightstand, zeroing in on the balled up sparkly bundle I'd tossed there the night before. She lifted it up and shook it out, the shimmering gown unrolling in her hands. She studied it for a moment before turning back to me.

"Hotel stuff, huh?"

"It's not what you think."

She turned it to the side, exposing the broken strap and ripped side. "Like it rough these days, do you?"

"It's not like that at all."

"Who's the girl?"

"I'm holding it for a friend."

"Whoever she is, I'd say she's a skinny little thing with a nice figure, expensive taste in clothes too."

"She told me it cost her a week's pay."

"Yeah, maybe if she makes Hedy Lamar like money. This is an original Chanel. They don't come cheap."

"I'm sure it's a knock off."

Rosie tossed the dress on the bed. "Frankie, there are two things I know, men and clothes. That's no knock off. Your little girlfriend has expensive tastes."

"She's not my girlfriend."

"Whatever. It's none of my business if you have a little something on the side. We're not married. You're allowed to do your thing. I just need to know you're going to be there when I need you."

"When you need me?"

"Look, Frankie, I know you got sore at me last night. We both said some things, but the bottom line is, we have a connection. We always have, and we always will. I'm sorry if it seems like I'm not playing straight with you, but you've got to believe me, I never meant to lie to you."

"It was just an accident, huh?"

"I've been on my own for a long time. Sure, there have been men, but they all wanted something from me. They all wanted what they could get from me, to control me and keep me in check. You're the only guy I was ever with who wasn't like that. You're the only one I could ever trust."

I had nothing.

"Maybe I haven't been as forthcoming as I should have, but it's only because, for so long, the only person I could trust was me, Frankie. I've been going it alone for such a long time, it's hard for me to trust in someone else."

Again, I bit my lip, part of me wanting to believe her.

"I need you, Frankie. I need your help. I don't think I can get through this without you."

I would have given a million dollars to believe any part of what she said.

"We need a plan," I came up with.

Rosie shot me that smile. "You always need a plan."

It was Rosie's idea to have lunch in the hotel restaurant. I argued that it would probably be a smart idea for her to stay out of sight, but she argued back that she couldn't stand to be cooped up in her room. Besides, she said, even with Martin and his thugs on the prowl, she figured she'd be safe with me at her side. Sometimes there's just no arguing with Rosie, and you have to resolve yourself to the fact that she's going to get her way.

The restaurant is located off the main lobby, back toward the right wing of the hotel. It's set up like an elegant ballroom, crystal chandeliers, impressive woodwork, round tables set with fine china, sterling silver utensils and Waterford water glasses. The perfect place for a mug like me to grab a quick bite.

Our waitress sauntered over to our table with a wry smile. She glanced over to Rosie and then to me. "Busy guy," she remarked. "Can I start you off with something to drink?"

Alice Seymour looked nice in her work attire, white shirt and bow tie, black skirt, comfortable shoes. Her brown hair was perky short and combed straight, bangs across the forehead over a pair of thick framed glasses, oval and gray, making her brown eyes appear larger and darker than before. The glasses, or lack thereof, were what threw me off earlier, they were the missing piece I couldn't place, and the reason I'd thought there was something different about her I wasn't used to seeing.

Her face was fresh and soft, a youthful and bright expression, off-set by dark and knowing eyes that sparkled with energy. Her thin pink lips were curled up in the slightest of smiles, placed perfect-ly between high creamy cheeks and under a slim and delicate nose, centered above a gentle, feminine chin.

Her figure was no longer hidden under the long nightgown, and, even in her work clothes, you could see the hint of generous curves flowing under the unflattering fabric. Her chest was pronounced, downright large in comparison to her small frame and it looked like she wore her shirts a few sizes too big to detract attention from it. It made me wonder how I hadn't noticed her before.

"Hello, Alice," I said, emphasizing her name and making sure she knew I'd made the effort to find it out.

Alice looked down to the name tag pinned to her shirt and then back up at me. "I'm impressed. You're a regular Sherlock Holmes."

"I'd love a glass of wine," Rosie said, ignoring the banter between Alice and me.

"Anything in particular, red, white?"

"Surprise me, Hon. Something imported, France maybe."

Alice nodded and scribbled something on her pad. "McKeller?"

"Coffee, black, please."

"Coming up," she said with a grin, turning away and heading off to the kitchen. My eyes followed her away, watching as she sashayed her way back across the room.

Rosie cleared her throat. "Excuse me. I'm over here."

"What?"

"Really? You're going to flirt with some bimbo while I'm sitting right here?"

"I wasn't flirting. She's a coworker of mine."

"OK, whatever. She's too short to be the girl with the gown. Just how many gals do you have down here?"

"It's not like that."

"Fine, be that way. We have more important things to deal with right now. I'm hoping my package comes today so I can get this business with Blake over with and be on my way. What time does the mail get delivered?"

I shrugged. "This isn't Baltimore. We're just a sleepy little beach town. The mail comes whenever the mailman gets around to delivering it."

She let out a sigh. "Honestly, I don't know how you can stand to live here."

I ignored the dig to my adopted hometown. "There's still the matter of speaking with the sheriff."

"Yeah, I was kind of hoping you could run interference on that one, maybe buy me some more time."

"This isn't a parking ticket we're talking about. This is murder. The sheriff wants to talk to you. There's no getting around it."

Rosie sighed again. "I really don't understand where that concerns me."

"Look, Rosie, I've tried to keep you out of this as best I could. Maybe the sheriff doesn't know your actual connection with Ralphy, but there's a good bet he suspects something is there. The way you've avoided him so far doesn't help your case any. I think it's time to come clean, get it over with. If you had nothing to do with it, you have nothing to worry about."

"I don't have anything to tell him."

"You could try the truth for a change. You don't even have to mention the books. Tell him how Martin is an ex-boyfriend with a history of putting his hands on you. Tell him how you came down here to get away from him. Tell him how he sent Ralphy to come down after you."

"That doesn't look so good for you or me," she pointed out.

"Hiding facts in a murder investigation doesn't look so good either."

"I just need more time, Frankie."

Alice was back with our drinks. She placed a glass of red wine in front of Rosie and slid a saucer with a coffee cup in front of me. "Are you ready to order?"

"I want a salad, maybe something with shrimp on it. You do have shrimp, don't you?"

"Of course," Alice replied. "What kind of dressing would you like?"

"Oh, I don't care, anything. Italian, maybe. On the side. I'd like extra tomatoes and hold the cucumber. Can I get walnuts in that?"

"That shouldn't be a problem. I'll check on that for you."

"I don't know what there is to check on. You either have walnuts or you don't, right?"

"I'm sure we probably do. I just have to check with the chef."

"What kind of place doesn't have walnuts?"

"I didn't say we didn't have them. I just need to check, is all."

"Sweetie, you do whatever you have to do. Just make sure I get walnuts on my salad."

"Relax, Rosie," I chimed in. "She said she'd check on it."

"I don't need to relax. What I need is walnuts on my salad."

"If they have them," I said, slow and clear, "I'm sure they will take care of it for you."

"You don't have to be a jerk about it, Frankie. I'm just trying to explain it to your little friend."

Alice turned toward me. I could see the fire burning in her eyes but she was keeping a lid on it. "What can I get *you?*"

"A BLT on rye would be great. Thanks, Alice."

She jotted something down, collected our menus and headed off without another word.

"What was that all about?" I asked.

"Nothing. I just want walnuts on my salad. Is that a crime down here?"

"I don't know. Is it a crime if they're out of walnuts?"

"Why are you taking her side? I just made a simple request. I didn't need the back talk."

"It's walnuts, Rosie. Lighten up." Deep down inside, I was really hoping the kitchen was out of walnuts.

Rosie got her walnuts. She wasn't so happy with what she perceived as wilted lettuce in her salad, though, and sent the first one back. Alice was courteous and polite about it, taking the offending salad away and replacing it with a fresh one in hardly any time.

"Thanks so much, Hon," Rosie said with a forced smile.

"Of course." Alice smiled back. "Is there anything else I can get for you?"

"Maybe a fresh glass of wine. Something good this time. Not that swill you gave me before."

"I'll get right on that."

It was like watching two prizefighters sparring in the center of a ring, Rosie getting in her jabs, Alice fending off her blows, holding tight to her composure. Rosie's behavior reminded me of some of the things Alice had said about Rachel Miller earlier in the day.

The rest of lunch was largely uneventful, what with Rosie doing her best to avoid talking about anything of relevance, I was finally able to steer the conversation back to Blake Martin and his precious books.

"Just how much do you figure Martin is going to pay for those books?"

"Ten grand," Rosie answered flatly. .

"That's a lot of pesos. Do you think those books are worth it?"

"Oh, they're worth it, all right."

I signed for the tab and left a fat tip for Alice, small consolation for the attitude she'd had to put up with from Rosie. As we were walking out and into the main lobby, Rosie clenched hold of my arm, stopping me in my tracks. Across the large room, standing with his two goons, was Blake Martin, and he was glaring back our way.

"This is awkward," Rosie chirped.

"I'll take care of it," I said. "You head to the elevator, and I'll stay here and hold them off, keep them occupied. Get up to your room and stay put."

"You're the best, Frankie," she replied before scuttling off toward the lift.

Martin and his thugs made a move toward me, staring me down, moving in quickly. It just so happens, Simmons and three of his security team came walking across the lobby between us. I made a beeline toward them and gave a tug on Simmons' sleeve. As Simmons and his men came to a stop in front of me, Martin and his goons held up, waiting to see what I was up to.

"How's the senator?" I asked.

Simmons gave a single nod. "As well as can be expected."

"Good. Hey, do you remember how you told me to be on the lookout for any suspicious characters, anything out of the ordinary?"

"Yeah?"

"You see those guys over there?" I motioned to Martin with my eyes. "The one with the expensive suit, sissy mustache and the two gorillas?"

Simmons shot them a quick look. "Yeah, what about them?"

"I've been noticing them the last two days. They're always hanging out around the lobby, watching the comings and goings. There's something fishy about them."

"There's no law against hanging out and watching people."

"True enough. It's just that one of the housekeepers told me three guys were asking about the senator, where he's staying, what his itinerary was. I think it might be the same guys."

"Is that so?" Simmons was checking them out good now.

"I just thought it might be something you'd want to know about."

"Thanks, McKeller. Good work." He turned to his men and motioned toward Martin and his sidekicks.

"We're on it, boss," one of them said as they crossed the room toward Martin.

I stood watching as the security team approached a nervous looking Blake Martin. Quiet words were exchanged and badges were shown before Martin and his goons raised their arms and turned away from the government agents, allowing them to pat them down. Revolvers were removed and slipped into pockets and Martin and his guys were ushered away, past me, toward the back offices of the hotel.

As they came walking by me, Martin's eyes were locked on mine with a glare so hard it could crack granite. I returned his stare with my friendliest smile.

I crossed over to the front desk where Curtis was at his usual station.

"How's it going, Curtis?"

He gave me a worried look. "I don't know. There's a weird feeling to this place today, like something's going on. Tensions are running pretty high. Those government fellows are all on edge. You got any idea what's up?"

I shrugged. "Got me."

"Well, something's going on. I don't know what."

"Do you know if the mail came in today?"

"Yeah, they delivered it an hour ago."

"I'm looking for a package. It would be addressed to Miss Carter, I mean Miss Young. She asked me to pick it up for her."

"Yeah, I got something for her." Curtis disappeared into the back for a few minutes and reemerged with a small package wrapped in brown paper. It was addressed to Sally Young, at the Ocean Forest Hotel.

Chapter Twenty-Three

I took the package down to my office and opened it up. There were four books, leather bound ledgers, tied together with string. Opening up the first, I began pouring through the pages, trying to get a fix on what I was looking at.

It didn't take long to figure out. Blake Martin was a thorough guy and he kept impeccable records, the kind of records a guy in his line of work ought not to keep.

There were dates and amounts, large amounts, and plenty of names to go with them. Most of the names meant nothing to me but every once in a while I'd come across one I knew, usually from the Baltimore papers, city officials, politicians, important people in Maryland high society.

A lot of big names had their fingers in Martin's pie, and he had every payoff recorded, all his I's dotted and T's crossed. It was some pretty incriminating stuff, and I could only imagine he'd kept it for insurance purposes, a bargaining chip in case he ever found himself in a bind he couldn't get out of. It was the kind of stuff that would have a lot of important people come running to his aid if they thought there was even a chance of it leaking.

It made me wonder if Rosie's ten thousand dollar number might be on the low side.

I stashed the books in the back of my filing cabinet and locked up the office. Martin would have his hands full for the next few hours so I wasn't too worried about him for the moment.

As far as little Rachel Rae Miller was concerned, it seemed like she had things firmly in hand, and I doubted she needed any help from me. It wasn't exactly the kind of thing I wanted to be a party to, anyway.

There were still a lot of loose ends hanging about in the Ralphy situation, and I couldn't help but feel the best way to protect Rosie and myself was to start tying some of them up. The loosest of those ends seemed to be Marcus Fletcher, and the fact that he'd popped up out of nowhere. If I could connect him to one of the principals involved, it might be enough to fish out whoever was responsible. I was still hoping that would lead back to either Taylor Mills or Blake Martin, but I knew it was a long shot. At the very least, I still held out hope it wouldn't lead back to Rosie.

I took the short drive to the Sea Shade Motel. She wasn't much to look at, four narrow stories of faded white paint and what were once red shutters. Rustic and weathered, it was advertised by a quaint, hand-painted sign out front.

Five steps led up to a small front porch, a couple of wooden rocking chairs lined up in front of the railing. I walked up those steps and into the small room that served as the lobby and check-in area.

A middle-aged man with small spectacles and thinning hair stood in front of what passed for the front desk. He was talking to one of the last people in the world I expected to bump into.

Sheriff Talbert turned toward me as I came walking in and showed me his best frown. "Why am I not surprised?"

"It's nice to see you too, Sheriff."

"Would you care to tell me what in tarnation you're doing here?"

I glanced around, trying to get my bearings and figure out what was going on. "I was thinking about getting a room, a little getaway for the weekend."

"Is that right? You wouldn't be here to see anybody in particular, would you?"

"I don't know what you mean."

"Maybe an old Army buddy you served in the Pacific with?"

"You got the wrong guy. I served in Europe."

"Earlier this morning, a fellow called looking for an old Army buddy, a guy with a scar on his face. You wouldn't know anything about that?"

"Can't say as I do."

"And here you come strolling in here, out of the blue. Ain't that something?"

"What's going on, Sheriff?"

"Why don't you tell me?" He reached into his pocket and pulled out what looked like a Maryland Driver's license. I know because I have one just like it. "You wouldn't happen to know a guy named Marcus Fletcher, would you?"

I didn't answer. I wasn't sure how without digging myself into a hole.

"That wouldn't be who you're here looking for, would it?"

"I don't know what you're talking about," was the best I could come up with.

"What if I told you this Fletcher guy was from Baltimore, like you?"

"There are a lot of people from Baltimore."

"Yeah, and most of them seem to be in Myrtle Beach this week. As I recall, Ralph Henderson was from Baltimore too. So is that little girlfriend of yours."

Again, I decided to go with the tight lip.

"You might want to start coming up with some answers, McKeller."

"Do you want to tell me what's going on here?"

"I can tell you this; if you're here looking for Fletcher, you're a little too late. Marcus Fletcher has departed this world. He had a little help too, three slugs in the chest."

I took a shallow breath and let it out quick. "There seems to be a lot of that going around."

"And you seem to be right there in the middle of it, every time."

"It's not what it looks like, Sheriff."

"Well, you had best start talking because, from where I sit, it looks like you're in store for a long stretch in one of our deluxe jail cells, 'til I start getting some straight answers."

"I knew Fletcher from back home." I wasn't going to call the Sheriff's bluff. I could tell by his tone he meant business and I could feel the water I was in heating up rapidly. "I hadn't seen him in years."

"Until this weekend," Talbert pointed out.

I shook my head. "I still hadn't seen him. I heard he might be in town and I did a little homework. I figured out he might be staying here."

"So, you just stopped by to say Hi?"

"Fletcher had a connection to Ralphy Henderson. He was spotted with him at the Chesterfield Inn. I thought it was something I should look into."

"And just why would you be poking your nose in my murder investigation?"

"Self preservation," I replied. "As you so eloquently pointed out, my fanny seems to be smack dab in the middle of this mess."

"That it is, McKeller," the Sheriff agreed. "I think it's time you and me had us another nice long talk."

There wasn't much nice about it, but it was plenty long. Two and a half hours later, and the sheriff and I had just about as much of each other's company as we could handle. I opted for the truth angle on most everything I knew, holding back only on Martin's books and Rosie's plan to bleed him for money.

I told him about Rosie showing up at the hotel, her story about getting smacked around by Martin and running to me. I told him about Ralphy, how he'd been sent to get her before, how he'd shown up, about the trashed hotel room and our little scuffle at the Chesterfield Inn.

Sheriff Talbert sat with a cold expression on his face, chiseled marble that showed no reaction, as I told him about Taylor Mills and his crush on Rosie, of how I'd gone back to the Chesterfield and talked to the old man, how I figured out Fletcher was in town. I even admitted to the phone call to the Sea Shade, figuring there was a good chance Fletcher was holed up there.

"That's some right fine detective work," Talbert said when I was done. There wasn't an ounce of sincerity in his voice.

"It's the truth, Sheriff, everything I know."

"What else do you know about Taylor Mills?"

"Not much. He's some kind of Karate instructor. Why do you ask?"

"He's staying at the hotel, room 419?"

"Yeah, why?"

"We found his name on a matchbook in Fletcher's pocket with the number 419 scratched below it."

"So, there was a connection."

"It's about time I had a talk with your little girlfriend."

I nodded my agreement.

"That's quite a story you got there."

"Did you get anything out of Martin and his boys?" I asked.

"Those fellows make you look like a flock of stool pigeon dolls. They didn't own up to nothing, never even admitted they knew Henderson. Martin told me you and him had a riff over the girl, sometime back, says you're out to get him, that's why you set him up."

"What else is he going to say? He doesn't want to incriminate himself."

"He had some fancy lawyer from up north make some phone calls. I got a call from a judge out of Conway, said it was in everybody's best interest to let those boys walk."

"Martin has friends in pretty high places. That doesn't mean he's not a dirt bag."

"I wasn't much impressed with him, but that doesn't make him a murderer."

"I'll be honest with you, Sheriff. I don't know who killed Henderson. I figure Fletcher was the link, but I didn't get to him in time. I was hoping Fletcher would lead me back to the trigger man; he's the one who didn't make any sense in this deal, and he had a connection to Henderson. I was hoping he could tie it all together."

Talbert shook his head. "It sure does sound like you've taken it upon yourself to conduct a private investigation of an official homicide, McKeller. The last thing we need is for a private citizen, such as yourself, sticking their schnoz where it don't belong."

"I have a vested interest and a stake in this matter."

"And I can't help but feel if you would have come to me sooner, with what you knew, Marcus Fletcher might still be alive. At the very least, I would have had the opportunity to question him."

I started to say something, but Talbert cut me off, sticking a lean finger in my face. "You listen to me, McKeller! You are done in this matter. I will take it from here. If I so much as suspect you're poking your nose in my investigation, I will throw your ass in the slammer so fast it will make your head spin."

I bit my lip.

"If you think, for a second, I'm bluffing, you just go ahead and try me. I'll have your Yankee ass locked away 'til the cows come home."

"I get it."

"You better get it, McKeller. I have had enough of your nonsense.

You take yourself back to that fancy hotel of yours, and you tell that little girl I'll be along shortly. If she can't find time to speak to me I will issue a warrant for her arrest. You explain to that little gal that she does not want to go down that road."

"I will do that."

"In the meantime, you leave the police work to the professionals. Do you understand what I'm saying?"

I nodded. "I smell what you're stepping in, Sheriff."

"You sure as hell had better, else you'll be smelling a lot worse for a long, long time."

It was another one of those cheery get-togethers with the good sheriff I'd come to know and love, and I had that familiar warm and fuzzy feeling in my gut as I made my way back to the hotel in the Studebaker. I also had no idea where I was going to turn next. I thought Fletcher would have been my one real lead.

I suppose the thing to do would have been to heed the sheriff's firm request that I cease and desist in my personal investigation into Ralphy Henderson's murder, and now Fletcher's too, but I've never been very good at taking direction. The sheriff's threats had been clear enough, but I also had Rosie's wellbeing to consider, not to mention my own. I figured what Talbert didn't know wouldn't hurt me. I'd just have to watch my step from here on out.

It's not like my little meeting with the sheriff didn't turn up any useful information. There was the little tidbit of Taylor Mills' name and room number found on Fletcher's person. Maybe it wasn't a smoking gun, but at least it connected the two in some small way. The trick would be to take it and run with it, see how far it would get me. I just hoped there weren't any steep cliffs off in the distance.

Curtis flagged me down at the main desk as I came walking through the lobby.

"McKeller," he said. "Rachel Miller has been calling down, looking for you."

"Thanks." I nodded back.

"Isn't she the blonde who works in the restaurant?"

"Yeah."

"What she doing upstairs in a room?"

"I don't know. Reward for all her hard work?"

"She's been here, what, three weeks maybe?"

"Something like that."

"I've been working here ten years. Nobody ever offered me a room."

I shrugged. "Maybe you need to step it up a notch, Curtis, go that extra mile."

He had a quizzical scowl on his face when I left him.

I didn't feel like seeing little Rachel Rae just yet. As far as I was concerned, her dirty little business was between her and the senator, and I didn't want to get in the middle of it. It was one thing when she was the innocent victim of a dirty old man, but now that there was hush money involved, I was having trouble picturing her as the damsel in distress.

I was thinking a little visit with Taylor Mills might be in order, and I was waiting at the elevator when Alice Seymour came walking down the hallway, from the direction of the restaurant.

"Hi, Alice," I said, the best ice breaker I could come up with.

"McKeller," she said back. "Where's your little friend?"

"I don't know."

"Rachel in the morning, the leggy brunette for lunch? What do you have planned for dinner, an entire harem?"

"It's not really like that."

"OK, knock yourself out. I just hope you're taking plenty of vitamins. A guy needs his strength."

"Look, I'm really sorry about earlier. Rosie is kind of—"

"A bitch?" she suggested.

"She's a little high strung sometimes."

"Yeah, that's one way to put it."

"I don't know what that was all about. I'm sorry about the way she acted."

"Don't sweat it. Girls will be girls. When you look like she does you don't really need manners, do you?"

"Just the same, I do apologize."

"For what? You're just like every other guy out there. So long as they look like a million bucks, you can put up with anything, right?"

With those words of wisdom, she was on her way, off to wherever she was heading. As I'm prone to do, I watched her walk away. She had a confident strut about her, little feet powering her along, her shoulders dipping and rising with each step. I watched her until she disappeared around the corner.

"You going up?" Clifford had stopped the elevator in front of me and was waiting for me to board. "Something interesting out there?"

"I don't know," I answered. "Maybe. Take me up to the fourth floor."

I knocked on Mills' door and he answered it quickly with a look on his face like he was expecting someone else. "Oh, it's you."

I didn't wait to be invited and walked right in. "Fletcher is dead, but you probably already know that," I tried, deciding on the throw it on out there strategy.

"Sorry for Fletcher's luck," he replied. "Who was he?"

"Like you don't know."

"OK, I'll bite. What's this all about?"

There was a bottle of champagne chilling in a silver bucket on the table with two glasses set beside it. It looked like he was expecting company.

"Celebrating something?" I asked.

"A little afternoon refreshment with a friend."

"You wouldn't be celebrating the arrival of, say, something special in the mail, would you?"

"What's it to you?"

"I checked on the mail. It didn't come yet." I could see the disappointment in his face. "I guess you'll have to keep the bubbly on ice another day."

He didn't answer.

"Let's get back to Fletcher."

"Yeah, let's. Who exactly was the guy?"

"He was a private investigator out of Baltimore."

"Huh? That's your racket, ain't it?"

"It used to be. You never crossed paths with Fletcher?"

"Never heard of him."

"That's funny, because he had your name and room number in his pocket when he was bumped off."

That caused him to hesitate a moment. "Ain't that a coincidence?"

"Yeah, I'm sure the sheriff thought so too."

"Look, I don't know this Fletcher guy from Adam. I've got no idea why he had my name on him. He never got in touch with me."

"You can go with that. There's a good chance the sheriff might buy it."

Mills was giving me a look like he wanted to use another one of his Karate chops on me. "If you're trying to spook me, it ain't working."

"No, no spooky business here. I'm just telling you how it is. We've had two murders here in Myrtle Beach since you got here. That's about two more than the yearly average. You have a roundabout connection to the first one, him being the primary threat to Rosie. The second one was found with a big fat clue in his pocket, a clue in the form of your name.

"The sheriff is going to want to talk to you, that's a given. You can stick to your story. Who knows? Maybe the sheriff will believe you, or you can come clean with me and, just maybe, I can help you out with this."

"And why would you want to help me?"

"Call it my generous and giving nature. You're going to have to meet me half way, though. I need to know just how deep you go in all this."

"I go as deep as Rosie needs me to go."

"Deep enough to bump off Ralphy, maybe Fletcher?"

"I never met either one of those guys. I sure didn't kill them, but I'll give it to you straight. I offered to go see Ralphy for her." He held up his hands. "I wasn't afraid of that big lug. I've taken care of bigger."

"Rosie said no?"

"Rosie told me to cool my heels. She said she had it under control, but if she needed, she'd let me know. I would have taken care of that big ox but good."

"Yeah, you're quite the tough guy."

He gave me a smirk. "I seem to remember taking care of you easy enough."

I ignored the remark. "You say you never met either one of them?"

He shook his head. "I never even heard of the Fletcher character 'til you came barging in here."

"Rosie never mentioned his name?"

"Never."

"How do you figure he ended up with your name and room number in his pocket?"

"I wouldn't know. Maybe you gave it to him."

"Why would I do that?"

"It's no secret you and Rosie were an item. Maybe you weren't so keen on me being in the picture. Maybe you were looking for a way to get rid of me and have Rosie all to yourself. Maybe that's what you're doing now, trying to rile me up and scare me off. It ain't working. I don't scare so easy."

"So, you and Rosie, you're a couple, are you?"

"Maybe not in so many words, but we got something special, me and her. I'm the one she comes to when she needs something. She knows she can count on me."

"How long have you known Rosie?"

He shrugged. "Three or four months. What's the difference?"

"I've known her a lot longer."

"Yeah, so what? From what I hear, she dumped you."

"Yeah, she did," I agreed. "Do you want to know why?"

"What do I care? It's ancient history as far as I can tell."

"She dumped me because she didn't need me anymore, because she found something better."

"It ain't like that between me and Rosie."

"You think so, huh? You two got plans? How's it supposed to work? After she gets the money from Martin, are you two supposed to go riding off into the sunset? Is that what she told you?"

He didn't answer.

"No, I'm guessing she didn't. With a lap dog like you, she wouldn't have to make any promises. She'd just have to bat her eyes and shoot you a smile every now and again, maybe tell you how much you mean to her. That would be enough to keep you in line. You'd just assume she was taking you with her."

"Why, I ought to ..." he made a move toward me but I laughed it off.

"Don't take it so personal. You're not the first guy to fall for her charms. Trust me, I know firsthand."

"You don't know nothing from nothing."

"Yeah, but I do know Rosie. Do you really think she's going to have a place for you after she gets her hands on that money? Ten grand is a lot of cash, but it's not enough for two people to run off and live like kings."

"Ten grand?" he repeated.

"She didn't tell you? How much did she tell you she was getting? Three? Five? Makes it a lot easier if she has to pay you off cheap, huh?

I'll bet she didn't even mention the two grand she already got off him." I could tell by the way his face was lighting up red I was right on the mark. "Kid, she's been playing you from day one. That's what she does. It's her nature."

"You're wrong."

There was a light tap at the door. We both looked to the door and back at each other. I motioned to the chilling champagne on the table. "I guess the other half of your party has arrived."

He was clenching his jaw tight.

"Maybe this would be a good time to find out just where you stand with Rosie."

The tap at the door was back. He made no move toward it, so I took it upon myself to let her in.

"Frankie? What are you doing here?" she asked as she came into the room.

"Just having a little heart to heart with your boyfriend."

"I told you, it's not like that," she answered.

"Yeah, maybe you ought to tell him that. Seems Taylor here is under the impression that you two are running off to La La Land once you get the money. He seems to think you two are heading for the big Happily Ever After."

Rosie turned to him and gave him her best sympathizing look. Every inch of him looked knotted up tighter than frayed shoe laces. "Taylor," she sighed.

I lit up a Lucky Strike and sauntered over 'til I was standing between them, looking Mills in the eye and blowing smoke in his face. "I was just trying to give him a solid dose of reality, a little lesson on how things tend to go down where you're concerned."

"You don't have to be mean about it," she told me, pushing me aside and taking my place in front of Taylor Mills. "You know how much you mean to me, Taylor. I couldn't have come this far without you. You've been my rock, my closest confidant.

"Our friendship is something I will always cherish, and there will always be a special place for you in my heart."

"This would be what they call the big blow off," I added.

"Frankie!" she snapped back at me before turning back to the young man. "I will always care for you, and I can never thank you enough for being there for me when I needed a friend. We have a special bond between us, something we will always have."

"But ..." I threw in.

Rosie shot me a hard glare that softened when she turned back to Mills. "You know how highly I think of you, but this was never destined to be forever. We're heading in two different directions."

"But, Rosie ..." he said, all sad and sappy.

"It wouldn't work, Taylor. You have a life back in Baltimore. I can never go back there, not after this. Once I get that money, I'll be a marked woman. I could never ask you to live like that. I don't know where I'll be going or how I'll survive. That's no life for us."

"We could make it work, Rosie."

"No, I couldn't ask that of you."

"You wouldn't have to ask. I'll go anywhere with you. I'll do whatever I have to."

"I'm sorry, Taylor. Where I'm heading, I have to go alone. It's the only way."

Tears were misting up in his eyes. "I love you, Rosie."

"I love you too. That's why it has to be like this. You've done too much already. You have to go back to your life up in Baltimore. My path leads in another direction."

"But, Rosie ..." he tried again.

"Please don't make this any harder than it has to be. You know how difficult this is for me."

Mills started to say something, but she placed her open palm on his cheek and he grasped it with two hands, clutching to her like he couldn't let go.

"I'm sorry, Taylor. I never meant to hurt you." She pulled her hand away, and he was left gasping for words he couldn't come up with. "I think it would be best if you caught the next train back to Baltimore. Never forget how much I care for you."

The performance over, she turned and walked out of the room, closing the door behind her.

I put my smoke out in the ashtray and gave him a long look. He looked broken and dejected, a shell of the man I'd seen when I walked through the door earlier. It was a familiar look and one that made me feel for him. It was a look I'd seen in my own eyes back in the day.

"Don't feel bad," I told him as I moved toward the door. "It's more than I ever got when she dumped me."

He didn't act like he even heard me as I let myself out.

Rosie was waiting for me in the hallway, leaned against the wall with one foot hiked up. The soft demeanor she'd shown Mills had hardened into something stiff and rigid. "Was that necessary?"

"Who are you kidding? We both know I did him a favor."

"What was that all about? Did you feel the need to see him humiliated, or did you just want to test me, prove that I was telling you the truth?"

"Maybe a little of both."

"Are you happy now?"

"Not particularly, but at least we all know where we stand now."

"Do we? Where do we stand now? Do you believe me now? Did I prove to you I'm being straight with you?"

"Not even a little. The only thing you proved is that you don't need Taylor Mills anymore. That, and you're still a damn fine actress."

Rosie let out a huff and started to storm away, down the hall, toward the elevator.

"Marcus Fletcher was found dead in his hotel today," I called after her. She stopped in her tracks and turned around.

"That's the man you asked about at that bar. I told you I don't know who he is."

"Yeah, I remember."

"I still don't."

"Well, he's dead, just the same."

"Too bad for him."

"The bodies are starting to pile up pretty high."

"What does that have to do with me?"

"I guess that remains to be seen."

"Frankie, why do you hate me so much?"

That one caught me off guard, and I had to think for a second before I could answer. "I don't know. Maybe because, as much as I want to, I can't make myself hate you. Maybe because you made me hate myself so much."

It was all she needed to hear. She turned back away and headed off, to places or persons unknown.

Chapter Twenty-Four

I'm not going to lie, part of me felt like a heel. Another part of me got a certain amount of satisfaction in seeing Taylor Mills get the heave ho. I'd gone up there to try and connect Mills to Fletcher, but I'd accomplished none of that. I'd left more confused than when I started, and it seemed like things had deteriorated into utter confusion.

It was my tried and true method of throwing mud against stuff and seeing what gets dirty. This method had about the same success rate as rolling dice. I wasn't sure what to think. I was pretty sure, however, that I needed a stiff drink.

The Brookgreen Room was empty but for a lone figure at the bar, slumped over his Martini and using his swizzle stick to chase an olive around his glass. Jonathon Masden was dressed in a tweed suit that looked tailor made and his hair was only slightly unkempt. Despite all that, he looked like he was on his way to getting good and snockered.

Something was still nagging at me from the events of the previous night and morning, and I thought maybe it would be worth a little prodding.

"Kind of early to be getting started, isn't it?" I asked, planting myself on the stool next to him.

"What's it to you?"

"Not a thing, I'm just saying—"

"Do I know you, young man?"

"Not really. I was at the party last night. I saw you there." This didn't seem to impress him much. "I recognized you from the movies," I added.

This caught his attention and he seemed to sit up a little straighter on his stool, an easy smile forming on his lips. "It's always nice to meet a fan."

"That was some party, huh?"

Masden took a sip of his Martini. "Quite."

"It got a little crazy at the end there."

"You could say that."

"You're friends with the senator; has he ever pulled something like that before?"

Masden gave me a look. "I'm not all that comfortable discussing the trials and tribulations of friends."

"I can understand that. It's just that I work security here at the hotel, and I couldn't help but wonder if the senator has a history of that kind of behavior."

"I'm not sure the senator's behavior, or lack thereof, has been established. As near as I can tell, the matter is now between the senator's people and the young lady in question."

"Yeah, I guess so. Just the same, have there been incidents like this before?"

He hesitated before answering. "I am not aware of any such incidents."

"And if you were, I'm guessing you wouldn't blab about it."

"Discretion is the better part of honor."

"I got there kind of late. How were the senator and the girl getting along before it all went down?"

"Well, I wasn't paying all that much attention, having pressing matters of my own, but it seemed like Rachel and the senator were getting along splendidly."

"Yeah, I heard something about those pressing matters. I guess they were pretty hard on you, huh?"

"I don't see where that is any of your concern."

"No, I don't suppose it is. What can you tell me about Stuart James?"

"He's one of the finest American writers of his generation," Masden answered immediately.

"Yeah, I've read his stuff. Have you known him long?"

"Long enough."

"What kind of guy is he?"

Masden sucked down the last of his martini and motioned to the bartender for a fresh one. He turned back to me and gave me a long look before replying, "Stuart James is the lowest form of scum I have ever had the dismay to encounter. He's a spineless and ruthless pig, and I wouldn't trust him with your wallet."

"He had nice things to say about you too."

"I'm sure he did. I almost forgot to mention that he's a miserable gossip."

"You two don't get along?"

"On the contrary, we get along quite fine."

"I sense a little bad blood."

The bartender had dropped off Masden's latest drink, and he took three large gulps from it. "I used to be one of the biggest stars in all of Hollywood."

"I remember. What happened?"

"To put it plainly, I got old."

"It happens to all of us, if we're lucky."

"In Hollywood it's not the luckiest of fates. I was down on my luck, so to speak. Parts for a distinguished gentleman of my caliber were few and far between. There was a script. It happened to be penned by my good friend, Stuart James.

"The lead character was a dashing, if somewhat aging, society patriarch who falls in love with a beautiful young chambermaid. It was like it was custom written for me.

"My agent went to the studio and argued on my behalf, convincing the studio head I would be perfect in the role. Even the director agreed that it seemed tailored to my unique talents."

"What happened?"

"Stuart James happened. He argued they needed a bigger name, someone more in the spotlight."

"Why would he do that?"

"Stuart James only does things for one reason, personal gain. He thought a bigger name would guarantee larger box office returns. As he was guaranteed a stake in the picture, he wanted to make sure his profits were maximized. He thought a bigger name star could do that."

"Some friend."

"Precisely. Since then, our friendship has been strained, to say the least."

"So, he's a pretty greedy, is he?"

Masden smiled. "Aren't we all?"

"Did you get a chance to talk to the girl, earlier, before it all went down?"

"I spoke to her briefly, earlier in the night. It turns out she was a fan of my movies when she was a little girl. How sad is that?"

"How about James? Did you see him with her that night?"

"It seems like I saw the two of them off conversing in some corner at some point. Of course, for most of the evening she was on Wright's arm."

"You don't know if she was a fan of his work as well, do you?"

"I wouldn't know, but if she can read, there's a good chance she's read Stuart's books. Most everyone has. Even you," he pointed out.

"Yeah, I guess that's true."

From there, all Jonathon Masden wanted to talk about was his glory days, rehashing the important moments of his career. Not being much of a movie buff, I decided to forgo the walk down memory lane after a quick belt of bourbon.

As I was leaving, I turned back to him for one more question. "Right before it all happened with the girl, you came into the room with Luis Middleton. Where were you guys coming from?"

Masden gave me an odd look. "Did I?"

"Yeah, you did. It looked like he might be reading you the riot act."

"Oh, yes, of course, I remember now. I had run down to my room for cigarettes. It's not like I couldn't use a break in the proceedings too. I ran into Luis in the hallway on my way back.

"It was a little odd, actually, a bit out of character for Luis. He apologized to me for some of the things he and the others had brought up. He said he was genuinely sorry for calling me out in front of the group, said he should have taken me aside. Then he proceeded to lecture me on my extravagant lifestyle."

"Nice guy," I replied.

"The pompous ass. Who in the hell is he to stand in judgment of me? He's so high and mighty. Let me tell you something about Luis Middleton. That golden goose company of his isn't doing as well as he likes to let on. Word is, they over extended themselves when all that government money was flowing in during the war. From what

I hear, Luis and his board of trustees are hanging on for dear life, about ready to go belly up. He can talk as big as he wants but I see right through his little facade."

With that, he turned back to his Martini.

I was thinking a little talk with Rachel might be in order, and I was mulling things over in my mind, things that didn't seem to quite fit together, trying to figure out what it all meant. If I had been paying attention, I'd have had a better heads up about Blake Martin and his goons coming down from the other direction.

Before I knew what was happening, his thugs had grabbed hold of each of my arms, stopping me in my tracks and holding me in place. Martin came slowly down the steps until he was square in front of me with a satisfied smirk on his face. Without a word he gave me a hard slug to the gut that sent me doubled over and wheezing.

"You're a pretty funny guy," he said.

"Yeah," I choked out. "That Clown School is finally paying off for me."

He slugged me again.

"That was a cute little trick, selling me out to the sheriff and then again to the Fed's."

"I'm a tricky guy."

"I guess you thought it would keep me out of the picture but good."

"I figured you'd show back up. You're like a bad rash."

"When I get done with you, you're going to wish all you had was a bad rash. You're going to wish you hadn't put the finger on me, too."

"Yeah, and I'm thinking you're going to be wishing you had those books of yours. Pretty interesting reading, if you go for that kind of smut."

I had his attention.

"We can play this a couple of ways," I continued. "First off, you can go ahead and work me over, teach me a lesson for being such a bad boy. Of course, if it goes down like that, I can't guarantee those books of yours won't end up in the wrong hands. There's no telling who might get to read them."

I could see the wheels in Martin's brain churning. "And the other way?"

"You call off your dogs here and let me be on my merry way. Once I feel like you've earned my trust, we can talk about you getting your books back, safe and sound."

"Do you have the books or does Rosie?" he asked.

"What's the difference? If you ever want to see them again, you're going to have to do this my way."

Martin was almost biting through his lip. "OK, I'll listen. What's your proposal?"

"I propose you back off before you make me angry. Now that I've seen what's in those things, I've decided to change the rules around. You remember back in the day, when I was the pathetic loser and you had all the cards? Guess what? Tag, you're it."

"Maybe I should just have my boys beat the dog piss out of you 'til you tell me where they are."

It was my turn to smile. "I think I've already demonstrated a friendly relationship with both the local sheriff and the federal agents. I'm guessing you wouldn't like it if those books were to end up with one of my buddies."

Martin gave a motion, and his goons let up on their hold on me. I shook my arms loose and straightened my jacket.

"That's better. Here's what we're going to do. You, Laurel and Hardy are going to go back to your room and wait for my call. I'll give you the where and the when, and I'll tell you how much to bring. In the meantime, you be thinking numbers, big numbers."

"You might want to be real careful, McKeller. You might feel like you're holding all the cards right now, but things tend to change real quick sometimes."

"Yeah, don't they? You might want to be real careful too. You're on my turf now."

He nodded slowly a couple of times. "When can I expect this call?"

"For your sake, you better hope it's after I'm in a much better mood. Otherwise, it's going to get awfully expensive for you."

"What assurances do I have you won't pull a fast one?"

"That's the beauty of my plan, Blake," I said in my friendliest voice. "You don't."

If looks could kill I would have been a goner. It looked like it took everything he had to stand down. I had him over a barrel, and I was relishing the moment, enjoying my little payback from days gone by.

The truth was, I was faking my way through the whole thing. He had me cornered, and I had to bluff my way out of it, hoping he wanted his books back more than he wanted to see me six feet under. I knew I had the upper hand, but if he hadn't forced it I'm not sure I would have come up with the whole go-wait-in-your-room bit. I was more than a little surprised he went for it.

"Don't keep me waiting too long," he said with what snarl he could muster. "I'm not a patient man."

"They have pills for that," I told him as I made my way up the steps and away from them.

With Martin, I was buying time again, the only thing I'd been doing since he'd shown up. I knew, sooner or later, the bills for all that bought time were going to come due.

Chapter Twenty-Five

With Martin out of my hair, for the time being, I decided to pay my little visit to Rachel Rae Miller. Some things nagged at the back of my brain that I needed to see about. I wasn't sure exactly what was going on there, but I couldn't help but feel something wasn't quite right.

She answered the door in the same sweater and slacks I'd picked up for her earlier, her hair pulled back tight. Her right cheek was still pink and splotchy and the small ring cut had scabbed over.

"Hi," she said when she answered the door. "I thought you bailed on me."

"I'm not sure it would matter either way."

"What's that supposed to mean?" she asked, shutting the door behind me.

"Just that you seem to have things under control."

"I know what you must think of me. I'm not that kind of girl."

I gave a long look to little Rachel Rae. She didn't look so young and little anymore. "What brought you to Myrtle Beach?"

"What does that have to do with anything?"

"I'm just making conversation. It occurs to me I don't know much about you."

She shrugged. "There's not much to know. I'm a small town girl. I've always loved the beach and thought it might be fun to live here."

"And that was what, two, three weeks ago?"

"Something like that, I guess."

"How do you like it, so far?"

Rachel smiled. "I like it. It's everything I thought it would be."

"It's not a little slow paced for you?"

"Slow paced? Like I said, I'm a small town girl at heart." It made me wonder about the expensive designer gown but, I chose to keep it to myself.

"How's the face?"

She reached up and gingerly touched the cut on her cheek with her fingertips. "It hurts but it's all right."

"I was just wondering, right after it happened, you told me Wright slapped you across the face. When you spoke with Simmons, you said he punched you. Which was it?"

"Does it make a difference?"

"Probably not. I'm just trying to get a clear picture of how it all went down."

She thought for a second. "He had me down on the bed and I was struggling to keep my dress up. It felt like a punch but, now that I think about it, it was more like a backhand. Yeah, he hit me with the back of his hand."

"He was on top of you and he caught you on the right side of your face, so if it was with the back of his hand, he must have hit you with his right."

Rachel nodded. "Yes, I remember distinctly, he backhanded me with his right hand." She gestured with her own right hand, mimicking the way she was hit. "It about knocked me silly. Things get kind of blurry from there."

"I'll bet."

"Look, McKeller, I know what you must think of me, but it's not like you think."

"I don't think anything."

"I just wanted you to know, I'm not taking any money from him. I thought about it, tempting as it is, but I don't want his money."

"I wouldn't blame you if you did."

"Well, I'm not. I just wanted you to know."

"You should get some rest," I said, making my move toward the door.

"You're leaving already?"

"Yeah, some of us still have to work for a living."

"I was kind of hoping you might hang around and keep me company awhile."

"Thanks but I've kind of got some stuff going on."

"Rain check?"

I ignored the invitation and glanced over to the Stuart James book on the nightstand. "How's the book?"

She looked back at it and back at me. "It's good. Ever read it?"

"Yeah, I have, as a matter of fact." I took my leave.

From there, I could have gone a couple of different directions. I needed to get with Rosie and put together some kind of game plan where Blake Martin was concerned. Checking up on Taylor Mills seemed like a good idea too, just to see if he was planning on packing up and heading home. Instead, I decided to head up to the Penthouse Suite to see how things were going on the senator's front.

Simmons answered the door and let me in. The senator was sitting on the sofa in his pajamas. He looked rattled, his hair tussled, dark circles under his eyes. He was staring off, twisting and toying with the wedding ring on his hand.

He didn't seem to notice as Simmons ushered me into one of the side bedrooms where we could talk privately.

"How's he doing?" I asked when we were alone.

"He's a mess. He still can't believe it happened."

"Did he give you his side of the story?"

"He doesn't remember much. He was pretty drunk. He remembers the girl inviting him into the bedroom. He remembers walking in with her. The next thing he remembers is waking up on the bed."

"She invited him?"

"That's what he says, but like I said, he was pretty drunk. Says he could barely walk when she led him back there, tripped over a nightstand in the dark."

"The lights were out?"

Simmons shrugged. "I guess so."

"They were on when we went in."

"Somebody must have turned them on, maybe the girl."

"I heard she turned down your offer."

Simmons seemed to fidget. "She said she didn't want his money. She wants a private sit down with the senator, one on one. Nobody else in the room."

"Does that seem a little strange?"

"Everything about this seems strange. I know you're not a big fan of the senator but, despite what you may think, he's a good man. Not a perfect man, he's had his share of indiscretions over the years but never anything like this."

"Does something seem not right here?"

"Like I said, all of it seems not right."

"When does she want the meeting?"

"Tonight."

"Any idea what she wants?"

"Not money, apparently. Maybe she wants to see him grovel. Maybe she wants to slap him across the face."

"What do you know about Stuart James?"

"I used to read his books. I see him at some of the senator's little get togethers, keeps to himself, for the most part. Drinks a lot but, then, so do the others. Why do you ask?"

"I don't know."

"You got something on your mind, McKeller?"

"The girl, Rachel. Did you know she'd only worked here a few weeks?"

"No."

"Maybe you guys should check that stuff out before you go offering to start writing checks."

"What are you saying, this is some kind of setup?"

"I don't know. If she doesn't want money, it doesn't really make sense, does it?"

"Plus, how would she know he was going to be here? We kept a pretty good lid on it 'til the last minute."

"I didn't know until two days before," I pointed out. "What about the guests? When did they know?"

"The senator and his friends have been planning this for some time."

"So, Stuart James would have known?"

"It's conceivable but where's the gain? The girl isn't asking for money."

"She's going to be alone in a room with a U.S. Senator. We don't know what she's going to ask for."

"What do you think we should do?" Simmons caught me off guard, asking for my opinion.

"Stall her."

"Stall her?" he repeated.

"It's one of my go to moves. In the meantime, I'd check out Mr. Stuart James as thoroughly as I could, personal, financial, ulterior motives. I'm assuming you guys have those capabilities."

"Yeah, I think we might be able to handle that."

"Keep me posted on what you find. Until then, I'd put off the meeting between Rae Rae and the senator as long as I could." I was halfway out the door when Simmons stopped me.

"By the way," he said. "Those guys you pointed out turned out to be dead ends, thugs down from Baltimore but no connection to the senator we could find. They're clean."

"Clean might be the wrong word, but I'd keep an eye on them just the same. There's something fishy about those guys."

Chapter Twenty-Six

What I really wanted was a day off. My plate was piled pretty high, and I didn't have much of an appetite. As if I didn't have enough worries with Rosie, Blake Martin and the dead bodies of Ralpny Henderson and Marcus Fletcher, now I found myself in the center of sleazy political intrigue I wanted no part of. Unfortunately, for me, I was head of security at the Ocean Forest and I couldn't help but feel this thing had gone down on my watch. That put me in the middle of it.

My primary concern was still Rosie and everything swirling around her. As usual, I felt like I didn't have the slightest grasp on what was actually going on. In lieu of a break, I decided on a brief stop at my room for a splash of cold water on my face.

I was standing over my sink, staring into the mirror, cold water dripping down my chin. My thoughts were a hodgepodge of question marks and innuendos, snippets of everything I'd seen or heard over the last few days. I was having trouble piecing them all together and making any sense out of them.

Looking into my own eyes, I was struck by my features, the unspectacular and familiar parts that make up Frankie McKeller, the ones I'd been looking at all my life. I looked somehow different, tired and haggard, aged in a way I hadn't noticed before. It made me wonder when it happened, when life had begun to sneak up on me and rob me of what little youth and exuberance I once possessed. I felt worn out, withered and spent. A nap seemed like a good idea.

The knock at my door snapped me back into the moment, and I knew there would be no rest for me just yet. There never is for the weary.

I'd barely cracked the door open when the blow to my chest sent me flying backwards, falling back into the room. I was sprawled out on the floor, lying on my back, as Taylor Mills stepped into the room and closed the door.

"I gave at the office, if you're soliciting donations," I said.

"You think you're pretty slick, don't you?" he answered.

"I don't know, As far as slick goes, I figure I'm pretty average." I started to get up but he slammed the bottom of his foot into my shoulder, knocking me back down.

"Funny guy, McKeller." For good measure, he gave me a swift kick to the side of my head.

I was cringing in pain, trying to shake loose the cobwebs that suddenly filled my skull. "Was there something in particular you wanted?"

"She had to say those things because you were there. She didn't mean it."

"Oh, that? Yeah, with Rosie, sometimes it's tough to figure out what she means, but I think she was pretty clear on this one."

There was another kick to the chest, this one knocking the wind out of me.

"You don't know what we have. You don't know what it's like between us."

"You'd be surprised," I managed to grunt out.

"It's all your fault. Rosie and me, we had plans. We were going places."

"Maybe this is a conversation you should be having with Rosie," I suggested.

"If it weren't for you ..."

I had a pretty good idea what was coming next so I rolled off to one side, just missing his next kick. I reached up and grabbed him around the knee, pulling him toward me and knocking him off balance. He managed to catch me in the side of the head with his other knee but I held tight to his leg, wrapping myself around it and pulling him down on top of me. With all his Karate expertise, I figured the closer I got him, the better chance I had of nullifying all that technique he brought with him.

He gave me a chop to the back of the neck as he fell over, one that sent shards of pain down my spine. I countered with an elbow to the jaw and his head jerked backward with a groan. I'd got him good and I wasn't about to let up.

Before he could respond, I turned into him and let loose with a series of jabs to his stomach, mustering all the strength and leverage I could find. Mills deflected my hand on the third punch and rammed his upturned fist into my face, catching me just below the left eye.

I fell back and he was on his feet in a flat second, poised in a Karate stance, ready to let loose with an ass kicking I figured I wasn't going to forget very soon. I'm no dummy and I know a lost cause when I see one.

I rolled over on my side and tried to climb to my feet, trying to get out of his range before the inevitable. I'd barely got to up past my knees, my back to him, scurrying to get away. He sent his foot jabbing into my kidney and the force of his kick sent me flying forward, over the nightstand and into the wall.

Over my shoulder, I could see him coming at me, and I knew it wasn't going to be pretty. He had blood lust in his eyes, and I got the feeling what he was about to do was going to leave some serious marks. Instinctively, I reached down and grabbed hold of the lamp on the nightstand. I waited the one second it took him to close in, and when he was within arm's reach, about to unleash his furry on me from behind, I whipped around as quick as I could, bringing the lamp with me in a violent swing that I put everything I had into.

I caught him on the side of his face and, at first, I thought I might have taken his head off. It snapped to one side and his body froze in place before crumbling to the floor. Taylor Mills was lying on the ground, bent and motionless, a frail moan emanating from his curled lips. There was a gash across his cheek and his eyes were rolled back in his head.

"Stupid kid," I grunted, as I threw the lamp off to the side.

I stumbled into the bathroom and splashed some more cold water on my face before filling a glass and going back out to Mills. He was still lying on the floor, groaning in semiconscious pain. I dumped the glass of water on his head and he bounced back to life, shaking his head and coughing.

While he was coming to, I went over to my dresser and pulled out my trusty .45. If he still felt like a fight when he came around, I was going to make sure the odds were leaned more in my direction.

It looked like he was about coherent again.

"Do you want to tell me what this all about, junior?" I asked, holding the gun at a visible but nonthreatening level.

"You ruined everything!" he screamed back.

"Yeah, and you ruined my day too. I was in a pretty good mood 'til you started kicking me around like a soccer ball."

"I came here to break your stinkin' neck."

"That's a good way to kill a guy. Is she really worth life in prison, maybe worse?"

"You don't understand what she means to me, what we mean to each other."

"Maybe you just don't understand Rosie like you think you do."

"How's that?"

"Look, don't feel bad. I've been there before. You can never compete with her first love."

"You?"

"I chuckled. "No, not even. Rosie's first love is Rosie, always has been."

"You don't know her like I do. She's not like that. She's sweet and kind and vulnerable and she's in over her head. She needs me and I don't plan on running out on her just yet."

"Kid, you got it bad. Take it from one who knows. Rosie has one agenda. That's to get what's best for Rosie. To do it, she'll do anything she has to. She'll chew you up and spit you out if that's what it takes."

It was Taylor Mills' turn to chuckle. "You think you have her all figured out, don't you? She must have done some number on you. You're so blind with it you can't see her for what she really is. She's a lost kid, McKeller.

"Yeah, maybe she doesn't always make the smart decision. Maybe she doesn't always lead with her head, but her heart is in the right place. Rosie is something special and I, for one, plan on seeing this through with her."

"Even if she doesn't want you along?"

"Rosie doesn't know what she wants. My guess is she's afraid I'm going to get hurt along the way. She's looking out for me but I don't need looking out for."

"What you need is a seeing eye dog."

"Rosie is special, McKeller. A girl like that comes along maybe once in a guy's life. You blew your chance with her. Don't blow mine."

He had that familiar look in his eyes, the one I recognized from my own face some time back. It was hard not to feel sorry for the dumb lug.

"Take my advice, Taylor. Give it up. You're barking up a Redwood, and you can't win. Take my advice and walk away."

"So you can have her all to yourself?"

I shook my head in disgust. "You just don't get it, do you?"

I was about to go into a lecture on the do's and don'ts of Rosie, but before I could get rolling with it the phone rang, and I crossed the room to answer it.

"Yeah?"

"McKeller, it's Curtis from the front desk."

"I know who you are, Curtis. What's up?"

"I've got Sheriff Talbert down here and he's piping mad. He says he wants you and the girl down here, pronto."

"All right, tell him to cool his heels. I'll be down in a few minutes."

"I don't think I want to tell him to do that. I'll just say you're on your way."

"Suit yourself," I replied, hanging up the phone and turning back to Taylor Mills. "Look, as much as I'd love to hang around and discuss the pros and cons of life with Rosie, I've got stuff to do. I trust you can see your way out?"

Mills made a big production of getting to his feet and making his way to the door. As he left, he turned back to me and said, "I'm never giving up on Rosie."

Dumb schmuck.

I swung up to Rosie's room to collect her before going down to meet the sheriff. She answered the door in a lime green dress, slightly off the shoulders, cut low in the front, puffy and frilly at the bottom.

She stood leaning in the doorway, peering out the cracked door. There was a soft, distant look in her eyes.

"I wasn't sure we were still on speaking terms," she said in a quiet voice.

"Sure we are. Why not?"

"I got the feeling you aren't too fond of me."

"You have a tendency to get under my skin from time to time."

"So, where does that leave us?"

I took a deep breath and let it out slow. "Well, let's see. Your boy-friend holds a bit of a grudge and stopped by my room to show me some of his Karate moves. I had to knock him down a few notches.

"Your ex paid me a little visit too. He was going to have his goons show me a few moves of their own until I told him I had his precious books. I've got him on ice for now."

"You have the books? Where are they?"

"They're in a safe spot."

"Take me to them."

"Right now we have another appointment. The sheriff is waiting downstairs to talk to you about a couple of dead bodies."

Rosie went to shut the door on my face but I stuck my foot in the way. "You can't dodge him forever, Rosie. You're going to make it worse on yourself."

"I don't have anything to say to him."

"Look, if you don't want to find a murder rap hanging around your neck, you're going to have to talk to him. The longer you avoid him, the worse it looks."

Rosie bit her lip and seemed to mull it over for a moment. "All right. Let's go talk to the sheriff."

Talbert was waiting in the lobby. He chose to stand beside one of the overstuffed chairs that most people prefer to relax in. His look was cold and stern as we came walking up.

"Young lady, I was beginning to wonder if you were real or not," he said.

Rosie held out her hand, which the sheriff gave a quick, half-heart-ed shake to. "Oh, I'm real all right. It's nice to meet you, Sheriff."

"Maybe we could start off by you telling me exactly what you're doing here in Myrtle Beach."

Rosie gave a shrug to her slight shoulders, and her eyes got all wide and innocent. She cocked her head to one side and flashed him her best little girl smile. "What can I say, Sheriff? I didn't mean to bring any trouble down here with me."

"I'm sure you didn't." he answered, unimpressed with her sweet and innocent routine. "I think it best if you start at the beginning."

"Is there something I can help you with, Sheriff Talbert?" Bunte-meyer, my boss, said, as he came walking up, inserting himself into our conversation.

The three of us gave each other looks before I said, "No, we're good here, boss. Everything is under control."

My boss didn't look convinced. "Is there something I need to know about?"

"I'm conducting a murder investigation," Talbert offered. "I was just asking a few questions."

"Murder investigation?" Buntemeyer's face went white as a ghost. "I hope you don't believe our hotel has anything to do with it. The last thing we need is any sort of scandal involving the Ocean Forest."

"Don't worry, Mr. Buntemeyer," the sheriff assured him. "I'm just taking care of some routine questions. There's no reason to believe the hotel's reputation is at stake."

"That's a relief," Buntemeyer said. "But may I offer you one of the hotel's meeting rooms? So much more private, you know," he added, glancing around as if afraid some guest was going to be offended by a murder investigation in the lobby.

Rosie was nothing if not a pro. She walked the sheriff through her ordeal, starting with the abuse she'd endured from Martin up in Baltimore. She seemed almost to break down into tears as she described the fear and misery he'd put her through. She told Talbert how, in a desperate attempt to escape his abuse, she'd run away, down to Myrtle Beach, seeking help from an old and trusted friend.

She was nearly sobbing when she told him how Martin had sent Ralphy down to bring her back, how he'd ransacked her hotel room, how I had gone to confront him in her defense. A single tear rolled down her cheek as she told him how she'd been hiding out in fear, how she found out about Ralphy's murder.

The sheriff didn't look particularly moved, which is surprising, as I'd seen lesser performances in Hollywood melodramas.

"How about this other fellow, Fletcher? Did you know him?"

"The private investigator?" She shook her head. "I'd never even heard of him until Frankie asked me about him the other night."

"Did you have any contact with Henderson since he came down looking for you?"

"No, not at all. Frankie kept me out of sight. I never even saw him."

"How about Blake Martin?"

"Like I said, Frankie has been keeping me under wraps, for my own protection. You don't know Blake. You don't know what he's capable of."

"You think he's capable of murder?"

"There isn't much he isn't capable of, Sheriff. He's a very bad man."

"If he's so bad, how did you end up getting involved with him?"

Rosie sighed. "I was naive and stupid," she answered, two things Rosie never was.

Talbert continued to grill her for the next half hour and Rosie seemed honest and forthright in her answers, disregarding the little bit about Martin's books and her plan to embezzle extort money from him. By the time he was done, Sheriff Talbert didn't seem too satisfied with her story. He seemed as on edge and agitated as always.

"I don't know what all's going on here, young lady, but if I find out you're holding back with anything, this is going to turn into the most unpleasant vacation you've ever had."

"Who said it was so pleasant to this point?" she answered with a coy smile.

"You need to make yourself available if I have any further questions."

"Of course, Sheriff. Anything you need."

"I'm finished here, for now. Miss Carter, be sure to keep yourself available if I have anything else. That goes for you too, McKeller."

"Sure thing, Sheriff. Just give me a buzz if I can help."

Buntemeyer was waiting in the hall when we came out of the room.

"If you're done here, can I have a word with you, McKeller?" my boss asked.

Rosie cut in. "Actually, Frankie and I had something we need to take care of."

"Is it hotel business? After all, you are still on my payroll, aren't you?"

"Last I heard," I answered before turning to Rosie. "We can take care of that other thing later. It's not going anywhere for now."

Rosie looked like I'd punched her in the gut. It was obvious she wanted me to take her to Martin's books.

"I'll give you a call when I get done with work," I told her before walking off with Buntemeyer.

"Do you want to tell me what's going on?" he asked once we were alone.

"Trust me, Boss. It's nothing you need to be concerned with."

"Exactly who is that girl, and what does she have to do with all this?"

"I guess that's the hundred thousand dollar question, isn't it?"

"Look here, McKeller, I hope you have this thing in hand. The hotel cannot be party to any shenanigans. We have a lot of important people in house."

"Don't you get yourself worried, Boss. I've got things under control," I lied.

"Speaking of our important guests, do you have any idea what's going on with the senator and his people?"

I shrugged. "Why do you ask?"

"Senator Wright canceled his afternoon reception and his dinner function this evening. There's rumor he's planning on checking out early."

"Maybe he's under the weather."

"His people are acting strange, like something is up. You don't know what's going on?"

I shrugged again. "State secrets, maybe?"

"Just what do I pay you for, anyway? You're my head of security. I expect you to be on top of all the hotel's goings on. If there's a problem with the senator and his people, I expect you to be there to resolve the issue."

"The senator has his own people for that."

"You know, I'm beginning to question your value to this institution. Do you realize how important the senator's business is to both the finances and the reputation of this hotel?"

"Do you want me to go up there and beg him to stay?"

"What I want is for you to find out what the problem is with the senator's stay and to use every resource available to this hotel to correct it. Is that clear, McKeller?"

"Crystal."

Chapter Twenty-Seven

The last thing I wanted to do was poke my head back into Senator Wright's dirty little mess. I had enough going on with Rosie and Martin and had very little interest in diverting my attention to anything else. That said, Buntemeyer made it pretty clear where he wanted my priorities to lie. As I was pretty fond of little things like food in my belly and a roof over my head, I figured maybe I could dedicate some of my time to trying to help resolve the issue.

First I had to figure out just what was going on. I thought Stuart James might be able to help me out with that.

It took me awhile to track him down, but I finally caught up with him on the back veranda of the hotel. He was kicked back in a lounge chair in his shirt sleeves, enjoying a Lime Daiquiri. They were all the rage this season, the idea imported up from Cuba, crushed ice and lime juice mixed with a generous portion of rum.

"Care for a drink?" he asked me as I pulled up a chair beside him.

"No thanks. A little too fruity for my taste."

He took a leisurely sip. "If it's good enough for Papa Hemingway ..."

"One writer to another," I added.

"Oh, don't get me wrong. Hemingway is a hack. A bunch of melodramatic dribble sprinkled with a heavy dose of testosterone. I don't know why anybody bothers to read his garbage."

"Do I sense a smidgen of professional jealousy?"

"In my day, I could drool better prose in a semiconscious drunken stupor."

"So can Hemingway, from what I hear."

"I met him once at a literary dinner in New York. He's a loud arrogant and abrasive man with an ego the size of Manhattan and an attitude to match."

"I know the type."

"The smug bastard, he actually paid me a compliment. He said I had a fresh and vitalic literary voice. He told me he enjoyed my second book immensely,"

"I can see why you dislike him so much."

"He also said I had yet to tap into my writing talents, that I had merely scratched the surface of what I was a capable of achieving."

"Everybody's a critic."

"The thing is, he was wrong. I had mined those fields for all they were worth, scratching every ounce of literary means I could come up with. I figure, at best, I had three good books in me, maybe one great one. I wrote six."

"You're saying the well has run dry?"

"I'm saying the well dried up long ago, and I've been licking the walls for every bit of moisture I could find ever since. Hence, my new career as a Hollywood screenwriter. Anybody could pound out that tripe."

We were interrupted by Alice Seymour who came walking up with a fresh daiquiri in her hand. It wasn't uncommon for servers from the restaurant to pick up tables on the veranda when business was slow.

She was still in her work clothes and shot me the slightest of smiles as she handed James his drink.

"Ah," Stuart remarked. "Twenty minutes, on the dot."

"You said to keep them coming," she replied with a smile.

"That, I did, my dear. And for your efforts ..." He reached beside his chair and produced a copy of his book, *The Last of the Best*. It was the same book I'd seen in Rachel Miller's room.

James pulled out a ballpoint pen and scribbled something on the first page before handing it to Alice. "A little something for your troubles."

"Thanks, Mr. James. I'm looking forward to reading it. I hear it's good."

"It's my masterpiece," he responded. "But it pales in comparison to your beauty."

Alice gave a snicker and shook her head. "OK, I'll be back in twenty minutes with another drink. You want anything, McKeller?"

"No, I'm good. Thanks."

"Pretty smooth lines," I said to James after she was gone.

"Mine or hers?"

"Hers are nice too, but I was referring to yours."

"What can I say? What good is it being a best-selling author if you can't flaunt it once in a while?"

"Do you give out many of those?"

"Let's just say, I travel well stocked. Consider it a form of romantic currency, better than a calling card. I find it doesn't hurt to point out to members of the fairer sex that I used to be someone important."

"And that works for you?"

"Well, if you give out enough of them it increases the odds, but you'd be surprised. Some women are impressed with a man in print."

"How about Rachel Miller? Was she impressed?"

"The girl from the party?"

"Yeah. You did give her a book, didn't you?"

"Yes, I believe I did. It was before the party, though, earlier, when she was working the reception."

"And was she impressed?"

James gave a shrug of one shoulder. "Eh, you win some and lose some. As I recall, she seemed grateful but not overly impressed. She did promise to read it."

"Did you talk to her long?"

"No I can't say I did. It was fairly evident from the beginning she was more impressed with power than talent."

"Why's that, because she ended up with the senator?"

"Well, there's that but even before the party I could see she was more interested in the power broker types. I saw her flirting shamelessly with Jonathon Masden at the reception. Movie stars tend to garner more attention than us mere writers, even washed up ones. I also saw her having a heart to heart with Middleton sometime after, Steel tycoon that he is. I suppose she was weighing her options. Of course, when the senator's attentions became available, all bets were off."

"She took a pretty quick liking to him, huh?"

"And alas, I had no shot after that."

"So, you never met her before yesterday?"

James chuckled. "No, I'm afraid we run in different circles."

"How about Masden? Do you get the sense he knew her before

this weekend?"

James looked confused. "How would he? She works at the hotel, right?"

"I was just asking."

"As far as I know, we all met her for the first time yesterday."

I left Stuart James with more questions than answers. For a brief minute I had suspected he might be involved somehow with Rachel Miller. Super sleuth that I am, I'd thought her having a copy of his book might connect the two but, if he was giving them out like candy to every pretty girl he met, the connection seemed vague at best. It made me realize just how little a grasp I had on what was going on around me.

I decided to swing by my office to get my head together and decide what to do next. Outside my door, I was fidgeting with my keys when I heard the unmistakable sound of a voice coming from the other side. It didn't take long to recognize the voice.

My door was unlocked and I cracked it open a hair, leaning an ear against it.

Rosie was on the phone, talking quietly. I could hear the sound of shuffling papers as she rifled through my desk.

"They have to be here somewhere," she said. "Of course I'm sure. Where else would he hide them? It's not like he's the brightest bulb on the tree."

That one hurt.

"I'll find the books and I'll meet you at your hotel. We can call Blake from there. We don't need Frankie anymore."

I felt like I'd been on the business end of a swift kick to the doo-dads.

"No, don't worry about him. We'll have the money by tonight. We can be in California by this time tomorrow."

I heard her close a drawer.

"No, Honey. Taylor won't be a problem. I took care of that. I told him it was over."

She paused for a few moments.

"I don't care what he thinks. You know you're the only one for me. You always have been. There's no need to worry about Taylor. He can't cause us any problems. He's not a threat."

I heard the filing cabinet drawer open.

"I've got them," she said. "The big dummy left them right here in his filing cabinet. He didn't even try to hide them."

Another swift kick to the nether regions.

"I love you too, Baby. This will all be over soon. Nothing can stop us now."

A surge of panic swept through my body and I wasn't sure what to do. Part of me wanted to barge into the room and confront her with what I'd heard. Another part of me wondered if that might be the stupid play. After all, I still didn't know who she was talking to.

I closed the door as gently as I could and dashed over to the utility closet two doors down. It was where the maid service kept their cleaning supplies, and it was about twice the size of my office. It was always left unlocked, and I opened the door and slid myself in, leaving the door cracked open enough to see through.

After a minute or so, Rosie went walking by, and I waited a few moments before poking my head out. Her back was to me, and she was walking away, down toward the staircase. I waited until she turned the corner before slipping out and following.

She had a pretty good head start, and I moved as fast as my bum leg would allow me to make up ground. By the time I got to the bottom of the staircase she was already in the lobby. I wobbled my way up, two stairs at a time.

Rosie was crossing the lobby, heading to the front door, by the time I got to the top, Martin's ledgers clutched to her chest. I was moving in behind her, keeping her in sight but not letting myself get too close.

I was halfway across the lobby when someone grabbed me by the arm.

"We need to talk," Simmons said, holding me in place.

"Not now."

Simmons' grip tightened on my arm. "Yes, now. The girl wants to meet with the senator this afternoon."

I was trying to worm my way past him, but he held tight to my arm, and I only managed to ease us closer to the door. We were close enough that I could see out the front, and I watched helplessly as Rosie got into a waiting cab.

It was the same cab that was always waiting out front. The one driven by Omar Best.

"I checked into Stuart James, like you said. I didn't find anything out of the ordinary."

"Yeah, forget James. He's a dead end," I replied as the cab drove off.

"You heard what I said, right? The girl wants to meet with Wright this afternoon. The senator wants to get it over with. I don't know how long I can stall him."

"Something's not right with this set up," I told him. "How about Jonathon Masden? Can you do a check on him?"

"I can but I have a pretty good idea what I'll find. A former big time movie star who's down on his luck and looking to make a comeback."

"Maybe a guy like that would like to have a United States Senator in his pocket."

"The senator is a powerful man, but he doesn't make a lot of casting decisions. I'm not sure how much weight he carries in Hollywood."

"I've got a sneaking suspicion someone is in on this with the girl, someone who knew the senator was going to be here this week."

"And you're basing this on what?"

"Call it gut instinct."

"You don't have a clue, do you?"

"I have suspicions."

"McKeller, you're wasting my time. You know, I did a check on you too. Born and raised in Baltimore, you worked as a longshoreman out of high school, until the war, where you were wounded at Omaha Beach. You spent nine months recovering from your injuries before enrolling in something called The Staley School of Private Investigation. After that, you opened a little office in downtown Baltimore where you barely scraped by.

"You came down to Myrtle Beach for a wedding in September of forty-six and somehow had a hand in solving a murder. For whatever reason, this seemed like enough for the management at the Ocean Forest to offer you a job. You've been here as house detective since."

"You left out the part where I took Janet Antlitz to the Junior Prom."

"You might be a big wig down here in the sticks, because you fancy yourself as some kind of half assed Philo Vance, but I work for a

United States Senator."

"You're the one who came to me," I pointed out.

"I thought maybe you had your ear to the ground down here. I thought you could be of some help. I think we can handle it from here."

"Suit yourself. I never asked to be a part of this anyhow."

"I expect any information you have or think you have to remain confidential. The last thing we need is people talking out of school."

I was getting the big blow off, which should have suited me just fine. After all, I never wanted any part of it. I had bigger fish to fry, and I'd always seen the senator and his problem as an inconvenience, an obstacle in my way while dealing with Rosie and everything that came with that.

A smart guy would have left it there, happy to be done with it. I've never been what you call a smart guy. Maybe my ego was a little bruised.

Simmons had turned his back to me and was walking away. I shouldn't have cared.

"You're right," I said, loud enough to catch his attention. It was enough to make him stop and look back. "You're absolutely right. I'm a low budget hack out of Baltimore that has no business poking his nose in the affairs of a United States Senator. I don't have the background or the experience, and to be quite frank, I don't give a rat's ass if the senator can't keep his pants on.

"The thing is, this is *my* hotel, *my* responsibility. If it goes down on my watch, that makes it my business. So you go ahead and take that meeting with Rachel, but you better tell the senator to bring his checkbook because she wants something, and I'm guessing it's not going to come cheap."

Simmons had nothing.

"Now, if you don't want to go in there with nothing but your nuts in your hands, you'll play this the smart way. Keep Wright on ice for a while. In the meantime, you do your little background checks on everybody involved, all the principles. Especially Jonathon Masden and little Rachel Rae Miller. She has a connection with one those people. I'm sure of it."

"What makes you so sure?"

"For someone who holds the senator's virtues in such high regard, you're pretty quick to bail on him when things get rough. Don't you think it's a coincidence that Rachel Rae shows up just before the senator's visit? Don't you think it's odd that a man like that could just black out and snap, attack a woman out of the blue?"

"I'm listening."

"How about the fact that the senator was blind drunk and walked into a dark room, but when we went in, seconds later, the lights were on."

"The girl probably turned them on."

"The girl was cowering in the corner. She'd just fought off a rapist and was screaming for help. Do you think she had the where with all to turn on the lights?"

Simmons didn't answer.

"Did you get a look at her face? She's got quite the bruise on her right cheek, along with a little cut where a ring caught her."

"So?"

"When I asked her about it, she said Wright backhanded her across the face. They were face to face and he hauled off and back handed her. She even showed me how he did it."

"So what?"

I stepped in close to him and brought my right hand slowly across his face, back hand style. "He would have done it like this," I explained.

"What does that have to do with anything?"

"How long have you worked for Wright?"

"Four and a half years."

"You're a pretty observant guy. Does he wear a ring?"

"Yeah, his wedding ring."

"And what hand is that on?"

Chapter Twenty-Eight

I don't know how sold Simmons was with what I gave him, but it was enough to peak his interest. It was enough to keep me in the loop too, a place I wasn't sure I wanted to be. My concerns still lay with Rosie, and she was off to who knows where?

At the front desk, leaning against it and wondering what to do next, it felt like I was holding a ton of bricks over my head, waiting for them to collapse on top of me.

There was a new player in town and Rosie was off to meet him, the two of them plotting to relieve Blake Martin of his bank roll. It might be the mysterious and familiar stranger I'd seen around, the thin guy in the conservative suit. I was pushed out of the picture and once she got her money, I'd likely might never see her again.

I should have been relieved by the prospect. It's not like she brought anything but trouble when she showed up in my life. I wasn't ready for that.

There was no logical reason for it. I didn't even like her anymore. She wasn't the woman I'd been crazy about for all this time. Maybe she never had been, but that didn't make it easy to let her go now, not like this.

I reached over and picked up the telephone from the front desk and dialed Blake Martin's room.

"Yeah?" he answered.

"It's McKeller."

"I figured."

"How are you enjoying your stay?"

"How about we do away with the chit chat, and you get to the point?"

"Come on, Blake. You're going to make me feel like you don't like me anymore."

"Have you thought this out, McKeller?" he growled.

"Not much to think about. It's pretty black and white from where I stand."

"Exactly where is it you stand, McKeller? How do you think this thing is going to play out? Do you think you and Rosie are going to ride off into the sunset? Is that how you see this going down?"

I didn't answer.

"We both know Rosie pretty well. I'm not sure you can count on the happy ending. The thing is, once she gets that money, I'm guessing she's going to take a powder. That's just Rosie looking out for Rosie. That's the way she is.

"Where does that leave you? Once she's gone, she'll be pretty hard to track down. It might take me years. You, on the other hand, where are you going to go? You have a pretty sweet set up down here. I doubt if you want to kiss it goodbye, not even for Rosie."

"Are you threatening me?"

"Threat is such an ugly word. I prefer promise."

"Let me make you a promise. You're going to regret making that threat. I promise you that."

Martin laughed. "All right, McKeller. If you say so. I was just trying to give you a little friendly advice. We'll play it your way."

"Yeah, we will. In fact, I'm going to go ahead and start keeping that promise right now. The price just went up. Ten G's, cash on the barrel head."

"Where am I supposed to get that kind of money down here?"

"That's not really my problem, is it? If I were you, I'd start making some calls."

"You are making a mistake, McKeller. A big mistake."

"Yeah, well, that's what I do. It's a little late in the game to start changing my ways now."

"I'm going to need time for that kind of dough."

"Time is one thing you don't have a lot of. There's a place downtown called Peaches Corner. You can't miss it. Be there at noon tomorrow, with the money."

"Peaches Corner? Where is it?"

"You're a smart guy. Find it." I hung up the phone.

It wasn't at all the way I had wanted the conversation to go. My plan had been to feel him out before he got the call from Rosie, but he pushed me over the edge and I faked my way through it. I had no idea how someone would go about getting ten thousand dollars to Myrtle Beach, but I was hoping it would keep him busy for a while. I was hoping it would buy me enough time to find Rosie.

"Howdy, McKeller," a familiar voice said from behind me. I turned around to find Clifford, the elevator operator, walking past, in full uniform, reporting in for work.

"Hi, Clifford. You have a sec?"

"Yeah, sure. I'm just heading over for another eight hour shift in the box. Got to enjoy the fresh air while I can. You can't imagine how that thing gets to smelling, all those people going up and down."

"Do you remember when we were in there, and you stopped to pick up Rachel Miller? She was all dolled up in her party dress?"

"Oh, yeah. I remember. She was looking pretty good. She was on her way up to the senator's party."

"Yeah, that's right. You don't remember what floor you picked her up on, do you?"

"Sure I do. The same floor I always pick her up on. The fifth floor."

I turned to Curtis, the desk clerk, who was busy with paper work behind the desk. "Curtis, I need a list of everyone staying on the fifth floor."

"I'm kind of busy, McKeller. Can't you go through the book and get it yourself?"

"I'll owe you one, Curtis. I'm kind of busy myself," I said as I slapped my fedora on my head and headed for the front door.

"I have important hotel business to take care of," he pleaded.

"This is more important. Call it a matter of national security. I'll pick it up when I get back."

I walked out the front door and trotted down the steps. Sometimes things just go your way, like fate is looking out for you.

I'd barely got to the bottom of the stairs when I saw a lone vehicle rambling down the long stretch of Woodside Drive. Even off in the distance, I recognized Omar Best in his beat up old cab, returning after his latest run, back to his usual spot in front of the hotel.

He pulled up, and I went over and leaned into the open passenger window. "How's business, Omar?"

He shrugged, pulling out a newspaper and making himself comfortable in his seat. "About like usual."

"You just picked up a girl, a brunette, here at the hotel."

"Yeah. Pretty little filly. She wanted to go downtown."

"Where'd you drop her?"

He shrugged again. "Took her to the Starlight Inn. Hope that's all right. I know it's not the Ocean Forest but that's where she wanted to go. I don't expect the Starlight's stealing a lot of your business."

"That's fine. Thanks, Omar."

"You take care, McKeller."

Chapter Twenty-Nine

The Studebaker Coupe the hotel allowed me use of was running well, and I was putting her through the paces as I sped through town, on my way to find Rosie. I had no idea what I was going to do when I found her, but I knew I was running out of time. I'd have to wing it, shooting from the hip, once I'd tracked her down.

The Starlight Inn sat just outside the center of town, a modest five story structure two blocks off the ocean. It was nothing fancy, but it was clean and kept up, affordable and convenient, a popular place for vacationing families.

I pulled the little Coupe into one of the side parking spots and sat for a few moments trying to prepare myself. There was no telling what I was going to find inside. I tucked my trusty .45 in back of my belt. It gave me a false sense of security.

I caught a flash of movement across the street, heading for the front of the Inn. I recognized him instantly and wasn't overly surprised to see him moving toward the front entrance.

Taylor Mills looked lost and forlorn, maybe a little nervous. He was taking slow and careful steps, never taking his eyes off the front of the hotel.

I hopped out of the car and rushed over to cut him off, meeting up with him just before he got to the front steps.

"Looking for somebody?" I asked.

"What's it to you?"

"Did you follow her here?"

"None of your business."

"You know she's in there with another guy, don't you?"

He gave me a look.

"Of course you do. You've followed her before, haven't you?"

Again with the look.

"Any idea who he is?"

Taylor shook his head. "I've seen the two of them together a couple of times."

"Thin guy, hat, conservative, pinstriped suit?"

"Yeah, that's the guy. Who is he?"

"I don't know exactly," I answered. "Insurance, maybe."

"What's that supposed to mean?"

"It means Rosie isn't the kind of girl to take chances. She likes to hedge her bets. In case you or me weren't enough to help her out, she had to have a backup plan, somebody she could count on to bail her out."

"I asked her about him once, the guy in the pinstripes, after I saw her talking to him at the hotel. She told me he was an old friend, someone from her past. She said he was in love with her and he'd do anything for her."

"Is that the way you want her talking about you down the road?"

"Of course not."

"What was your plan, Taylor? Were you going to barge in there and cut loose with your Karate moves?"

He didn't answer.

"You'd end up looking pretty silly if it turns out he's the one who put a couple of bullets in Ralphy Henderson and Marcus Fletcher. Those moves of yours aren't much use against bullets."

"I ain't afraid of nobody."

"That's your first mistake. Guess what, kid? No matter how tough you are, there's always somebody down the road who's tougher, somebody who's willing to take it a step farther. How far are you willing to go? Are you willing to kill a man? Is she worth that?"

Taylor swallowed hard, perspiration beading up on his forehead.

"That's what it's going to take, you know. The bar has been set. Two men are dead. It's blood for blood time. You go in there, you better be willing to go the distance because these people aren't playing games."

His eyes shot to the hotel and then back at me.

"Your second mistake was trusting Rosie. She's in this for one thing, what's best for Rosie. She'd step on either one of us to get what she wants, but you know that already. Even if you don't want to admit it.

"Look, you're a decent kid. It's not too late for you. Cut your losses and go home. I wish somebody would have given me this talk awhile back. It would have saved me a lot of grief."

"You just want me out of the picture."

I chuckled. "Take a good look around you. I'm not the one holed up in a hotel with Rosie. I'm on the outside looking in, like you. Face it, we both got played.

"She's poison, Taylor, straight poison from the start."

"That's a little harsh."

"Trust me, she's the cross bones on the label. I should know. She's been in my bloodstream since the day I met her. I've been infected for years, and I keep coming back for more. Don't make the same mistake. Get out while you can."

"I love her, McKeller."

"Well, if your mind is all made up," I said, reaching back under my jacket and pulling out my gun. I held it out in the flat of my hand, for him to take. "You're going to need this."

Taylor stood looking at it, the sweat coming down harder from his forehead.

"Go ahead, take it. You're going to need it. This isn't fun and games. Two men are dead, and if you don't want to be number three, you better be ready to pull the trigger."

Taylor Mills looked younger and more frail than I was used to seeing, his eyes wide with fear, locked onto my .45, but he made no effort to reach for it. I could almost see the wheels in his head turning, trying to decide his next move.

"Go home, Taylor. It's over." I stuck my gun back under my coat. "Rosie made her choice and you weren't it. Neither was I."

"What are you going to do?"

"I'm going to go in there and find out who the guy in the pin-stripes is. I've got a sneaking suspicion I already know."

"Are you going to kill him?"

"I hope not. Rosie's not worth it."

He stumbled off, a broken man. He didn't know it, just then, but he got off lucky. After he took his lumps, he'd be fine.

After he was gone, I lit up a smoke and stood leaning against the front of the building, figuring out what to do next. I was half wishing Taylor Mills had taken my gun and gone in himself. It would have saved me a lot of trouble.

I strolled into the front lobby of the Starlight Inn like I didn't have a care in the world. I had been piecing things together in my pea brain, trying to figure things out, and I thought maybe I had.

The thin man in the conservative pinstriped suit had looked familiar all along, but I just couldn't place him. Taylor said it was someone from Rosie's past, someone who was in love with her and would do anything for her. Rosie had given me the last clue days before.

A middle-aged woman was sitting behind the front desk. Her smile brightened as I approached.

"Hello, Sir. Welcome to the Starlight Inn. How may I help you?"

"I'm looking for one of your guests, I think he's staying here. Medium height, thin, usually wears a conservative pinstripe suit and a hat, fortyish ..."

"We have quite a few gentlemen staying here," she pointed out.

"Maybe you could check your guest list. I'm looking for a guy named Oscar Carter."

"Oh, sure, Mr. Carter. He's staying in room 207. Would you like me to ring him and tell him you're here."

"No thanks. I'll surprise him."

The dumb lug was even registered under his real name. Why wouldn't he be? It wasn't like anyone was looking for him.

I turned and started toward the stairs but stopped and looked back at the woman behind the desk.

"Could I use your phone?"

"Sure, Honey. Whatever you need."

Room 207 was in the middle of the hallway, on the right hand side, as you came off the staircase. I stood outside the doorway for a few moments, gathering my thoughts and trying to decide how bad I was screwing up. After convincing myself it was the right move, I knocked on the door.

There was movement on the other side, and I could hear muffled voices. I reached back behind me and gave my .45 a reassuring touch and knocked again.

"Who is it?" Rosie asked from behind the door.

"Avon Lady," I replied with an edge to my voice.

The door opened just far enough for Rosie to stick her head out.

"Frankie, what are you doing here?"

"I could ask the same thing. Are you going to ask me in or is this a private party?"

She stepped back and opened the door farther, hanging her head and refusing to look me in the eye. My hand was under my sports coat, gripping the handle of my pistol as I stepped in. I'd have been better served to have it out.

The cold barrel of a handgun was pressed against my temple before I had crossed the threshold.

"Hi there, McKeller," a familiar voice said. "Long time no see."

"It's been awhile, Oscar."

I got a glimpse of him as he guided me into the center of the room, Rosie closing the door behind me.

"Let's get those hands where I can see them," he said. I complied, raising my hands in the air.

"Rosie mentioned you lost a lot of weight," I told him. "I didn't even recognize you."

"Well, I recognized you from the get go. I've been waiting a long time for this little reunion."

"Yeah, I guess we've got a lot of catching up to do."

"I don't imagine there will be much time for that. I'm on kind of a tight schedule these days."

"You've been pretty busy," I agreed. "Ralphy Henderson, Marcus Fletcher ..."

"All leading up to the one I've been waiting for," he added.

"You flatter me, Oscar. I would have thought you'd forgotten about me long ago."

"Oh, no." He snickered. "You were the main reason I wanted to come down here. I've been waiting a long time to settle this score."

Rosie was off in the corner with her head slung low, like she wanted no part of what was going on. Oscar was up close to me, his head at my shoulder, his .32 pressed hard against my temple.

"For what it's worth," I offered. "I always felt bad about the way we did you back then. It always gnawed at my gut, the way we played you."

"Well then, even Steven. As long as you feel bad about it, I guess we're all square, huh?"

"It was a pretty crummy thing to do. I'm not going to lie."

"I paid you good money, McKeller. I trusted you. I came to you for help."

"That's right, you did. As I recall, you came to me because things weren't so great with you two to start with. It's not like it all began with me."

"Is this necessary?" Rosie asked.

"What's wrong, not in the mood for a little walk down memory lane? You had a little something to do with all that too," I tried.

"We have things to do, Oscar. We have to get the money from Blake and get out of here."

"Try calling him again," Oscar said. "He'll answer this time."

"Maybe he won't," I added. "Maybe somebody already called him and made arrangements to meet. Maybe he's out getting his money together for the big trade off."

I saw stars when he slugged me on the side of the head with the gun. It knocked me sideways, and I had to struggle to stay on my feet. I pulled up to find him standing in front of me, aiming his revolver straight between my eyes.

"You called him?"

"When I realized Rosie had taken the books I figured I was being pushed out, but I also figured Martin didn't know that. I made a call and set up a meeting."

"You're not very bright, are you, McKeller?"

"That seems to be the general consensus."

"All you did was inconvenience us. We still have the books. The ball is still in our court."

I was holding the side of my head where he whopped me. Blood was beginning to trickle down the side of my face. "Yeah, it was just a stall tactic. Figured I could buy a little more time."

"Time is a precious commodity you're about out of," he said with a grin. "Either way, you've come to the end of the line." He motioned to Rosie. "Call Taylor Mills. Get him over here. Tell him you've reconsidered and you need to talk to him. It's time to start tying up loose ends."

Rosie looked at me and back at him. "I don't want any part of that."

"It's a little late to get all squeamish on me, isn't it?"

"I didn't sign up to be a party in any murder. That's all you, Oscar. I just wanted to get the money and start a new life."

"Sometimes you have to push things along. Make the call."

Rosie looked uneasily around the room. "I need to get some air," she announced, grabbing her bag and storming across the room to let herself out.

"Rosie!" Oscar called after her. She was already out the door.

"That throws a monkey wrench in the plan, huh?"

"She'll be back. She knows what has to be done."

"So, this is the big plan, huh? You kill me and Mills, make it look like I did him in?"

"Simple but effective. Once they find you with the murder weapon in your hand, it will be easy to link you to the first two. Open and shut case."

"And if Rosie doesn't call Mills?"

"It just creates more work for me. I'll take care of you and go get him myself if I have to. Either way, you're found dead with the murder weapon, but she'll call. She'll do what has to be done."

"So, let me see if I got this right. After Rosie dumped me, she hooked up with Blake Martin. She dumped you soon after, when he put her up in her own place.

"You went a little nuts, lost your cookies over her. That's when you lost all the weight. Rosie said she didn't hear from you for a long time, didn't know how you found her. I'm guessing that's where Fletcher comes into the picture. It was his kind of job, tracking down a cheating wife for her distraught and disturbed husband. Knowing Fletcher, I'm guessing he bled you pretty good. Once he sees those dollar signs, he tends to sink in his hooks."

"I like the way you still refer to him like he was still here."

"Once you found her again, you managed to weasel yourself back into her life. It would have been pretty easy by then. Martin was using her as a punching bag, and she was probably looking for all the allies she could get. This is about when Taylor Mills joined the party too. Rosie always did like to increase the odds wherever she could.

"Somehow, you two put your little heads together and came up with this blackmail scheme. You figured you could roll Martin for a sweet little bankroll, but you had to get him off his own turf. I'm guessing it was Rosie's idea to come to me. She remembered me as the heartbroken sap who was willing to cross any line to be with her. I was the perfect mark to play middle man, maybe even do the dirty work, if she could convince me."

"The idea of coming face to face with you again was pretty appealing on my end too," he admitted. "I still have unfinished business with you. Not only did you play me for the jerk, but things were never quite right between Rosie and me after you. I always felt like I owed you something a little extra."

"So you two came down here and fed me her sob story, about how Blake Martin was abusing her, and she wanted to get some pay back. When Ralphy showed up, you were hoping I would step in and take care of it for you.

"Were you the one who called him and gave him the number of her old hotel room or was it her?"

"Does it matter?"

"It would have been you. You needed to get him back in my face, show me what a threat he was to Rosie. The thing is, he didn't create the big squall you were hoping for. When he didn't find her, he went back to the Chesterfield, content to wait her out until Martin showed up. That's why you trashed the hotel room. It was to give me a little nudge in the right direction, show me how dangerous he was."

"She even tried to come out and ask me to kill him but I wasn't that far gone anymore. Instead, she convinced me to talk to him, to try and convince him she had blown town. You figured there was a good chance one of us wouldn't get out of that hotel room alive."

"Worst that can happen, you're up for murder and Ralphy is dead. Either that or you're dead and Ralphy is out of the picture."

"But it didn't go down like that and you had to clean up the mess yourself. Ralphy knew where she was the whole time. The thing you didn't count on was Marcus Fletcher showing up. He got wind of what you were up to and saw a big payday in his future. It was right up his alley, blackmail, corruption. He decided to play both sides of the fence.

"He met with Ralphy before I did, and I'm guessing he offered to deliver the whole works to Martin and his thugs. As far as I know, he might have come to you too. That was Fletcher's style. Anything for a quick buck. The sleazy bastard would sell out his kid sister for two bucks. Who knows what he would do for the kind of money you and Rosie were looking at.

"To this point, nobody even knew you were in town, nobody but Rosie. You were the Shadow, the Invisible Man. When I mentioned Fletcher to Rosie, it sealed his fate. Maybe you were going to do it anyway. You knew he'd met with Ralphy. He was too dangerous to have around."

"Maybe you're not as dumb as I thought, McKeller."

"As long as I was still in the picture, why not use me, right? I was the perfect middle man between you and Martin. He was already on his way to Myrtle Beach when Ralphy met with Fletcher. There was no time for him to tell his boss anything about you being involved. To Martin, it looked like it was me and Rosie. Why not let me take all the chances?"

"And when it was all over, on the small chance you'd still be alive, you'd still be here in Myrtle Beach. Rosie and me would be long gone. Your goose was cooked either way."

"You were never going to let it end that way. You still wanted to get me for breaking up your perfect little marriage. I don't know how Taylor Mills ended up down here. Maybe Rosie was telling the truth, and he followed her down. My guess is she brought him along for a little extra insurance. Either way, he's your last play once you get the money. He's the red ribbon on this package, him dead, me holding the gun. Everything nice and neat for the local law authorities."

"You've got to admit, it falls nicely into place."

"You made one mistake, Oscar. The same mistake we all made."

"Yeah, and what's that?"

"You trusted Rosie."

"You don't know her the way I do."

"That's what people keep telling me. Maybe I know her better than you think. She's the same girl you hired me to follow all that time ago. She's the same one who hooked up with me and let you pay our bills while we were running around together."

He had his gun aimed square at my face, his finger clenched around the trigger. I could see the anger growing in his face, the hatred in his eyes.

"She's the same girl who dumped me for Martin when she thought he could give her more," I continued. "She played us both, right from the start. You were a money pouch to her. I was the one who gave her the freedom to do what she wanted without cutting the purse strings. When Martin came along, he was the best of both worlds. She didn't need us anymore."

"You don't know what you're talking about." His hand was

clenched so tight around the revolver his arm was shaking.

"If he had treated her better, she'd still be with him. Until something better came along, anyway. How did it happen?

"You showed up on her doorstep, flowers and candy? One day she took you inside. She confessed how he treated her, how he hit her. She told you how sorry she was for everything she'd done, how she'd made a mistake by leaving you. She told you how much she loved you, how you had always been the one for her.

"Is that when she told you about her plan? Is that when she brought you in on this?"

"Just shut up, McKeller!"

"She told you everything was going to be fine, like back in the old days. Let me ask you something, Oscar. Just how good were things back in the old days? How long was it all peaches and cream before things started to go sour?

"You don't know nothing about back then."

"I know there was a reason you hired me. I wasn't the beginning of your problems, Oscar. I was just the first one you could put a face on."

"Things are different now. You don't know how it is."

"I know she's playing you again. Instead of paying her bills, she's got you doing her dirty work. Two men are dead because of what Rosie wants, maybe two more to cover her tracks. She played us both, Oscar. She's been playing us all along."

"It's not like that."

"Yeah? What's it like then? How does this play out? Are you two going to pick up where you left off all those years ago, everything all hunky dory? My guess is Rosie's gonna be fine. She'll start a new life somewhere, but someone is going to be left holding the bag. Do you care to guess who that might be?"

"You're talking out your ass, trying to buy yourself more time," he said.

"Where are the books, Oscar?"

He didn't answer but his eyes got all wide and confused.

"They wouldn't be in her bag, would they? The one she grabbed when she ran out of here?"

His head darted about the room, eyes wide and frantic, the gun still trained on me. "She wouldn't..."

"She did. She's gone, and she took the books with her, leaving you to clean up her mess, again."

"No, it's not like that."

The pounding on the door caused him to look over. "Open up! Sheriff's Department!"

It was my chance to make a move.

As Oscar turned the gun toward the door, I lowered my shoulder and bum rushed him with everything I had. The gun went off as I collided with him and we both went barreling into the wall, him face first, me behind him. He was squeezed in between the wall and me, fighting to bring the gun around, but I had him by the wrist and had his arm wedged against the wall.

With my free hand, I started giving him upper cuts to the kidney, one after another. He was grunting in pain with each one, trying his best to turn the gun on me. His head turned around and our eyes met, his burning with hatred.

"I will kill you," he groaned as he managed to gain some leverage and bring the gun barrel closer to my head. He let out an animal-like grunt and managed to gain another inch in my direction, the gun almost aligned with my face, his arm shaking in my grasp with the force of his strength.

I was losing my hold on him, and I could feel him slipping away, gaining the advantage. He was drawing on every ounce of strength he had and was inching the barrel closer to his target, me trying desperately to hold him off but losing my edge one deadly inch at a time.

"I will kill you," he grunted again, and there was no doubt he meant it. Everything I had done to him, all those years ago, was boiling over inside of him, filling him with a rage like I had never before witnessed. He was determined I was going to die right then and there.

I had other thoughts.

I had wedged my free arm from between us and had managed to bring it up, over my shoulder, bending it at the elbow and pulling it back toward my far shoulder.

"I don't think so," I said, as I thrust my elbow into his face with all the strength I could muster.

There was the sound of bones cracking, and he let out a girlish whimper as his body went limp and the gun fell from his hand, all of him sliding lifeless down the wall.

The sheriff and his deputy were pulling me off him, the room a blur of exhausted energy and adrenaline. Oscar was lying crumpled against the wall, blood gushing from his face, his nose a twisted and broken knot in the center of his skull.

"What's going on here?" Talbert yelled, pushing me back, away from the unconscious Oscar.

"There's your murderer, Sheriff," I explained. "His name is Oscar Carter. He's Rosie's ex-husband."

"You have about two seconds to tell me what's going on here, Mc-Keller."

I was spent and breathing heavy, trying to catch my breath and stop the room from spinning around me, but I managed to spit it out in bits and pieces, how I had spotted him but didn't recognize him, how I ended up at the Starlight. I told him everything I could think of, even blurting out about Rosie and the books.

The sheriff and the deputy were both looking at me, taking it all in with shocked looks on their faces when I caught movement. Oscar had come to and made a quick move for his gun, still lying on the floor.

Without thinking, I reached behind me for my gun, pulling it out at the same time he was raising his. There was no time to think or aim, only react.

Shots were fired from both sides, the sheriff and deputy diving for cover. When it was over and the smoke cleared, nobody was more surprised than me that I was still standing. Oscar was slumped over against the wall, his arm lying across his lap, the gun dangling from his fingertips.

I had to check myself three times to make sure I wasn't hit. Even after the sheriff and Deputy Dale checked me out, I wasn't a hundred percent convinced, but somehow I had come through unscathed. Battered and bruised, I was still in one piece with nothing in the way of new entrance wounds. Oscar Carter didn't get off so lucky.

The investigation later discovered that I fired three times. I had no recollection. Two of my slugs ended up in the wall beside where Oscar was perched. The third found its way to his gut.

He was out cold but breathing when they carted him off to the hospital.

Chapter Thirty

By the time I got back to the hotel all I wanted was a hot bath and a good night's sleep. Every muscle in my body ached and my bad leg was throbbing like it might fall off. I was limping my way past the front desk, hoping to sneak by and make it up to my room, when Curtis, the desk clerk, stopped me.

"Where have you been, McKeller?"

"I was out getting my hair done."

"Simmons has been calling down for you all afternoon. He says he needs to talk to you."

"If he calls back, tell him I moved back to Maryland."

"He says it's important."

I took a deep breath and let it out slow. "Did you happen to make that list for me?"

He handed me a sheet of paper with a scowl on his face. "You know, I'm not your secretary."

"If you were, you'd make a fine one." I was scanning down the list of names when I looked back up at Curtis. "You haven't happened to see Taylor Mills lately, have you? The guy in 419?"

"He checked out a couple of hours ago."

"Good."

"Left in quite a hurry. Didn't even stop to pick up his messages."

"Messages?"

"Well, just one, really."

"What was it, from who?"

"I don't know," he said, rummaging through some slips of paper, looking for the message. "It was from some woman. Something about meeting her at the Sea View Inn."

205

I felt a knot clench up in my gut. "Rosie," I muttered.

Curtis had found the slip of paper he was looking for. "Yeah, that's her name. She said it was urgent and she needed him to meet her right away."

So, she had gone and done it, just like Oscar said she would. She'd sold me out, along with Taylor Mills, setting us up for what was supposed to look like a murder suicide. You think you know somebody.

"Speaking of urgent," Curtis said. "Simmons seemed to want to talk to you pretty bad."

"Call him and tell him I'm on my way up."

Curtis cleared his throat. "I'm not your secretary, McKeller."

"No, but if you were ..."

Simmons opened the door with a stack of papers under his arm. "Where have you been?"

"I had to see a guy about a dog."

"I have no idea what that means, but I can't put off the Miller girl any longer. She's demanding to speak with the senator."

I motioned to the papers he was holding. "Are those the reports I asked for?"

"I took the liberty of doing checks on everybody who attended the party," he replied, handing me the stack.

"Anything interesting?"

"The usual stuff, criminal records, financial holdings, tax returns."

"Criminal records?"

Simmons shrugged. "Nothing too exciting. Stuart James did a night for drunk and disorderly and indecent exposure. Got loaded at some party and decided to take his clothes off."

"Glad I missed that little shindig," I answered, shuffling through the pages.

The plush sofa looked particularly inviting. and I couldn't resist, making my way over and plopping myself down on it. I spent a few quiet minutes pouring over the papers, searching for anything I could use. There wasn't much there.

I did catch a few interesting tidbits. I found out Johnathon Masden was about as broke as everyone said and that Stuart James was well off but not rich, by any measure. I found out that Roger Middleton was holding his empire together with spit and glue, and that

Thomas Gladding had more money, and businesses, than God.

I reached into my coat and pulled out the list of names Curtis had made for me, the people staying on the fifth floor. It wasn't much, but it was all I had.

I looked up at Simmons. "What do you say we throw ourselves another little party?"

"I'm not sure I'm feeling very festive."

"That makes two of us. Let's do it any way."

"What did you have in mind?"

"All the principles, everyone who was at the party. Let's get them all up here."

"The senator?"

I shook my head. "I don't think there's any reason to bother him."

"I don't know about this, McKeller."

It was my turn to shrug. "If you'd rather, you could just let Rachel Miller have her meeting with the senator."

"All right. We'll play it your way."

I had two shots of the senator's bourbon while I was waiting for the festivities to begin. One by one, all the players were ushered into the suite, courtesy of federal agents, everyone minus the senator himself.

Roger Middleton was the first to pipe up. "See here, what's the meaning of all this?"

"Don't get your shorts in a bundle," I told him, standing up in front of the group. "We're all going to have us a nice little chat."

"This is highly irregular," Stuart James added.

"So is conspiring extortion on a United States Senator."

Rachel Miller stood up, hands on her hips. "I demand to speak to Senator Wright."

"Sit down, sweetheart. Nobody's talking to the senator. We're going to settle this right here, between us."

She shot me those puppy dog eyes. "I don't understand, Mr. McKeller."

"You can bat those eyelashes all you want, Honey. It's not going to do you any good. Now, sit down like a good little girl."

Rachel sat down.

"Mystery writers have an old saying," I began, addressing the room. "Follow the love. Follow the money. I don't imagine there's much love lost in this crew."

There was a murmur from the peanut gallery.

"Something seemed fishy about this whole deal from the start. A pretty young girl shows up and gets a job here at the hotel, just before the senator is set to show up for his big soiree. She ends up at the senator's private party, and by the end of the night, she gets herself attacked by him, very nearly defiled.

"It could be quite the scandal if it ever gets out, the kind of scandal that can derail a promising political career. Unless, of course, this scandal could be hushed up."

"What are you accusing me of?" Rachel gasped.

"Of being a lousy waitress, among other things."

"Is that a crime in this state?"

"No, but it is a little curious. Why would a girl come in and start a new job but show almost no interest in making money at it?

"It's my understanding that you've shown very little interest in working in our fine restaurant downstairs. They say you gave away tables regularly, that you've been known to give up entire shifts."

"Is that a crime?"

"No, not at all. It makes a guy wonder, though. It's almost like this girl had another source of income, like she didn't need the money."

"Maybe I'm independently wealthy."

I looked down at the stack of papers in my hand, the ones with the financial records of everyone in the room. "No, we both know that isn't the case. Maybe you were just banking on a bigger payday."

"I didn't ask for any money. In fact, I turned it down."

"Yes you did. Makes a guy wonder about that too. Maybe you had a bigger prize in mind."

"Maybe you're fishing for straws."

"And maybe I might catch a few. Like I said, you showed up here, conveniently, just before the senator, looking for work but you didn't seem to need the money. You also didn't take advantage of the free lodging the hotel provides its employees."

"I don't like sharing a room."

"No, you wouldn't. You wouldn't be much for the dorm setting. A girl like you has expensive tastes. She would prefer a nice room in a luxurious hotel. It's kind of tough to afford on a waitresses salary, though.

"Clifford, our elevator operator, reports he picks you up and drops you off regularly, on the fifth floor. The thing is, there's no Rachel Miller registered on the fifth floor, or anywhere else in the hotel, for that matter. Makes a guy wonder where you keep coming and going from."

"You do a lot of wondering, for a house dick."

"I'm a curious kind of guy. There were other things I wondered about too. I wondered how if, like you said, the senator was directly in front of you when he backhanded you across the face, how you got that ring cut on your left cheek."

"His ring caught me on the cheek. What's the big mystery about that?"

"Do you remember, you showed me how he did it. You said he backhanded you with his right hand."

"Yeah, so?"

"The thing is, the senator doesn't wear a ring on his right hand. His only ring, his wedding ring, is on his left hand."

Rachel looked flustered. "I got confused."

"Oh, you got confused all right, but then, that's easy to do when you've been coached on what to say."

"You don't have any proof."

"Proof of what, Rachel? What is it I need proof for?"

"It sounds a lot like I'm being accused of something."

"Yeah, it sure does, doesn't it? Let's forget all that for now. Let's talk about what really happened in that bedroom. Senator Wright says he remembers walking into a dark room with you. The next thing he remembers is coming to on the bed, you in the corner, screaming bloody murder.

"Liquored up like he was, he would have been an easy mark. His drunks were legendary, as everyone in this room knows, his, so called, friends. What if, when you two walked into that dark room, there was already somebody else in there, waiting? What if this somebody hit the senator with something just as he came walking in with Rachel, something like a telephone maybe?"

"This seems a little far-fetched, doesn't it?" Middleton asked with raised eyebrows.

I shrugged. "Maybe. Maybe not. The senator was barely conscious from the booze as it was. One good slug on the side of the head and he'd be out cold. Long enough to toss him across the bed, to rip Rachel's dress from her body, to backhand her across the face for effect."

"That's preposterous!" James said.

"Is it? The senator said he walked into a dark room with Rachel. Moments later, when we came rushing in, the lights were on. Why do you think that was?"

"How would I know?"

"You're the writer. You're the one with the imagination. What do you think? A girl is attacked, almost raped. She struggles against her attacker, manages to hit him with the phone on the night stand, knocking him briefly unconscious. We rush in and find her, moments later, cowering by the side wall. She's hysterical and, yet, somehow, she had the where with all to turn on the lights. And where is the light switch?"

"I'm sure I don't know."

"It's in the same spot you find every other light switch in every other room in America. It's just inside the door. Why would she go to the door, turn on the light, and then go back over by the bed, where her attacker is still lying? If she made it to the door, why wouldn't she continue out and make her escape? Why would she go back into the room?"

No one said a word.

"Maybe she wasn't trying to get away. Maybe she and her accomplice turned on the light so they could organize things, make sure everything fit with her story."

"Why would someone go to all that trouble?" Stuart asked.

"Blackmail. Good, old-fashioned extortion, American style."

Thomas Gladding spoke up for the first time. "You've already established Miss Miller didn't ask for any money. In fact, you said she turned down a substantial offer."

"Rachel Miller and her cohort weren't after money. They were looking for something else, something a United States Senator would have in spades. They were looking to gain his influence."

"Are you saying someone in this room was working with Miss Miller?" Stuart James asked.

"That's exactly what I'm saying. Someone with the power and money to bring Rachel Miller to Myrtle Beach, to set her up in a hotel room, maybe even buy her some expensive clothes to entice her into the deal."

"That's ridiculous," Middleton snorted.

"Is it? How does young girl afford a designer gown on a waitress' salary? Especially when she doesn't work so hard at it."

"Gladding replied, "I'm guessing a young lady with Miss Miller's obvious charms could certainly find eligible men to shower her with expensive gifts. That doesn't prove anything."

"Maybe not, but explain this: who knew the senator was going to be here this weekend? I didn't even know until just before. The only people who knew of his plans to come to Myrtle Beach were his staff and his friends, the ones who were invited. I'm going to go out on a limb and say his staff had nothing to gain."

Everyone in the room looked nervous and uneasy, nobody more so than Roger Middleton. I walked over until I was standing directly in front of him.

"Mr. Middleton, I couldn't help but notice you wear a ring on your right hand."

"So does most everyone in this room." he snapped back.

"Yes, but most everyone in this room doesn't own a struggling Steel company. Most everyone in this room isn't vying for a contract on the bridge in North Carolina, a contract Senator Wright has a large say in."

"Have you lost your mind?"

"That's debatable, but are you going to sit here and tell me you didn't come down here with the express purpose of convincing Senator Wright to give that contract to your company? Your company is over extended, on the verge of bankruptcy. Since the end of the war, business is down. Those military contracts have dried up and you're left holding the bag.

"You needed something, anything to keep your company afloat. Maybe this bridge in North Carolina wouldn't be enough to save your empire, but it's a start. Maybe it would lead to bigger and better things. Maybe once you got your foot in the door, you could convince Wright to throw some more business your way."

"No!"

"Admit it, Middleton, you would have done anything to secure that contract, to save your company."

"OK, so I wanted the bridge deal. So what? Why wouldn't I?"

"When you couldn't bribe your way into that contract you decided to fall back on plan B, the girl you planted here at the hotel."

"No, it's not like that. I never did any such thing. I wanted that contract. I wanted it bad. I needed it but I would never—"

"Sure you would. You would and you did. This is all part of your plan to get Wright to hand you the deal you need to save your dying company."

"You're wrong. I didn't," he pleaded, desperation in his eyes.

I reached into my coat and pulled out the list of names Curtis had jotted down for me. "You might have gotten away with it but you made one bad mistake." I held up the paper for dramatic effect.

"This is a list of all the rooms registered on the fifth floor, the floor Rachel Miller was seen coming and going from. All the rooms are registered to legitimate guests, all except one.

"What is it with you guys with money? You could have paid cash but you just can't stand the thought of paying out of your own pocket. You've got to put it on the company tab."

"What are you talking about?"

"Every room on the fifth floor is registered to a person's name, all but one. It's registered under a company name. Maybe you didn't think anyone would notice. Maybe you thought no one would put two and two together. You never expected anyone to notice where Rachel Miller was staying."

"Let me see that," Middleton said as he stood up and ripped the paper from my hand, scouring over it with his eyes.

As he read the document, the desperate look on his face changed to shock, then confusion. Slowly, a slight smile began to form on his lips. By the time he looked back up at me, he was grinning broadly.

"This is it? This is what you've got on me?"

"Maybe it's not a smoking gun, but it's enough."

Middleton began to chuckle. Before long it was a full blown belly laugh. "You are an idiot."

"Excuse me?"

"Breckenridge Steel? Breckenridge Steel?"

"Yeah?"

"My company is called Middleton Steel. It's named after my great grandfather."

"What?"

"You might have wanted to check that out before you started throwing around accusations. Breckenridge Steel might be the one steel company in America that's in worse shape than my company. They've changed hands three times since the war ended. The last I heard they were getting bought up by some conglomerate."

"That's impossible."

"I think you've wasted enough of our time, Mr. McKeller."

People were rising from their seats, heading toward the door, some of them laughing out loud, laughing at me and my incompetence.

"It all made sense," I muttered to myself. "It all fit."

The crowd was making its way out the door and into the hallway. I was standing in the center of the room, staring down at the piece of paper, my head spinning with confusion. It didn't make any sense. Then it hit me.

I ran out the door to catch up to the crowd. They were standing down by the elevator, waiting to be picked up.

"Wait!" I yelled after them.

"Is there something else you wanted, McKeller?" Middleton asked, still chuckling.

"Simmons, can you find out who bought Breckenridge Steel?"

He had followed me out of the room and was standing beside me. He gave a shrug of one shoulder. "Sure, I guess. Why?"

"Do you want to tell him, Mr. Gladding?"

Gladding gave me a hard look. "Don't you think you've made enough of a fool out of yourself for one day?"

"I notice you wear a ring on your right hand too."

"Do you really want to do this again?"

"I'm going to guess Breckenridge Steel is owned by Skyline Industries, one of your many buy ups."

"And what if it is?"

"It would mean you're the one who put up Rachel Miller."

"And why would I do that?"

"For the same reason I thought Middleton did it."

"There's a flaw in your theory. I don't want the bridge contract. Breckenridge Steel is a dying institution. I bought it to dismantle it, to sell it off. I got it cheap enough that I can still turn a profit by liquidating its assets. I'm not looking to rebuild it."

"Of course, that's why you charged the room to the company. It's going belly up, so why not run up its losses as much as you can? I imagine you're putting a lot of things on the Breckenridge tab before it goes under. No matter how many millions you have, it still feels good to save a few bucks where you can. Any losses you can show will benefit you in the long run, right?"

"Do you have a point, McKeller?"

"You rich guys love to save a penny, don't you?"

"I'm a busy man. I have things to do."

"I had it backwards, didn't I?"

"I think we're all in agreement that you had it much more than backwards."

"You didn't want the bridge contract."

"I already said that."

"You wanted to make sure Middleton didn't get it. His company is going down for the third time and you saw a juicy profit on the horizon. That's what you do, isn't it, buy up failing companies?"

Gladding didn't respond.

"That's what this was all about. You had to make sure Middleton Steel didn't get that contract. That would have kept them afloat, jacked up the price. Without that deal, Middleton was finished and you could pick it up at a bargain."

"Prove it."

I turned my attention to Rachel Miller. "What were you supposed to say to the senator, Rachel? What did Gladding want you to tell him?"

"I don't know what you're talking about," she replied.

"All right, fine. You don't have to answer to me. I hope he's paying you well. Have you ever testified before a senate committee? They can be pretty brutal."

Rachel turned to Gladding. "What's he talking about?"

"Who do you think you're dealing with?" I added. "You tried to blackmail a United States Senator. You don't think this is going to end here, do you?"

"He's bluffing," Gladding assured her.

Rachel's cool demeanor had melted away, and I could see the fear in her eyes.

"You're looking at hard time in a federal prison. This is extortion, conspiracy, maybe treason."

"I didn't do anything," she said in a trembling voice.

"You don't have to tell me. You'll have plenty of chances to say it to the senate investigators. I imagine it will be a pretty big deal, newspapers, radio—"

"You never said anything about that," she said to Gladding.

"Shut up. He's trying to get under your skin."

"It's out of my hands," I assured her. "What do you think, Simmons? Do you think there might be some people who would want to speak with Miss Miller?"

"I think you'd better come with me, young lady," Simmons told her.

"What? What is he talking about?" She was still speaking to Gladding.

"Keep your mouth shut," Gladding replied. "They've got nothing on us. It's all circumstantial."

"Well, we probably don't have much on you, Mr. Gladding," Simmons said. "But Miss Miller, on the other hand—"

"What's that supposed to mean?" she squealed.

"It means somebody has to take the fall, Rachel. You were the one who took him in the room. You were the one we all saw," I said.

"I don't understand."

"Don't worry. The money will be there when you get out. You'll probably still be young enough to enjoy it."

"I'm not going to prison."

"Shut up, Rachel," Gladding said.

"I didn't do anything wrong."

"Just keep your mouth shut."

"Yeah, listen to Gladding. He doesn't want you to implicate him. He wants you to take the fall. That's what he's paying you for."

"It was his idea. He told me to do it."

"Shut up, you stupid dame!"

"Nobody was supposed to get hurt. I didn't know he was going to hit him. He told me it would be quick and easy," she pleaded. "I was just supposed to get him alone."

"Stupid bitch!"

"I think you two should come with me," Simmons said.

"I was just supposed to get him into the bedroom. I didn't know what he was going to do."

"Keep your yapper closed," Gladding said to her. "They got nothing on us."

Simmons had Gladding by the arm, leading him back to the suite; another had Rachel. He was walking them down the hallway. I couldn't resist getting in one last jab.

"Hey, Gladding," I called after him. The three stopped and looked back at me. "Who's the idiot now?"

"This is nothing," he said with a smirk. "My lawyers will have this cleared up before you can whistle Dixie."

"Yeah, well, I'll start whistling, just the same."

Chapter Thirty-One

Sleep didn't come as easy as I thought it might that night. My body was exhausted and worn down, every inch of me aching for rest, but my mind had other ideas. It wouldn't let go for the life of me.

Every time I felt like I was about to drift off I'd be awakened by another rogue thought, an image of Rosie, another nagging detail in the twisted saga that constituted our demented relationship.

I'm not going to lie. There were still feelings there, buried under the slime and manure she had dumped on top of me for all this time. There was even a part of me that wanted to find a way to forgive her for everything she'd done, to justify her actions in some way. That's how it was with Rosie.

Try as I might, there was no getting around this one. Rosie had crossed a lot of lines this time and there was no making it right in my head. It didn't make it easy to let her go. I still had that little part of me that wanted to be with her, wanted to bask in the glow of her, open up my innards and give her another shot at ripping them out again.

I never claimed to be the sharpest knife in the drawer.

I woke up early the next day, not sure I'd gotten anything in the way of sleep or rest. I went through my usual routine of cleaning up and getting dressed, brushing my teeth and shaving, while trying not to look at myself in the mirror. Nothing about me felt anything but remorse and sorrow, glum and dejected.

I wasn't sure what I was going to find as I made my way downstairs. There was no telling if Rosie would still be around, if maybe she'd flown the coop or been hauled in by Sheriff Talbert. I shouldn't have been so surprised to find her standing at the front desk when I came around the corner. She's resilient like that.

She was having a heated conversation with the desk clerk, her large shoulder bag slung over her shoulder. She was dressed in a sleek tan dress that hugged her figure like I'd wanted to since the first time I saw her. Her raven hair was down long and straight, shimmering in the morning light. She was in a pair of high heels that looked like they were made for the express purpose of showing off those long lovely legs.

"Are you sure there are no messages for me?" she was saying.

"No ma'am," Curtis answered.

"For a Sally Young or a Rosie Carter?"

"No ma'am, I've got nothing."

"How about for Frank McKeller?"

Curtis gave her a funny look. I had come up behind her by this point. "That's awfully neighborly of you to check my messages like that."

Rosie turned around with surprise. "Frankie?"

"Surprised to see me?"

"No, not at all. Happy, in fact."

"I thought you might be."

"What happened yesterday, after I left?"

"You didn't hear?"

"No. I was afraid Oscar might do something crazy."

"Oscar's in custody, probably recovering from that gunshot I gave him."

"I'm just glad you're all right."

"I'm sure you are."

She gave that look, the one that's supposed to turn me to butter. "I didn't want to leave you like that, Frankie. Honest, I didn't. You know how much I care about you."

"I bet you were up all night worrying."

"I was," she tried.

"Yeah, I saw that message you left for Taylor Mills, about meeting you at the Sea View."

"I didn't want to do that. Oscar made me."

"Give it up, Rosie, it's done. It's over."

"What are you talking about? I still have the books. We have to meet Blake. Once we have that money we can be together, you and me."

"There is no you and me. There never was."

"What are you talking about? Of course there is. We can finally be together, like we always wanted."

"This thing has run its course, Rosie. There aren't going to be any happy endings, not where you and me are concerned."

"Why are you saying that? You know how much I care about you."

"Rosie, there's only one person on this planet you give a squirt about, and it's not me."

"Oscar, is that what you think? You think I'm in love with Oscar?"

"No, I know that's not the case."

"Then who?"

"I'm looking at the only person you ever gave a damn about."

"That's a hell of a thing to say to an old friend, somebody you shared so much with."

"You never shared anything with anybody, Rosie, and we were certainly never friends."

"How can you say that, Frankie, after everything we've been through?"

"Everything you put me through is more like it."

I saw a look in her eye I'd never seen before. It was a mix of confusion and frustration, an angry glare like she knew she'd lost her hold on me. I could almost see the wheels in her head spinning around, trying to figure out how to get it back.

"It doesn't have to be like this," she said.

"I think maybe it does. I think this is the way it was always going to end up, right from that first time you turned around and spoke to me."

"You're talking crazy, Frankie. What, you don't care about me anymore?"

"The crazy part is that I probably still might but I'm not stupid enough to let it get in the way, not anymore. I've been on the butt end of your games long enough. I've let you use me and abuse me. I've let you rob me of my dignity and my pride and any little bits of decency I had left inside me. I sat back and took it while you wrung me out and left me to dry."

"A little dramatic, don't you think?"

"That's rich, coming from you, the queen of drama."

"All right, I get it. I'm a bad person. Nobody held a gun to your head. You wanted this just as much as I did. You loved every second of it, the intrigue, the sneaking around, all the craziness that came with it."

"You're wrong, Rosie. I was never in it for that. All I ever wanted was to be with you. Call me stupid, but I always thought there was something more to you, something special. I always thought under that tough shell was a little girl with a heart of gold, a confused kid who just wanted to find her way."

Rosie laughed. "You're such a girl, Frankie. You try to come off all tough and macho but underneath you're just a sniveling little girl. What do you want me to say? I'm a bad person? I'm insensitive to your needs? OK, I am. Get over it. You think you're the first person to get their little heart broken?

"You needed me. You still do. You're the kind of guy who wants to be lead around by the nose, or whatever protruding appendage happens to be available. You wanted me to take charge. You reveled in it. You even loved it when I broke you into little pieces and left you back in Baltimore. That's your thing, Frankie. You're one of those people who need to be used by people like me. It gives you purpose and fulfillment and a reason to be all dark and brooding and wishy-washy.

"If it weren't for me, you'd still be up in Baltimore chasing around cheating husbands and wives for chump change, whining about how screwed up your life is. I gave you everything you needed, the good, the bad and the melodramatic."

"Wow, you're a bitch."

"Really? Is that what I am, Frankie? I guess that explains why you've been swooning over me since the day we met." She shifted her hip and struck a little pose. "And all this time I thought it was my sweet demeanor and sparkling personality that attracted you to me.

"I know what I am, Frankie, and I know what I have to work with. I am a realist. You only have so many options in this life. You can sit back and take what life throws at you, you can ride on somebody else's coat tails, or you can go out there and take what you want.

"I chose to go get what I want. You picked hanging on to my hem line. That's fine. It's who you are. Just don't start crying about it, getting all sappy and sentimental when we don't end up with the picket fence.

"You signed up for this ride and, all in all, it's been a good one. It doesn't have to end here. This could be just the beginning for us,

Frankie."

"Are you really that screwed up in the head?" I asked her. "Is that how you see this? Is this all just some big game to you?"

"Of course it is." She smiled. "And the one with the most chips at the end wins."

"I feel sorry for you, Rosie. I really do."

She let out a sharp cackle. "You feel sorry for me? You pathetic son of a bitch. Let me tell you something. I'm going to be fine. I know what I want and I know how to get it. I have a plan. What have you got?"

I looked long and hard at the pretty girl with the evil glare in her eyes. I hardly recognized her. "What have I got, Rosie? Not a whole hell of a lot.

"I've got an honest job and a roof over my head. I've got a handful of friends and a mother back home who thinks the world revolves around me.

"I've got a bum leg, a two-pack-a-day habit and a penchant for the booze that will probably keep me from ever getting ahead in life. I've got a history of bad choices and enough regrets to fill a dumpster, a lot of them with your initials scribbled on them.

"And I'll tell you what else I've got. I've got a thin streak of decency down my spine that keeps me from straying too far in the wrong direction and just about enough self-respect to be able to get out of bed in the morning.

"It's not much but it's a start and it's something to build on. From where I'm standing, it's a lot more than you've got."

She gave a slight sigh. Not the kind of sigh that indicates sorrow or regret, more the kind that reflects impatience or annoyance. "So, this is it?"

"I guess so."

"Well, we had a good ride. I'm going to miss you, Frankie."

"I don't know how good the ride was, but I doubt if you'll miss me all that much until you need something again."

She shook her head slowly, side to side. "Now what?"

"I'm going to need those books," I told her.

"Over my dead body."

"I think there's been enough of that, lately."

"Those books are my ticket, Frankie. I need those."

"It's done, Rosie, finished. Talbert knows the deal and if you try to put the pinch on Martin, your goose is cooked, if it isn't already. I'm surprised he hasn't come looking for you by now."

"Nothing is done until I say it's done."

"If Oscar hasn't started singing your name already, he will be by the time he comes to."

"You don't know Oscar."

"Maybe you overestimate the hold you have on us mere mortals."

"I doubt that. Besides, what do they have on me? I didn't kill anybody. Oscar is my ex-husband. He's crazy with jealousy. I had no idea what he was up to."

"That's not the way I see it. You had to get Ralphy out of the picture. You were hoping you could convince me to take care of that little problem, but when I didn't come through for you, Oscar was your next choice. He was love sick and desperate to get back with you. I doubt it took a lot of convincing on your part. Probably just a few empty promises."

"No, it wasn't like that. Oscar acted alone. I didn't even know he was in town until he called me up yesterday. He was acting crazy. I was afraid for my life."

"You might want to work on that story some more before you give it to the sheriff."

"It's the truth, Frankie. I didn't know anything."

"Rosie, you were playing both sides against the middle, hedging your bets and keeping your options open. You didn't care who did your dirty work as long as it got done."

"No, it wasn't like that."

"When I spotted Oscar in Atlantic Beach you went out of your way to keep me from going after him. You stalled me long enough for him to get away. You said you never saw him but you knew he was in a pinstriped suit."

"No, that's not the way it happened."

"What about Marcus Fletcher?"

"I never even met Fletcher."

"He was a thorn in your side and he was onto your little plan. You needed him out of the way. Maybe you were hoping he'd just go away but, when I mentioned his name, you knew I was putting the pieces together. You couldn't afford to let me get to him. You wanted to keep me in the dark. That's why he turned up dead the next day."

"I didn't even know who he was."

"Yeah, that's what you told me when I brought up his name. You didn't know anything about him. The funny thing is, when you talked to the sheriff, you told him Fletcher was a private eye out of Baltimore."

"So?"

"I never said anything about what he did for a living, Rosie. I just gave you his name. How would you know what he did if Oscar didn't tell you?"

Rosie didn't have an answer. She stood there looking up at me, big brown eyes searching for a crack in my exterior, a weakness she could capitalize on. I could tell by her face she was coming up empty.

"You made two grand off the deal, the money you took from his safe. It's more than you deserve. Knowing you, I'm guessing you still have whatever jewelry he gave you. Cut your losses and play it smart.

"You didn't pull the trigger, you've got that going for you. If you slip out of town now, there's a good chance you can get away without having to answer any questions. When Sheriff Talbert comes sniffing around, things are going to start pointing in your direction. You don't want that.

"I'll stall him as best I can, try to buy some time before he comes looking for you."

"You would do that for me, after everything that's happened?"

"I'm a sucker like that. You were right about one thing. I do love you, Rosie. I have from the second I laid eyes on you. I don't like you very much, but I do love you."

"I love you too, Frankie."

I tried to smile, but there wasn't much in the tank. "I believe you do, Rosie. In your own twisted and psychotic way, I really believe you do."

She leaned in and gave me a soft kiss on the cheek, her lips all warm and full of life. Sparks went off in my brain, but I fought them off and stood there and took it, soaking in the warmth and the smell of her for one last time.

"Thank you," she whispered.

I had nothing.

Rosie turned and began walking away and I watched her go, long dark hair dangling down her back, trim figure snuggled into that wispy beige dress, those long legs with their lean perfect calves. She was across the lobby and almost out of sight, seconds away from vanishing from my life forever. I couldn't let it end like that.

"Rosie," I called after her.

She stopped and turned around, her eyes wide with hope and wonder. For a split second she was that girl I met in some gin mill back in Baltimore, the one I'd been smitten with from the moment I first saw her.

"Aren't you forgetting something?" I asked.

There was a distant smile on her face and she gave a small shrug of her shoulders. "You can't blame a girl for trying," she sighed.

She walked back over and reached into her shoulder bag, pulling out Blake Martin's ledgers and pressing them into my chest. I took the books. She turned and walked away. That was that.

Chapter Thirty-Two

I don't know how long I stood there at the front desk, staring down at the books in my hands, wondering how many mistakes I'd made over the previous few days, the previous years too, for that matter. I was caught in one of those moods, a mix of melancholy and regret, part of me wanting to chase after Rosie, another part glad to be rid of her.

It took a lot for me to snap myself out of it. I still had things to do.

"Curtis," I said to the desk clerk. "Can you get Simmons on the horn for me? Tell him I'm on my way up."

"Are your hands painted on? I'm not your secretary, you know."

"So I've been told," I answered, heading for the elevator.

Simmons answered the door of the suite in his shirt sleeves, his tie loose around his collar. It looked like he'd had a long night.

"How did it go?" I asked, seeing my way past him and into the room.

"Just dandy."

"Did you get everything settled?"

"As settled as it's getting."

"What does that mean?"

"It means the senator, thanks in some part to you, will be spared the embarrassment of an ugly scandal. He won't have to worry about having this unfortunate situation held over his head for favors either."

"The girl and Gladding?"

"I suspect they're both on their way home by now."

"So, no charges are being filed?"

"All parties decided the matter was best left alone."

"Just sweep it under the carpet, right? Rachel Miller and Thomas

Gladding walk."

"No matter how you slice it," Simmons replied. "It doesn't bode well for the senator's reputation. Nothing good can come from a public trial."

"What the voters don't know can't hurt the senator."

"Look, Wright's not a bad guy. He's done a lot of good during his first two terms. I'll admit he's had some questionable decisions where his personal life goes, but that's no reason to throw away a promising career."

"Got to love politics."

"I think this latest fiasco went a long way in opening the senator's eyes. He got a good scare this weekend, and I expect we'll see a change in the way he handles himself in private."

"At the very least, I'm sure it will make him more careful in the future."

"We had a talk. There are going to be some changes."

"So, that's it, huh? The girl and Gladding get off scot free."

"You put a pretty good scare into the Miller girl. She rolled over with everything she had. She'd of tried to pin the Lindburg kidnapping on him, if she could.

"Turns out he recruited her a few months back, showered her with a lot of expensive gifts, made a lot of big promises. He told her she'd be set up for life, all she had to do was go along with his little plan."

"How come nobody ever offers me deals like that?"

"You haven't got the figure for it," he replied with a grin. "I doubt if Gladding will be getting any more party invitations from the senator. Their relationship is strained, to say the least. In fact, the senator is already talking about putting together a special senate committee to investigate the business practices of the country's larger conglomerate companies. I wouldn't be surprised if Gladding's Skyline Industries wasn't one of the first they look at."

"God bless America."

"I owe you one, McKeller. So does the senator."

"I'll keep that in mind when income taxes come due."

"I don't suppose I have to mention it, but this entire ordeal is not for public consumption. We'd just as soon forget about the whole ugly mess. We'd appreciate it if you could keep it under your hat."

"You don't have to worry about me. I don't have much in the

way of friends, and I don't like reporters. Who would believe me, anyway?"

"Well, we are grateful for your help in the matter."

"Just another day in the life of a house detective," I told him. I stopped for a second and gave him a look, a thought crossing my mind. "Exactly just what does this job of yours encompass?"

Simmons shrugged. "Whatever needs to be done."

"So, you're like an official government law officer?"

"Yeah, I'm a U.S. Federal Agent."

"That means you carry a gun, question suspects, arrest people?"

"Of course."

"I know you're assigned to the senator's security detail, but if you came across a crime, you'd be obligated by duty to do something about it, wouldn't you?"

"It comes with the badge. Why do you ask?"

"I was thinking about that favor you said you owe me."

"Yeah?"

I handed him the stack of ledgers I was carrying under my arm. "What do you know about racketeering?"

"I know it's a federal crime," he said as he opened the page of the first book and began reading.

Chapter Thirty-Three

Peaches Corner sits right off of Ocean Drive, next to the water, practically across the street from what passes for a downtown in Myrtle Beach. It's a cozy little diner, famous for burgers, dogs and French fries, popular with the young locals and a place most families make sure to visit while vacationing at the beach. It was where I told Blake Martin to meet me at noon.

The place had the comfortable feel of an outdoor pavilion someone decided to enclose and turn into a restaurant. Everything in it was bare wood and worn, a long counter running along the back of it, heavy wooden tables scattered across the front. Martin was seated with his two thugs in one of the far tables, Coca Cola bottles in front of them. I walked over, books in hand, and sat down across from them, plopping his books in front of me.

"How do you like the place?" I asked.

"It's peachy," Martin answered with a snarl.

"Hence the name."

"Let's get to it."

"Here they are," I replied, motioning to the stack of ledgers.

"How do we do this?"

"Look, Martin, I feel like we got off on the wrong foot, way back when. I guess there's been a lot of water under the bridge since then, but I'm willing to let bygones be bygones."

"What are you jabbering about?"

"I'm simply extending an olive branch."

"What?"

"It's an old saying."

"What do you want, McKeller?"

"That's just it. I don't want anything."

"What are you trying to pull? You told me to bring the money ..."

"Yeah, I've reconsidered. I don't want your money. You can keep it. You can have the books too."

"What gives?"

"Nothing. I was thinking about what you said, about back in the day, when I was that pathetic loser you'd see in the barrooms when you were out with Rosie. What was it you said, you offered to take care of me but Rosie felt sorry for me?"

He didn't answer.

"I figure I owe you for that, for not sending one of your boys to have that talk with me and taking care of me. I owe you for a lot back then. Consider this my payback."

"I don't get it."

"What's to get? These books are your property, and I think they should be in your possession. It's as simple as that." I pushed the stack of books toward him.

"Just like that?"

"Look, do you want them or not?"

"Yeah, I want them. In fact, there isn't a whole lot I wouldn't do to get them back. I figure that's what this is all about. You figured out what you're up against, and you got cold feet. Maybe you're smarter than I gave you credit for."

"Okay, let's go with that."

"Don't feel bad, McKeller. You're making the smart move. You know I would have had to come after you once I got them back. It would have just been a matter of time. You and Rosie never would have been able to enjoy the money. You'd have been looking over your shoulder forever."

"You're not a very gracious winner, are you?"

"I'm just pointing out the facts. I am who I am, and you are who you are."

"You have no idea who I am, Martin. I'm just figuring it out for myself. I can tell you one thing, though. I'm not that busted wreck you used to see at the bars, drinking his sorrows away, brooding over his lost girl. That guy is dead. He died a long time ago.

"If you want to think I'm doing this because I'm so afraid of you, go ahead. The truth is, I don't want your money. I never did. It might sound good, but the problem is, I'd never be able to get the stink off my hands once I took it."

He made a flinch like he wanted to reach across the table and grab me by the throat, but he held himself back.

"Take your money and take your books," I said, standing up from my chair. "You have yourself a nice life. I wish you the best of luck. I get the feeling you're going to need it."

I turned and walked over to the counter, settling into a stool and watching the action behind me. Simmons and his team had started moving in the moment I stood up, and they had the table surrounded, guns out, by the time I sat back down. It didn't take but a second for Martin to figure out what was going on. He turned his head toward me and shot me a glare that could melt lead. I smiled back with my friendliest smile.

There was a lot of commotion as Martin and his men were ushered out and into custody but, all in all, it went pretty smoothly, just like we planned it. I turned back to the counter to find a young waitress standing, stunned, watching the happenings around her.

"Can I get a cup of Joe?" I asked her.

She managed to pour me a cup of coffee and set it in front of me without spilling too much of it.

"Can I get you anything else?" she asked in a shaky voice.

"Yeah, let me try one of those hotdogs you're so famous for."

Chapter Thirty-Four

The next day I was sitting in the hotel restaurant, at a table by myself. I'd just finished off a corn beef sandwich and was nursing a cup of java. My mind was wandering over recent events and I was taking a cold hard look at some of the choices I'd made.

All things considered, I'd come out of it relatively clean. Sheriff Talbert had some issues with how I'd handled things, but then, he usually did. After a while he even stopped hounding me about where Rosie was.

It didn't matter. When he came to, Oscar Carter took the heat for the whole thing. He confessed to both murders and declared Rosie had nothing to do with it. If that isn't true love, I don't know what is.

Last I heard he was serving consecutive life sentences.

Blake Martin was indicted on federal racketeering charges. None of his big wig friends came to his rescue. He was given fifteen years but he only did two of them before one of his fellow inmates stuck a knife in his back.

Nothing ever came to light about Senator Wright's sordid adventure in Myrtle Beach. He never got to be president, but he was elected to another term. Before he could finish it out, he got caught red handed having an affair with a young staff member. When it went public, it ruined his career. I never heard his name again.

Simmons still works for the Feds. After Wright was outed, he took a job at the FBI. They say he works closely with J. Edgar Hoover as one of his right hand men.

Thomas Gladding fell into some trouble soon after leaving Myrtle Beach. It seems a senate committee appointed to investigate unethical business practices in America found he'd been employing some questionable methods while building his financial empire. Fines were levied and restrictions were enforced. He never served any jail time, but he lost millions and was forced to sell off many of his assets. By my standards, he died a very wealthy man, but it was never enough for him and those closest to him say he was angry and bitter for the rest of his life.

Rachel Rae Miller became a successful fashion model in New York City. I've seen her picture on the cover of magazines from time to time. They say she married a European designer and lives in some castle in the South of France.

Roger Middleton never got that bridge contract he wanted so bad, but he did manage to hold his company together by downsizing. They are still doing business today.

Stuart James went back to writing books. He wrote a mystery that made it all the way to number three on the *New York Times* best seller list. It was about a congressman who is accused of attempted rape and blackmailed before the day is saved by a veteran member of his security team. I never got around to reading it, but Jonathan Masden played the veteran agent in the movie. He wasn't half bad.

It would be years before I heard from Rosie again. Eventually, she would show back up on my doorstep, looking for help. That's just the way it is between me and Rosie. Once she gets in your system she's hard to get rid of.

I would never know, for sure, where she went or what she did after she left Myrtle Beach. When she finally showed back up, all those years later, she told me some stories but you can't go by that. Not with Rosie, anyway. She's not one to show her hand unless it suits her purposes.

For years, I'd find myself thinking about her from time to time. Sometimes it would make me angry. Other times it would make me sad.

Sometimes I would find myself wondering if things could have been different, if maybe I could have done more to make it work. I wonder if there was ever a chance for us, if we could have settled down under different circumstances, if we could have been happy together. I wonder how different my life would be if we had given it an honest try.

It's crazy, I know. Rosie does that to a guy. Rhyme and reason go flying out the window when she looks at you with those big brown eyes, and once you've peered into them, the way I have, it's tough to let it go.

But you can't make a house pet out of a tiger, and you can't harness the raw energy that is a girl like Rosie. All you can do is hang on for as long as you can. Once it's over, you think back fondly on the good parts and try not to get too worked up about the bad parts.

Being with Rosie was a roller coaster ride. The highs were as high as I ever got and the lows were sometimes too much to bear. I bought my ticket, and I took my ride and, in the end, I'm glad I got off when I did. I'm glad I got off while I still have a chance to salvage what's left of this big Merry-Go-Round we're all on.

"Do you want another cup?" Alice asked me, snapping me back to reality.

Alice Seymour looked good in her crisp work shirt and pressed black skirt. Her hair was in slight disarray and her face was somewhat flushed like she'd been running around, working her tables. Her narrow face looked impish and gentle, a small smile curling on her lips. She looked fresh and natural.

"Do you want another cup of coffee?" she asked again.

"What do you do when you're not working, Alice?"

"I don't know. Stuff."

"Do you want to go out for a drink sometime, maybe dinner?"

She glanced around the room like she was confused, like she was making sure I was talking to the right person. "Are you asking me out?"

"Yeah. I think I am."

"You buying?"

"Sure."

"Hmm," she grunted, leaning over and refilling my cup. "Ain't that something? A week ago you didn't know my name. Now you're asking me out to dinner."

"Is that a yes?"

Alice straightened up and stood looking at me for a moment, her smile growing bigger and friendlier. "I'll think about it," she replied, turning away and heading off, back to work.

She was going to say yes. I could tell. Sometimes a guy just knows.

The End

Acknowledgments

A special thanks to all the people who helped make Rosie possible. It's hard to believe we're already on number three in the series

Thanks to all my loyal readers, to those of you who took a chance on an unknown writer, plopping down your hard earned cash on a book you'd never heard of and stuck with it through the continuing adventures of Frankie. There are plenty of writers with more readers but none with better.

So many people have helped me along the way, these past few years, it would be impossible to list them all. Thanks to all the wonderful people who have given their support and encouragement, who've attended my many book promotions, who have opened their businesses to the cause, who've lent their advice and expertise, and or have been kind enough to tell a friend. A heartfelt thank you to you all.

A tip of my fedora to Dad, always my first editor and sounding board, and to my entire family for their unwavering support.

A shout out to my merry band of coworkers at the Marriott Grand Dunes and all of my friends at Foster's Cafe. To the City of Myrtle Beach and all the great friends I've made along the way, and to my extended family back up in Baltimore.

Of course, thanks to the good people at the Ingall's Publishing Group for making it all possible.

I only wish I had room to list everyone individually.

And, to Emine. *Seni Seviyorum.*

www.theoceanforest.com

www.ingramcontent.com/pod-product-compliance
Lightning Source LLC
Chambersburg PA
CBHW070104260626
47160CB00004B/1310